SPEED OF
FLIGHT

DOCTOR WHO – THE MISSING ADVENTURES

Also available:

SPEED OF FLIGHT

Paul Leonard

First published in Great Britain in 1996 by
Doctor Who Books
an imprint of Virgin Publishing Ltd
332 Ladbroke Grove
London W10 5AH

ISBN 0 426 20487 5

Cover illustration by Alister Pearson

Typeset by Galleon Typesetting, Ipswich
Printed and bound in Great Britain by
Mackays of Chatham PLC

Acknowledgements

I'm sick of mentioning Jim Mortimore first, so I won't. Oh, whoops, I have. What a shame. Thanks must go to Nick Walters, for sterling reading of the entire MS., usually in a very rough form, and many useful comments. To Simon and Rebecca at Virgin for putting up with delivery dates whose slow remorseless advance into the future resembled the motion of glaciers, only slightly more terrifying and quite a bit faster. To Barb and Simon, Nadia, Helen, Ann, Patrick and Martine, Denise and Jerry, and, last but not least, my mother, for putting up with being ignored for ages while the book got finished. To Bob O'Brien for ordering all my books for the school library (every little sale helps!).

And finally, of course, to Jim Mortimore for reading the book and making many useful suggestions whilst under great pressure to do at least 14,567,871,904 other things. Good luck with the music, mate!

I should add a thanks to Diana Swales for reading the first chapter of my last book (*BUGS: Out of the Hive*), for which I completely forgot to thank her in the acks there. Thanks anyway!

As the last chapters of this novel were being edited I heard the news that **Jon Pertwee** had died of a heart attack at the age of 76.

As a thoroughly professional and well-respected actor and showman, Jon Pertwee gave pleasure to millions of children and teenagers (including me) in his role as the third Doctor between 1970 and 1974. All the Doctor's mannerisms and figures of speech used in this book are his and always will be his, and it therefore seems only right that the book should be dedicated to his memory.

Prologue

They'd found the fallen sun at last, but Xa didn't care about that. All he knew, all that his blood and body would let him know, was that it was time for him to fight. By tonight, he would be Promoted – or he would be Dead, waiting to be buried in the earth of this alien Land.

He tried not to think about that.

He was standing up to his knees in the snow, at the farthest edge of the camp, facing the blackened stumps of the frozen forest and the icy wilderness beyond. A thin, ragged gap of light between the Sky and the mountains, far in the distance, was all that he could see of sunlight, of the Land that he knew. He wished he had never left it now, but it was too late to worry about that.

Behind Xa, in the freezing half-darkness, the campsite was full of noise and excitement, the clatter of metal pots, the hammering of tent pegs into the hard ground. The younger men were shouting, their high voices blending into a continuous, meaningless chatter. But the only sounds that mattered to Xa were the low grunts of the other bearers: the men his age, the ones whose size and strength made them possible opponents.

He shuddered with uncontrollable anticipation at the thought of the fight. It had to be soon. The long march, the company of the others every night in that small, smelly tent, had brought him to the end of his ability to resist the urge. His muscles were constantly tense, and the blood beat too hard through his arms and his legs and behind his eyes. Xa's hands clenched into fists, and then wouldn't unclench, the tendons standing out below the knuckles, his fingernails drawing blood from the palms.

He couldn't wear his gloves any more, despite the cold. He didn't even want to wear his thick fringelands coat: he was bathed in sweat beneath it, and the smell of his own body rose to his nostrils, as rank as that of an animal. He had seen the other bearers looking at him, and knew that they knew.

He wondered which one would be the easiest for him to kill.

He couldn't stop thinking about it. Couldn't stop imagining the musculature under the shaggy layers of their coats, the thick, warty skin, the blood beneath. Every minute, it seemed, he thought about ripping those coats aside, tearing through flesh and muscle and bone to rip out the heart. He thought of the taste of heartmeat, and shuddered again. He almost turned, called out the challenge – to one or any.

He had to fight.

He crouched down, plunged his bare hands into the snow around his boots, took a handful of the stuff and pushed it, hard, into his face.

The cold shock sobered him a little. He turned round, saw through dripping eyes the five younger men, the scholars, clustered tightly around a spot at the edge of the dome-shaped hillock that they had pronounced to be the fallen sun of this frozen land. They looked dwarfish and irrelevant to Xa's fight-driven mind, but he was desperate for any distraction, so he tried to make sense of what they were doing.

Xa could see the glint of brass in the lamplight, no doubt one of the many scientific instruments that he and the others had hauled in their wooden crates across half a Land of ice. Mr Epreto, the expedition leader, was very excited, almost dancing in front of the others, talking continuously. His movements were jerky, almost machinelike, and his face was so young and unformed that his jaw still jutted out, though he was trying to hide it with a beard. It was amazing that he could lead anything, amazing that he had the strength.

Suddenly Epreto stopped talking for a moment and

2

turned his attention to the slope. Xa saw the glint of brass again, heard a tapping sound, like a hammer hitting bedrock. The other young men applauded as if Epreto had performed a particularly clever conjuring trick. Once, perhaps, Xa would have been cheering with them. But now he could only think that they looked ridiculous, standing in the freezing air in their heavy coats and brightly coloured leather hats. Where was the point in the things that they were doing? Did it have any connection with life, with death, with the fight? Those were the only things that mattered, and, if the young men didn't realize it now, they would soon enough.

If only they would realize it *now*.

If only they would let him fight.

'Xa.' The word was a statement, not a question or a greeting. A statement of intent. Xa looked round, saw Tuy. Dark eyes, blazing with killing force. A heavy, muscular neck, no folds in the skin, no weaknesses.

The eyes were examining him.

'You would be a worthy opponent.' Again it was a statement, not a question. Xa felt the excitement shudder through him, suppressed an animal snarl.

'We gave our word,' he muttered, looking away. 'All of us.' But, even as he spoke, he knew it was hopeless. Yes, he had given a promise, in return for promised money, but what was his word now? What was money? These things were empty, empty as the grey sunless Sky above the icefields. The killing force was like a wind, a hot wind, stinking like the breath of an animal, blowing through his heart and his brain. Promises were nothing. Money was nothing. The fight was everything.

Tuy met his eyes. 'They've found what they wanted. They will not need so many bearers on the way back.'

Xa swallowed, looked away, forced himself to look, really look, at the landscape around them. Ice. Ice, huge broken ridges of it, lit by the faint pinkish-orange light seeping through the mountain gap from their own Land. In the valley between the ice ridges were the blackened bones of frozen forests, the trail that had taken them days to walk. And beyond that were the mountains themselves. Here they looked small, dwarfed by the ice ridges, but in fact they were vast, taller than any city or temple, almost joined to the Sky itself in places. Xa remembered the surface of the mountains: rough, dead clay, laced with slow, dark rivers of living clay, a mixture of the clay of his Land and the remnants of that of this alien Land. The two were always fighting, changing, dangerous.

Yes. It would be a long way home, on his own, even if he won the fight and gained wings. He couldn't fly forever. And what would he eat? The ground beneath his feet was frozen. Nothing lived in this alien Land: he had seen not one animal or plant since they had scaled the mountains. Worse, there was nowhere to bury and honour the dead. The loser would cease to be, as surely as if his body had been burnt. Thinking on it, the winner might well freeze, too, during the transformation, before the journey home even began.

To fight here would be insane.

But his mind and body sang with the need: fight, fight, *fight*.

With a supreme effort, Xa tried to forget his excitement. He struggled to concentrate his attention again on the younger men. Using torches to light the way, they had cleared some of the snow away from the side of the hillock. Xa saw that the surface underneath was dark with more than just shadows. He peered closer, saw Epreto break off a chunk of some glittering substance from beneath the hillock and wave it in the air. 'This is the proof!' he said. 'The clay itself is metamorphosed – melted and then fused solid! Only the heat of a sun could have done that!' The other young men gave a ragged cheer, and the low voices of the bearers joined in, Tuy's amongst them. To Xa it seemed painfully close, almost a challenge.

He felt his bloodlust returning. To avoid thinking about it, to avoid temptation, to avoid Tuy, he started forward, striding over the scattered boxes and the various pumps and gauges and equipment, steering between the half-finished tents. He imagined Tuy following him, imagined his ragged breath, his footsteps.

He forced himself not to look round.

'Is there anything you would like me to do, Mr Epreto?' he asked when he was close enough to be heard.

Epreto looked up, blinked. Close up, he seemed even more unformed: his face seemed tiny, his eyes huge, the jaws still full of a child's jagged cutting teeth. Xa almost expected to see the leathery surface of wings escaping from the little man's coat.

The eyes sized Xa up for a moment, then Epreto nodded. 'Yes, Xa. Get the heavy pick from crate seventeen and take a bigger piece out of this thing for me. I want to know what a sun is really made of.'

Xa went to the crates, found number seventeen tipped on to its side, the contents spilt out carelessly into the snow. There was a heavy pick there, half buried: he took it, hefted it, shook away the loose snow.

I could kill with this.

No. Not that, thought Xa, disgusted at his own perversion. To even think about using weapons in the fight, he must be further gone than he'd realized.

Just let me fight, he thought. Only let me fight, and everything will right itself.

Though he knew it wouldn't.

Xa's vision blurred: for a moment he saw images of blood, of Tuy's heart slippery in his grasp, the organ pumping Tuy's last blood and life into his triumphantly shaking hands. When his eyes cleared he was holding the pick above his head, ready to strike, but there was nothing in front of him except a brass thermometer, a pressure gauge, the empty crate, and the snow.

Shaking, Xa walked back to Epreto with the pick. The younger man didn't seem to notice his emotion; Xa imagined that he was probably oblivious of everything but the excitement of his discovery. He was pointing at a place where the black surface gave way to something paler, almost mirrored, though covered with pieces of ice and dirt. The lamplight glinted off it as if it were metal.

'There,' said Epreto. 'Break off a piece of that material.'

Xa raised the pick again, waited for Epreto to get clear, then struck with all the force of the frustration burning through his body. The impact jarred his bones, sent pain along his spine, but his fury only increased. He could see a gap in the silvery material, and something red inside – glowing red, like blood, lit from within.

He raised the pick, struck again – again – again –

There was a flash. At first Xa thought the light, the shock, the trembling ground, were happening inside his head. Then he saw Epreto stumbling, the snow breaking up over the surface of the dome and sliding down towards him. Someone shouted. Xa stepped back, felt the snow pummel him, push him towards the ground. He fought it, waving his arms and the huge pick, kicking at the heaving ground, screaming in fury and despair. To come this close to the fight and to die in an accident was impossible, unforgivably stupid. Why had he ever come on this insane expedition? What had he expected to gain?

Then the ground stopped shaking, and Xa felt huge, strong hands pulling him out of the snow. He was aware of fog rising all around him, a hissing sound like a steam engine in the factory. A figure formed out of the warm dark fog as he found his feet. Black eyes looked into his. 'You will be a worthy opponent. Remember that.'

Tuy.

The arms let him go, let him stand on his own. Tuy turned and walked away, his feet crunching in the snow.

Xa became aware that the hissing sound was still going on, that steam was rising around him. He remembered Epreto, but, before he could start to worry about the man, he heard the young voice shouting in renewed excitement.

'It isn't dead! Gentlemen, it isn't dead! This sun is still alive! This sun will be our greatest discovery!'

Xa turned, and stared amazed at the 'hillock', now becoming dimly visible as the fog of steam cleared away. It was no longer covered in snow, but was a bare metallic dome. What was left of the snow was steaming and sliding

6

across the surface, hissing as it did so. The metal glowed a dim red in places, and it was hot: Xa could feel the heat of it from four paces. It was like standing beside a furnace.

Epreto was closer, pushing aside the fallen shell of snow with his legs, dancing forward to touch the bright surface. He winced and jumped back, then rapped it with the small hammer he was carrying. It rang like a bell.

The ground shuddered again, and more snow slid off the metal carapace of the sun. Someone shouted, 'There is a crack! Look!'

Xa looked round, saw Mr Lofanu, Epreto's second-in-command, with his hand against what must be a cooler part of the metal. He caught at the surface, tugged, then shook his head.

'It won't move, sir.'

Epreto turned to Xa. 'Come and see if you can prise this open.'

Xa ran across the snow, slipping and sliding a little, until he reached the place where Lofanu stood. He could see the crack now: a vertical line, narrowing, then making a right-angled turn to the left. It looked like a door, slightly ajar. Xa gripped the edge of the crack with his hands. The metal was hot, but not too hot to hold. He braced his legs against the ground, pulled with all his strength.

There was a groan of metal, and the crack widened. Then, with a noise like a rifle shot, it gave way and Xa was pitched backward into the snow. By the time he'd got up, Epreto was already walking in through what was now an open hole in the side of the sun.

No. Not a hole. An open door.

For a moment Xa, with his dull, musclebound mind, couldn't grasp the significance of what he was seeing. Then he heard Lofanu speak. 'It isn't the sun at all. It's a building. It must have been built by the people who lived in this Land before it became cold.'

Epreto's excited voice answered from inside. It was blurred by metallic echoes, but Xa could just make out the words. 'There are more doors in here!'

Lofanu looked round, saw Xa. 'You! And you, Tuy!'

'Sir?' Xa managed the word with difficulty: the physical exertion, far from suppressing his desire to fight, had only made things worse. His body ached to finish the job it thought it had started. He tried to tell himself that what he had been attacking had been no more than a piece of metal, but his mood didn't change.

Lofanu was speaking, but Xa could barely follow the sense of it. Words weren't important to him now. Only actions were important.

'I need you to go inside with me. We have to get these inner doors open, and you and Tuy are the strongest. Can you manage it?'

Xa tried to think clearly. If he refused, he would have to say why: that he couldn't work with Tuy, couldn't be close to the man now, without a fight becoming inevitable. If he heard this, Lofanu would probably try to stop them fighting, because of the promise they had made. Xa knew that if that happened he would have to kill Lofanu, and that the other young men would then kill him with their rifles.

That must be avoided at all costs. There would be no fight then.

But all his thinking was no use: he heard himself saying, 'No,' the word almost a growl. It was as if he had no control over his speech any more, as if it was directed only by his anger and frustration.

Tuy spoke behind him, his voice unexpectedly light, almost laughing. 'Xa drank too much *zhamo* last night, sir. His head's not too clear.'

Yes, thought Xa. A good intervention.

How strange that the last friend he should make in his life was the man he was going to kill.

Lofanu's eyes moved between the two men, as if assessing something. But, whatever it was he assessed, he got the answer wrong.

'Follow me,' he said. 'Both of you.'

They scrambled through the open door. Lofanu went first, then Xa, then the three other young men, Jimbonu,

Gefen and Wutil. Xa heard Tuy scraping through the narrow doorway, suppressed the urge to snarl.

Inside, the light from their lamps glinted off metalled walls, shining in several colours like the body of a carnival float. As they made their way deeper into the chamber at Epreto's direction, Xa kept expecting the songs of the carnival to begin, and the thin, thrashing, metallic music: but all that he heard was their footsteps ringing on the floors, the creak of the lamps swinging, and their breathing echoing off the walls. Epreto tutted occasionally, said 'Turn here,' or 'Down this stairway.' Every so often he would pause and scribble on a pad. Looking over the young man's shoulder, Xa could see that he was making a map of the corridors and chambers they were passing through, annotating it in his tiny, scrawly hand, with arrows along the corridors and corkscrews to represent the stairwells.

Finally they stopped. 'We have made one full circuit at all the levels,' announced Epreto. He consulted his map, began drawing a web of lines across it. His breath made short-lived clouds of vapour in the air in front of his face, turned gold by the light of the lamp. 'There's a space in the middle,' he said after a while. 'And I think it's just one room. Look at the pattern of these doors. And these stairwells go down to it. Whoever designed this had a well-ordered mind.'

Lofanu was looking over Epreto's shoulder. 'I still don't see how it could be the sun, sir. With all these chambers inside it. This is a built –' he hesitated, then used the newer, more precise word instead '– manufactured thing.'

Epreto said nothing for a moment, just stared at his map. Then he said quietly, 'There's nothing else it could be, Mr Lofanu. Nothing else could be this shape, here and now. Why do you think otherwise? Why do you think it cannot be the sun, just because it is artificial? Are you afraid of people who could manufacture a sun?'

'I'm not afraid,' said Lofanu. But Xa could tell that he was. Fear was a scent to him now. 'I just don't see how anyone could survive the heat.'

'Obviously they didn't have to. The heat wasn't there on the inside, any more than the cabin of one of the new steam machines is as hot as the boiler, or the firebox.'

'Let's get on,' said Wutil. 'We need to finish making the camp before dark.'

'Do you really think that matters any more?' asked Epreto.

There was a brief silence. Then Epreto started walking, and the others followed.

Epreto consulted his map at every junction. Behind Xa, Tuy was a solid, constant presence, his footsteps sounding like those of a giant. Xa could smell the man now, and it was the same sharp, animal smell that came from his own body. His nerves tightened, as he realized they were really going to fight. That it was inevitable. His heart began thudding in his chest, his muscles bunched. It occurred to him that they *could* fight in here – it wasn't so cold, somehow. It would be safe to pupate here, to make the transformation after his victory.

He suddenly wanted to start talking. He wanted to babble at Tuy about how he'd worked as a sailman on a flyboat as a young man, and later as a haulier. How he knew all the winds, all the knots and hauls and names of the angles of sail. How he'd always wanted to fly, had always dreamt of flying, of being Promoted to naieen, but had never really thought about the man he would have to kill to get there. Never until now. And now he wanted to kill, and he wanted his new friend to die willingly so that he, Xa, could fly, could walk into the air with his new wings –

Tuy walked into him.

Xa turned, ready to scream in rage, to punch, to kick, to shout, to kill – but Tuy held up an open hand. 'Wait,' he whispered. 'Epreto mentioned an open space.'

'Not much further.' Lofanu's voice.

How much had Lofanu overheard? Xa wondered. Had he realized at last what was between Xa and Tuy, or had his remark been coincidental? Xa found that he didn't care any more. We will fight we will fight we will fight –

But wait. Tuy was right. Wait for the open space. Wait for the chance.

They descended another stairwell, into a narrow chamber where there was barely room even for Lofanu and Epreto to stand. Xa and Tuy were both forced to bend almost double. The walls were red and gold, a weavelike pattern. They seemed to pulse and change in front of Xa's eyes, to slowly close in on him and squeeze tight.

I must fight fight fight –

'This door should do it,' said Epreto suddenly. 'Open it please, bearers.'

Tuy stepped forward, gripped a wheel-like handle in the centre of the door. He tried turning the wheel, but it wouldn't move. Then he tried pulling. He pulled until the veins stood out like cords in his neck, his face twisted with pain.

Now, thought Xa. It would be so easy to start it now. It would be so easy to reach out, to grip Tuy's neck, to squeeze, to break –

He reached out, his hands shaking, and made himself take hold of the opposite side of the wheel. Added his strength to the pull.

The door wouldn't give.

But Xa wasn't about to let go of the wheel, unless Tuy did.

And he was sure from the bright fire in his eyes that the other man felt the same.

'I'm loath to burn it open,' commented Epreto. Xa could scarcely hear the voice over the humming in his ears. 'But it looks as if we have no choice.' He began to pull something out of a canvas sack he was carrying.

Tuy suddenly let go of the wheel, clearly exhausted. As he did so, the wheel lurched towards the side where Xa was pulling, with a sharp cracking sound.

Then it turned freely.

The door opened, revealing a huge space dancing with many small lights.

'Ah! Good!' said Epreto.

Gasping, Xa lay back. The exertion should have left

11

the need to kill momentarily in abeyance, but again it hadn't worked. His muscles remained clenched; his heart kept pounding. His vision blurred, then cleared again.

He realized that he would have to fight, fight *now*, or he was going to die.

He looked at Tuy, met the man's eyes.

Tuy nodded.

Lofanu and Epreto, oblivious, were advancing cautiously into the new chamber, their lamps held high. Wutil and the others were somewhere behind, on the stairs. Some tiny corner of Xa's mind reminded him that they were carrying guns, but he found that he didn't care any more. He stepped into the big chamber, acutely conscious of Tuy following, of the faint sound of the man's breathing.

There was a muffled click, and an uneven but none-theless painfully brilliant illumination suddenly filled the whole chamber. Xa could see many angular shapes, brightly coloured and covered in flickering lights, arranged in a rough semicircle.

It was truly like the carnival, thought Xa. Carnival time inside a fallen sun. He was dimly aware that he would once have been fascinated, or perhaps afraid, or even awestruck.

But none of those emotions mattered now.

He turned, looked at Tuy once more, peeled off his coat. Then he growled, deep in his throat, the wordless signal unmistakable.

Tuy seemed to hesitate, then growled back, removed his coat – and moved with surprising swiftness, his hands jerking forward to close around Xa's neck. Xa dodged just in time, then rolled through the open doorway and jumped to his feet inside the illuminated chamber. He had never felt more alive. Every muscle in his body felt springy, prickling with blood and excitement. His vision was unbelievably sharp: he could see the individual pores on Tuy's skin, four paces away. He could pick out individual filaments in both their scents, things that told him how fatigued Tuy was, how much strength was likely to remain in his body, how long he would take to die from certain kinds of wound. Most important of all, he could read the movements of the man's body, could see that he was going to –

'Stop!'

Epreto. But the voice was a rat's squeak, unimportant, unimaginably far below the plain of golden fire where Xa and Tuy were standing.

And Tuy was moving, leaping straight towards Xa, his legs swinging forward. Xa dropped, rolled to one side, kicking upwards as soon as he was on the ground.

The kick connected, and Xa thought he felt a bone breaking. He was almost disappointed. Was it going to be that easy?

Epreto, or perhaps one of the others, was still shouting. Meaningless sounds, insect's chittering.

Xa was on his feet, watching Tuy struggle upright, holding on to one of the strange cabinets for purchase. Something on the surface of the cabinet seemed to give way, and there was a sharp click. Then another voice spoke, booming like a priest's in a temple.

Perhaps there is a priest here, thought Xa vaguely. Which is as it should be. There should be holy witness.

Tuy was upright now, but it was clear that one leg was injured, if not broken. He smiled at Xa, then clenched his fists. Still dangerous.

Xa advanced slowly, carefully, watching every movement of his opponent's body. When he was still three paces away, Tuy jackknifed forward and to one side, a barely controlled fall, and pushed his head towards Xa's belly.

It was almost enough. Xa fell back, minimized the impact, but nonetheless fell to the ground, momentarily winded. Instantly Tuy was on top of him. The cold metal rang like a gong at their joint impact. Xa reached out, pushed his hands towards Tuy's throat, but the man caught hold of them, forced them back.

Then Xa realized.

The injured leg made little difference, now that Tuy didn't have to carry his own weight. And Tuy's huge arms

13

were stronger than Xa's, and, worse, he had the weight of his body behind them. Xa rolled, flailed, tried to get free, but it was no use. The big, calloused, hands came closer to his throat.

He was going to lose. He was going to die. With a cold shock of horror he realized that the Dead could never come here, that the loser would truly die. Forever.

Somewhere, the priest was still speaking, but Xa couldn't understand the words any more. He wondered if he ought to, wondered if this alien priest could offer him any comfort. He tried to listen, hear the words 'Sky' and 'launch'. But the rest was meaningless babble.

Tuy's hands were touching his skin now. With a supreme effort, Xa held them back, but he knew he couldn't keep up the pressure for long. Then bright light flared all around them, and the floor trembled. Xa heard Epreto shout, 'The sun is shining again! We will all die!'

No! thought Xa. We will not die! I will not die! I did not come here to die! I will launch myself into the Sky, as the priest says!

He bucked upwards, jolting Tuy's body back for a moment. Then he let go of one of those advancing hands, and punched his opponent in the throat with all the force he had. Even as Tuy's hands closed around his own throat, he felt them go limp. Tuy dropped back, choking, convulsing.

Now!

Xa rolled, rammed his knees into Tuy's belly, chopped at his throat again. He saw the windpipe collapse, the blooded saliva boiling out of the man's mouth, and knew the fight was over.

He became aware that a roaring sound had filled the room around him. The light was brighter. The floor had lurched sideways. Xa could hear Epreto screaming something, could see Gefen struggling with one of the cabinets, almost as if he too were fighting.

But none of that mattered.

Xa had won. Now he would be Promoted. Now he would go to the Sky.

Now he would fly, as he had always dreamt of flying.

He stood over the shuddering body of his opponent, flexed his hand sharply, felt the long claws break through the ends of his fingers. Blood oozed, but there was no pain. Not yet. The light around him was so bright that it seemed to burn his skin. Tuy opened his eyes, and there was no anger in his expression, only the shining light of the dying.

And Xa knew that he, too, knew the fight was over.

Epreto was still shouting. 'You fools! You have killed us all! The sun is alive!'

And the priest was chanting, over and over, 'Launch now. The Sky is broken.'

How appropriate, thought Xa, as he broke open Tuy's chest and ripped out his heart. The sun is alive and it's launching me into the Sky. And the beating flesh in his hands, the death in Tuy's eyes, only seemed to confirm that everything was as it was meant to be.

The Land

Book One

The Land

One

Captain Mike Yates arrived at Paddington Station feeling more nervous than he would have believed possible. His throat was dry, his face was flushed, and his hands were shaking slightly. He looked at the clock above the timetable and saw he had less than five minutes to spare. He looked over the heads of the crowd, searching for platform nine. He couldn't see it. Eight, ten, eleven, fourteen – no nine. Where had they put it, for goodness' sake? His heart began to race with something closely akin to panic. What if he couldn't find it? What if he was late? What would happen then?

He surveyed the station concourse. It was the busiest time of the day, and there were people everywhere, most of them in a hurry. Businessmen in city suits mixed with students in leather jackets. A solitary long-haired man was wearing a leftover-looking caftan. Yates noticed several people in anoraks or raincoats, although it was quite warm. He wondered if the forecast had mentioned rain and, if so, whether he would have to change his plans.

He shook his head, tried not to think about it. It was pointless making any plans at this stage, before he'd even made contact. And he wasn't going to make contact at all unless he could work out where platform nine was. He scanned the concourse again, and saw it – right between eight and ten, exactly where it should be. Somehow he'd missed it on the first pass. Mike rubbed his sweaty palms together and began pushing through the crowd.

This is ridiculous, he thought. I've got to calm down. I've faced far worse things than this on other missions.

Then Mike grinned to himself as he realized what he

had been thinking. Other *missions*. But, then, perhaps it was best to think of this as a kind of mission. He was here to make contact, to observe, to decide if the matter needed further investigation. The only difference was that he wouldn't be reporting this one to the Brigadier for action. He was going to have to make his own decision.

Which was probably just as well.

As Mike got closer to the platforms, he became aware of the familiar pungency of diesel oil. He could still remember when the smell of going somewhere had been the sulphurous burn of coal, accompanied by clouds of steam and black smuts. He wasn't sure that diesel was an improvement, but it certainly made it easier to keep your shirt cuffs clean. He glanced at his cuffs now, at the gold links. Then he smoothed his green sports jacket and straightened his tie. He wondered if he wasn't a little overdressed for the occasion – perhaps blue jeans and a sweater would have been better. He really had no idea. If only he'd had better information . . .

There I go, thinking of it as a mission again, he thought. All I need is my knapsack, my rifle and my two-way radio and I'll be ready for anything. He grinned to himself again.

A flash of blonde hair in the crowd caught his attention: he looked, but saw only a woman in a yellow summer dress moving through the crowd. As he watched, she met up with a tall young man in a velvet jacket and gave him a kiss. Mike quickly looked away, scanned the concourse once more, absurdly wishing he'd brought his binoculars. Not that they'd have made things any easier in this crowd.

Blonde with a black jacket, he thought. That's what they said. A blonde with a black leather jacket.

He glanced at his watch. Two minutes to six. They had said six o'clock, hadn't they? And it *had* been platform nine, not six or nineteen? He had another absurd idea: that he should have brought Benton and had him patrol the station, checking all the platforms and periodically radioing in his location.

Somehow, Mike didn't think the Brigadier would have approved.

An arm jabbed him in the back, and a familiar voice said, 'Oh, sorry.'

Mike turned, and saw Jo Grant.

They both started at once: 'What are *you* doing –?'

Jo looked up and grinned. 'Meeting someone.'

'And me,' said Mike.

Then he realized she was wearing a black leather jacket.

Blonde . . . black jacket . . .

Bloody hell!

On the platform behind them, a train hooted and revved its engine, making any conversation impossible for a few seconds. They just stared at each other. Jo was frowning, as if trying to puzzle something out.

Mike felt a slow flush creeping over his features. 'Uh – Jo,' he said when it was possible to talk again. 'This chap you were going to meet, was he supposed to be wearing a yellow carnation in his buttonhole?'

Jo stared at him. 'How did you know it was a chap?' Then she saw the carnation in Mike's jacket, and said, 'Oh, I see.'

'I thought Sergeant Benton looked a bit sheepish,' said Mike thoughtfully.

'It was Sergeant Bell! She told me that he had to come in from Reading, so . . .' She stopped, then blushed deeply and looked at the ground. 'We've been conned, haven't we?'

'Looks like it,' admitted Mike. 'Never mind. It could have been worse. The bloke you met might have been an Auton.'

Jo managed a grin, but Mike could tell that she was just as embarrassed as he was.

'Well,' he said after a moment, 'I reckon I know who's going to be on clean-up duty for the next couple of weeks, don't you?'

'That's the last time I go on a blind date!' said Jo suddenly.

And me, thought Mike. At least, it's the last time I go at John Benton's recommendation. He looked at a point somewhere over Jo's head, cleared his throat and said, 'I think in the circumstances the least I can do is buy you dinner.'

There was a slightly awkward silence. Jo also stared into the distance for a while, then said, 'Hang on a minute. I've got a better idea.'

The laboratory, thought Mike, looked pretty much as usual. The bench was covered with electronic clutter, plus a couple of clamp stands with flasks attached. The huge, dusty retort that had somehow survived the destruction of the lab at the Bedfordshire HQ stood, once more unused, on an equipment cupboard by the far wall. A thing that looked like an illuminated spinning top hung from the ceiling, flickering as it slowly rotated to and fro.

But the TARDIS was missing.

Mike shook his head slowly. The Brig was right: the time was fast approaching when the Doctor was going to disappear for good. Mike didn't really blame him. With all of time and space to wander around in, there couldn't be much of an attraction in working for UNIT in twentieth-century England.

He turned to Jo, who was standing in the doorway, her jacket over one arm. Underneath she wore a red dress, which Mike had to admit was rather smart. It also made her look . . . older, somehow. Well, Jo is changing too, he thought. We all do, in time. He gestured at the space where the TARDIS should have been. 'Gone again.'

'I don't suppose he would have wanted to go to the Last Days of the Raj anyway,' she said mournfully.

'Never mind, Jo. It wasn't a bad idea.' He glanced at his watch, saw that it was already almost seven-thirty. 'Come on, if we're going to eat anywhere before the crowds get in –'

He broke off as a familiar sound began, a wheez-ing, groaning noise that rapidly grew in volume as the TARDIS materialized in its usual corner of the lab.

After a moment the door opened and the Doctor emerged, wearing his purple jacket and a magenta shirt with a bright red collar.

'Doctor!' began Jo. 'You're just in time. We thought you might like to –'

'Captain Yates!' interrupted the Doctor. 'Good of you to join us! I see you're dressed for dinner already.' He looked Mike briefly up and down, then glanced at Jo. 'Yes, I think that will do. If you'd like to step this way . . .' He gestured at the open door of the TARDIS.

Jo and Mike looked at each other. Jo shrugged. 'Umm, Doctor,' she began. 'Where are we going?'

'Karfel, of course.' The Doctor looked from one to the other of them and frowned. 'I thought I'd told you about it.'

'Tomorrow! You said you might have the coordinates by tomorrow!'

'You mean it isn't tomorrow?' The Doctor looked at his watch, then at the clock on the wall. 'Oh, so it isn't. Never mind. You both seem to be all ready to go anyway.' He gestured to the open door once more.

'We were actually planning –' began Jo.

The Doctor raised his eyebrows at her.

'We had in mind the Last Days of the Raj,' said Mike.

'What? India in 1947? I don't recommend it. It was a pretty unstable time, you know. Now Karfel is a very peaceful place, and we'll be visiting it at the height of its civilization.'

Mike looked at Jo in bewilderment. She giggled. 'I think you two have got a crossed line.' She turned to the Doctor. 'We were talking about a restaurant. It's off the Strand.'

'They do an awfully good curry,' supplied Mike.

The Doctor frowned. 'Well, it's up to you, of course. But I think you'll find Karfel much more interesting.'

'Uh, where is it, exactly?' asked Mike.

'Oh, not far. It's in the same galactic cluster as Earth. And only about twenty thousand years in the future.'

Mike looked at the Doctor, then at the open door of

23

the TARDIS. He hesitated, then shook his head. 'Sorry, Doctor. I'm supposed to have permission from the Brig before I leave the country, let alone before I leave the planet. I'd love to come along, but I think I'll have to –'

Jo jogged his arm. 'Oh, go on Mike. Didn't you say you wanted to see the wonders of the Universe?'

Mike did vaguely recall making such a remark, perhaps on the way back from Kebiria. He had a feeling he'd meant it as a joke at the time. But on the other hand . . .

It *would* be nice. Just once. To see an alien world that wasn't geared up for war. To meet aliens who weren't preparing to invade Earth.

'Are you sure this is quite safe, Doctor?' he asked. 'There won't be any complications? I need to report for duty at six o'clock tomorrow morning, you know.'

The Doctor frowned again. 'Complications? My dear chap, I've no idea what you mean!'

Grinning, Jo walked past the Doctor and into the TARDIS. Mike hesitated a second longer, then went after her.

'Don't worry,' said the Doctor cheerfully as the door closed behind them. 'I've checked the coordinates three times. Nothing can possibly go wrong.'

Two

Herik Lofanu watched his old friend Epreto as he stood with his huge hands gripping the big ribbed wheel of the steamwing, and wondered why he didn't like him any more. He was huge now, so large that it was hard to believe that he hadn't been Promoted. He wore a beard almost down to his waist, laden with rings of rose-gold and beaten copper, and a green-and-white jacket, thickly padded and with an odd, ridged texture; a material said to be proof against bullets. But it was his eyes that gave it away, Lofanu decided. They were never still for a moment. It seemed to Lofanu as if they were always checking something: a transaction, a piece of machinery, a face.

He saw them check his face now, and shivered. If his old friend guessed . . .

He pushed the thought away. Nothing would expose his guilt more quickly to Epreto than letting it show on his face. Epreto was no longer looking at him, but was instead studying the view over the wooden rail of the observation platform. Suddenly he moved, the big hands releasing the seven brass valves that controlled the pipes to the buoyancy balloon. The platform started to sway, and Lofanu caught hold of the iron rail for balance. The hiss of escaping gas grew louder, until it was a nerve-tearing racket. The misty images of the naieen temples cling-ing to the Sky, far away in the blue air above the bal-loon, seemed to ripple as the stream of gas moved in front of them. Then, slowly, the big green-and-white canopy folded inward and draped itself over the bracing frame which surrounded the polished iron cylinder of the boiler. Two crewmen scrambled out along the rigging and began to fold and then cleat it into place. The boiler hissed once, jetting steam from its underside. Lofanu supposed the craft must be falling already, but it was hard to tell when they were so far from both Land and Sky. He looked over the edge of the platform at the canopy of the childforest far below, its green undulations broken by the high feathery blades of speartrees. From this height it almost seemed like moss: but wreaths of mist, slowly evaporating in the morning sun, destroyed the illusion by making clear the vast scale of the view.

Epreto's view, thought Lofanu. The world seen from high up, made small, and therefore whole. Analysed, understood, comprehended. Once, that had seemed a wonderful thing to Lofanu, but not any longer. He had seen the consequences of that kind of thinking, and wanted no more of it.

The crew were still folding the canopy around the boiler. 'Be careful with that!' shouted Epreto. 'Remember we can't land without it. This isn't a sailwing, you know.'

The two men glanced up at Epreto, said nothing.

Lofanu closed his eyes. The warm airstream blew across his face, its force changing with the rhythm of the steamwing's slow wingbeats. Lofanu tried to imagine that he was gliding, Promoted, a naieen. Above all things that were of men.

'Tell me your dreams, Herik.'

Epreto's voice. Lofanu jumped, said, 'I – I was just relaxing, Juliu. The wind is so pleasant – on the steamwing – and the steamy air –' He stopped, aware that he was talking nonsense.

'I asked for your dreams.' A pause. 'You don't tell me them any more, do you? You, or Gefen.'

Lofanu opened his eyes, saw Epreto gazing at him. He forced himself to meet the older man's eyes. 'Our dreams change as we grow older. We grow apart, I think, and they become impossible to explain.'

'Do you think so?' It was Epreto who looked away. 'Mine have never changed.'

There was a silence. The forest below was closer now, and from time to time Lofanu caught a glimpse of something moving – perhaps a balloon lizard or a crystalwing snake, fleeing as the steamwing's huge angular shadow fell across them. He wondered, as he always did, at the vast variety of life, all of it struggling to survive in this narrow, hot world so near to the motionless sun.

It was hard to believe that, if Epreto had his way, everything here would soon be dead.

Was that the dream his old friend was talking about? It certainly wasn't the way it had started. Not for the first time Lofanu considered the possibility of appealing to Epreto, of telling him the truth about his feelings.

What you intend to do is hideous, immoral. You mustn't do it, Juliu.

Yes, it would be so easy to say. But he couldn't say it. Couldn't take the risk. And the only other option was what he was going to do: betrayal.

'Down a little on the port wing, I think,' muttered Epreto suddenly.

Lofanu couldn't comment, steam aeropiloting not being a study of his. But his sense of balance told him that the craft was already stable. Why trim it? No doubt it was some complex factor about the machinery that only Epreto understood.

Suddenly he felt Epreto's eyes on him again. Again he felt that crawling sense of guilt, but he made himself turn to face the man once more. He had turned and was pointing over the opposite rail.

'Look there!' he said. 'Jerim birds!'

Lofanu stepped over the top of the stairway, looked where Epreto was indicating. He saw not one but a whole slow, stately flock of the green-tinted, rotor-winged birds, drifting just above the canopy, rotors lazily beating the air. 'You don't often see so many at once,' he commented.

'No,' said Epreto slowly, 'You don't.' A pause. 'Do you remember the day that we found the sun, Herik?'

Lofanu nodded.

'Do you remember us struggling with the levers? All of us pulling together?'

Lofanu frowned slightly. It hadn't been quite like that. He remembered Gefen and Epreto shouting. He remembered staring at the prone bodies of the fighters, one dead, one beginning to spin his transformation cocoon, and thinking that they would soon all be dead, cocoons or no. He didn't remember what Wutil or Jimbonu had been doing — hiding, quite possibly. He had a feeling that the thing had just stopped by itself; certainly all the lights had gone out. Later, when Epreto had claimed the credit for saving their lives, he hadn't objected, because he hadn't been sure what had happened. But he'd always felt that the man might be exaggerating, claiming more knowledge than he had actually gained, in order to enhance his reputation. In subsequent years, Epreto had made two more expeditions to the fallen sun, but it had been quite cold inside, and by the second time rusted, as if whatever force had been preserving it was gone forever.

If only it had stopped there, thought Lofanu. If only Epreto had been satisfied with the miracles he'd seen, and not sought to create more of them.

'I can see that you do remember,' said Epreto, breaking into Lofanu's reverie. 'I can see the memory on your face.' He touched Lofanu's arm. 'It's a shame we no longer work together.'

Before Lofanu could reply Epreto turned and left the platform, beckoning one of the crewmen up from below to take his place at the controls.

Lofanu wondered what Epreto had meant by his last remark. Did he know something? Had he guessed Lofanu's and Gefen's plans? Was it a warning — betray me and you will suffer?

He knew he should try to speak to Gefen — but how? Epreto had gone back down to the cabin where Gefen was. He clenched his fists, uncertain, watched as the pilot pulled back a couple of levers, heard a clatter of chains. The nose of the steamwing dipped sharply. Lofanu looked down at the forest, saw that they were almost brushing the tops of the speartrees.

'What's happening?' he asked the crewman who had taken Epreto's place.

The man didn't say anything for a moment, then spoke without looking at Lofanu. 'Coming in to land, sir.'

'But we're three hours early! Surely we're in the wrong place!'

But even as Lofanu was speaking he saw the gap in the canopy ahead, the wide, polished wooden platform that could only be the landing site prepared by the Dead. Lofanu felt a sudden sense of panic. Epreto knew — he had to know. Why else would he change his plans? Lofanu turned, almost ran down the steps that led to the cabin.

Inside, it was almost dark. For a moment Lofanu's sun-dazzled eyes could see nothing but a yellow mist. As they returned to normal, Lofanu could see the polished wood-and-brass fittings and the dim shapes of the three other men. Gefen was propped against the far wall: he briefly met Lofanu's eyes, but made no other signal. Epreto himself was crouched by the open door of the fire, next to the stoker, who was shovelling in extra fireclay. In the tiny room, the man was a shadowy giant, his gold beard rings glinting red in the light seeping up from the fire. The two new men, Jitil and Hanu, were sitting against the opposite wall of the cabin, the single porthole at their backs, dressed in farmer's leathers. Their rifles were across their knees, their faces alert but expressionless. It was almost, Lofanu thought uneasily, as if they were guarding prisoners.

He shivered.

Epreto glanced up, saw Lofanu in the doorway. He turned to Jitil and Hanu. 'I suggest that one of you remain with the steamwing,' he said. 'There is always the possibility of treachery of some kind where the Dead are involved. But I will need one of you with me.'

'Yes, sir,' replied the men in unison.

'Why are we landing so early?' asked Lofanu, stepping forward into the room.

Gefen looked up sharply. 'We are landing? Now?'

'Yes, yes,' said Epreto irritably. 'We're landing.'

Gefen looked at Lofanu. 'But you said the journey would take four hours! It's only –'

Jitil looked up. 'Mr Epreto gives the orders,' he said.

His hand was curled around the trigger guard of his rifle, and, though casually held, the gun was pointed in Gefen's direction. Lofanu noticed that Hanu's rifle was similarly aimed at him.

Lofanu felt dizzy, as if he were suspended by a thin wire over a vast chasm. He could almost *feel* the wire, there, cutting through his belly and making a cold incision in his heart. He turned, started towards the steps to the observation platform. Perhaps he could talk to the pilot. Persuade him to change the plan. Something.

Neither Jitil nor Hanu said anything to stop him, but he could feel the gun trained on the small of his back.

Halfway up to the platform, he heard those regular, heavy footsteps behind him.

'Herik.' Epreto's voice.

Slowly, Lofanu turned. He saw Epreto looking up at him. Looking up at him and looking through him.

And then Lofanu knew. Epreto knew their plans. Knew that they were going to betray him.

And he was going to kill them for it.

'Juliu, I –' he began.

There was a crash of metal, and the too-loud crack of a gunshot. A scream of pain, another thud, then silence.

'Gefen!' shouted Lofanu. Had Gefen tried to take on Jitil or Hanu? Or had the po-faced executioners decided it was time for the kill? He started to scramble down the steps. Epreto gripped his arm: he struggled free, with the strength of panic, and pushed past the man. He had almost reached the bottom when something hit him, hard, on the head. He half fell into the cabin. Dimly, he saw Jitil, still holding the gun. He tried to crawl aside, wondering if he could appeal somehow to Epreto. But hands grabbed hold of him. He struggled, fell against something wet and warm.

His hands were covered in blood.

'Gefen?' he asked. But there was no response. Was Gefen really dead? How could something like that happen so quickly?

He heard Epreto's voice. 'Knock him out for the time being. They won't come if they hear any more noise.'

There was no pain after that, only a huge ringing sound, like the bell at a naieen Temple.

Just for a second, Lofanu had the illusion that he could fly.

When Lofanu woke up, he felt sick and weak. His head hurt, and there was a strange, repetitive whooping sound in his ears. For a moment he was confused, wondering why he was outdoors, unable to understand the canopy of green branches he saw above him, the blue Sky streaked with bright clouds.

He tried to move his body and felt ropes biting into his arms and chest. Then he remembered.

The forest. The steamwing. Epreto.

Epreto, who must have been more ready for a possible betrayal than Lofanu had been ready to betray him.

Lofanu's arm was throbbing. He managed to raise his head, saw that his sleeve had been ripped away, and a long cut made along the flesh. Blood ran out over the wood, trickling towards a dark lump, a lump that was covered in far too much blood.

Gefen. Gefen's corpse. They'd killed Gefen. And he was going to die too. Without any possibility of meeting the Dead. Without any possibility of betraying Epreto.

Without any possibility of saving the life of the world.

Lofanu felt vomit rise in his throat and struggled to sit upright, only to feel the ropes bite into him again. Gefen was tied to a branch, his skull covered in blood, his eyes open, staring blankly. Lofanu was tied to the same branch as Gefen, and they'd cut him so that he would bleed.

Now he realized what the whooping sound was. It was coming not from inside his head, as he'd first supposed, but from all around him. They were here. The

31

children. He could see them now, their huge eyes peering from between the shadowy leaves, the grey fur of their bodies, the clumsy movements of their wings. Their mouths opening wide at the prospect of the feast.

It was then that he wished that Jitil or Hanu had just shot him. That he'd given in and watched whilst Epreto destroyed the world. That anything had happened, anything but this.

The children moved forward, all of a mass, in a rushing and whooping of wings.

Lofanu screamed.

Three

The TARDIS in flight made Mike slightly uneasy. The regular rise and fall of the time rotor, the faint, alien pulse of what he could only assume were engines, the bizarre geometry of the place with its machines and hexagons and roundelled walls, all conspired to remind him of what he usually managed to forget: that the Doctor, for all his human mannerisms, was an alien.

He wondered how often Jo remembered that, or whether she'd got so used to working with him that she just thought of him as human. She seemed relaxed enough, sitting reading a newspaper on a black tubular chair that wouldn't have looked out of place in some millionaire rock star's apartment. The Doctor stood at the console, occasionally adjusting a control, though Mike had no idea how he knew where they were going. The scanner was blank. Perhaps, he thought, it was like flying a plane by radar – but he couldn't see anything that looked like a radar display, either.

Suddenly the Doctor leant over the console and flicked a series of switches. The pulse of the engines changed, became louder.

'Coming in to land?' asked Mike.

The Doctor nodded, then frowned. 'Funny, I could have sworn –'

He didn't finish the sentence, because the sound of the engines stopped with a sudden thud and the floor of the TARDIS pitched to one side. Mike felt himself falling towards the console, but, even as he automatically began to roll in order to control the fall, the floor righted itself.

He ended up landing on his backside, hard. The floor jolted again underneath him, then was still.

He scrambled to his feet as quickly as he could. Jo was already standing. 'Doctor, what's happening?'

'Nothing to worry about,' said the Doctor. 'We just missed the ground by a few feet.' He frowned at the console, and added in an undertone, 'Funny, she doesn't usually do that.'

Mike glanced at Jo. 'Are you all right?'

She nodded. Then an expression of alarm crossed her face. 'Doctor! Look!'

Mike whirled round, saw that the scanner had come to life. It showed an extreme close-up of a hideous thing a bit like a monkey, but with long, carnivore's fangs. Its huge eyes were staring directly at the camera. Its body was partly out of focus, but it seemed to have wings. Some kind of bat? Mike looked at the Doctor.

'Don't worry. It's just an example of the local fauna. I expect we frightened it, appearing suddenly like that.'

'It doesn't look frightened,' observed Jo. The creature appeared to be trying to bite its way through the lens of the camera that fed the scanner. Mike could hear its claws scrabbling at the material, its snorting breath. He wondered how secure they were.

'Are there any more of them out there?' he asked.

The Doctor pressed a control and the view changed, to show several more of the creatures hunched around a carcass like vultures, their wide mouths dripping blood.

He heard Jo's intake of breath, felt her hand grab his arm.

'It's OK, Jo,' he said. 'We're safe in here.'

But Jo only gripped his arm tighter. 'It's a man!' she said.

And then Mike realized she was right.

The carcass looked human.

He swallowed. 'Doctor –'

'I can see, yes. But there's nothing we can do for the poor chap now. I suggest we –'

He was interrupted by a scream. A man's scream. 'Help me! Please help me!'

Mike looked at the Doctor again, then reached for his gun. But his gun wasn't there. He was dressed for dinner. This hadn't been supposed to happen.

The scream was repeated, incoherent now, pure terror.

'There must be another victim,' said the Doctor. 'Stay here, Jo. Captain Yates, look after her. I'm going to see what I can do.'

'Doctor! No!' Jo shouted. Mike too opened his mouth to object – surely there was nothing the Doctor could do, unarmed, against these creatures – but the doors of the TARDIS were already opening, and the Doctor was running through them, his hands rummaging in his jacket pockets as if searching for something.

Mike didn't hesitate. The Doctor was going to need help. He ran after him, and just made it outside before the doors closed. His momentum carried him forward beyond the narrow strip of solid ground where the TAR-DIS had landed into what seemed like a clump of large leaves, rather like those on a rubber plant. He toppled through the leaves. He reached out to grip them, but they broke away in his hands. He fell. He kept on falling.

Below was a drop of several hundred feet.

Mike seemed to fall in an impossible slow motion. He could see the Doctor below him, also falling. He could see projecting branches, long loops of coloured vines, huge, distant tree trunks. But there was nothing near enough to hang on to. No hope of stopping his fall. It seemed an impossible, an utterly stupid way to die.

There has to be something I can do, he thought. He looked down at the Doctor, falling perhaps a hundred feet below him, and saw that he had somehow managed to turn over in the air and was facing upward, holding something that looked like a fluorescent orange football against his chest. Mike tried to signal to him but all the Doctor's attention was on the 'football'. He appeared, bizarrely, to be talking to it.

Suddenly the thing seemed to explode. A blaze of brilliant colour rippled out across the Doctor's outstretched arms, then snaked its way beneath them, leaving a bright webbing across his chest. Another rippled down across his legs. The Doctor kicked his legs, rolled in the air, and the fabric – the bulk of which was now above his back – billowed out, shaping itself into wings and a broad, paddle-like tail. It was amazing – but it wasn't big enough. Mike knew about parachutes, and he knew that the Doctor couldn't even glide with the amount of surface area available.

But, whatever the theory, the Doctor was undoubtedly slowing down. In fact, he was swooping to one side, fully under control, and Mike, still falling, was rapidly drawing level with him. It occurred to Mike then that he wasn't falling anything like as fast as he should be, either. Was the air denser here, or something?

'Doctor!' he called.

The Doctor looked over his shoulder, raised his eyebrows. 'Captain Yates!' he barked. 'I thought I told you to stay with Jo!'

Mike was well below the Doctor by now. He watched helplessly as the bright orange wings tilted and the Doctor dived towards him. He saw a rope uncoil, apparently by itself, from the Doctor's waist. Mike tried to reach out and grab it, but the Doctor bawled, 'Keep still!'

The rope snaked towards him. It brushed against his neck, then wrapped itself around his chest, pinning his right arm to his side. It tightened until his arm was cramped and his ribs hurt at every breath. Above, the Doctor stretched out his arms and legs so that the wings and tail bloomed outward into something like a cross between a kite and a parachute.

'You really should have stayed put, you know,' commented the Doctor. 'I could have saved that poor chap who was screaming. I shouldn't think he's got a chance now. I can't fly up with you hanging on like that.'

As if to confirm his words, a hideous wail of agony echoed through the air, fading away to silence.

The huge tree trunks glided slowly past them, the nearest now several hundred yards away. There didn't seem to be any branches or vines at this level. Mike looked over his shoulder and saw the ground, approaching slowly. He could see huge ridges of roots, slimy-looking pools, and green things shaped like knife blades that seemed to be growing as he looked at them.

Or perhaps it was just that they were getting closer.

Mike braced himself for the landing, watching the lie of the land carefully as they covered the last few yards.

'Doctor, there's a ten-degree slope,' he reported.

'Ten point seven, on average,' responded the Doctor.

Mike curved his legs and tried to roll as his training demanded, but it was difficult, roped to the Doctor as he was. However, the impact was surprisingly gentle, and, though Mike fell awkwardly, it seemed, once more, to happen in slow motion. He hit warm mud, slithered a little, then stopped easily. But when he tried to get up he found himself flying again, and only the tether linking him to the Doctor stopped him from performing an ungainly somersault. This time when he fell he hit his head.

'Be careful,' said the Doctor who was extricating himself from the billowing fabric of his wings. 'You won't be used to the gravity here.'

'Gravity?' asked Mike, struggling to sit up.

'Yes.' The Doctor held up a finger, as if testing the wind. 'About one-sixth gee, I should think. The same as the Moon.'

Yes, thought Mike. That explained it. The fact that the wings had worked, and had even supported both of them. The soft landing. The fact that he'd almost fallen over trying to stand up.

The fact that they weren't both dead.

Mike tried again to get to his feet, but this time he moved more slowly, giving himself time to feel any imbalance and compensate for it. He made it, but everything seemed wrong, too light. It was as if he'd lost his sense of balance.

The Doctor didn't seem to be having any problems. He pulled a cord on the wings, and they collapsed back into the orange football, which then shrank slowly to the size of a golf ball, making a faint crackling sound as it did so.

'Where did you get the wings from?' asked Mike, wondering if the Doctor always carried a set, just in case he fell out of anything on a low-gravity planet.

'Oh, I picked them up in Oxford Street,' said the Doctor cheerfully. 'July 2108, in the sales.'

'Oxford Street,' said Mike flatly, rather wishing he hadn't asked. 'The July sales. In 2108.'

'Yes.' The Doctor flashed Mike a smile. 'I think they were rather good value myself. They're only rated for one person, and only up to one-eighth gee, too. But obviously there's a margin of error. Just as well, from our –' A pause. 'Now that's interesting.'

Mike took a step forward, cautiously, but this time didn't lose his balance, though it did seem to take a very long time for his leg to come down to the ground again. He saw that the Doctor had picked up a handful of a greyish substance that was clinging to the mud and was examining it with a penlike object. Looking closely, Mike saw the words, 'Xavier Eugéné Microscope "Et Fleur Lavalle . . ." ×3000' in the type of fancy gold script usually reserved for expensive watches. Obviously the Doctor had been busy in the 2108 sales.

'Spores,' he announced after a while. 'Probably fungal in origin, but they could be from the trees.'

Mike nodded, though he didn't see the relevance of the observation. He looked around, assessing the situation for himself. The ridged roots he'd seen from the air were high enough to block vision on the ground: to see any distance he would have to climb one of them. Above, it was hard to see anything clearly, though a patch of bright greenish light presumably indicated the top of the open space they'd fallen through. On the ground, between the roots and only feet from where he was standing, was a muddy pool. In the mud by the side of the pool was a piece of metal.

A piece of metal of a type that Mike recognized.

He bent down and picked it up, handed it to the Doctor. 'A spent cartridge case,' said the Doctor. 'Not an Earth make.'

'Where do you reckon it came from, then?' asked Mike.

'More to the point, Captain Yates, is to ask who fired the bullet? Was it one of the unfortunate chaps we saw by the TARDIS or was it –' He broke off.

'Whoever put them there?' asked Mike after a while.

The Doctor nodded. 'Quite. I think we need to get back to the TARDIS as soon as possible.' He put the microscope away in his pocket, together with the wings, which were now no bigger than a fifty-pence coin. 'I hope that Jo stays inside.'

Mike looked at his shoes, now half buried in the ashy mud, which was also coating his trousers up to the knee and the left sleeve of his green sports jacket. He was reminded of how inappropriately dressed he was for climbing a tree. He even still had the yellow carnation in his buttonhole.

'I'm sorry, Doctor,' he said. 'I don't know whether we can climb that far without equipment. It was several hundred feet, at least.'

'Just over a thousand, actually,' the Doctor replied absently. 'But I shouldn't worry.' He had climbed partway up one of the huge roots, and was staring up to and into the darkened forest. 'These trees all grow into each other. In fact, they're probably just one tree – like banyans on Earth, only rather bigger. We shouldn't have to do much climbing, as such.' He clambered the rest of the way up the root, then grabbed hold of a branch a couple of feet above his head and, without apparent effort, swung himself up on to it. A thin rain of displaced fragments – bark, fungus, dried leaves – fluttered down, very slowly.

Low gravity, Mike realized. The Doctor had evidently had practice in this sort of situation. But it wasn't going to be so easy for him. Slowly, he reached up for the branch, took a cautious grip.

'Well, come on, Captain,' said the Doctor, more than a little impatiently. 'What are you waiting for?'

Jo stared at the scanner until her eyes hurt, but there was no sign of the Doctor or Mike. Only the grisly remains of the corpse stared back at her, now free of the monkey-faced scavengers and covered instead by a writhing mass of insects and white, ropy worms.

She hadn't seen the Doctor and Mike at all since they'd left the TARDIS: certainly they hadn't gone anywhere near the body. And the final scream of the other man, the agony and terror of it, still echoed in her ears.

If only she'd been able to help.

She wondered if she should go outside now and try to find Mike and the Doctor. She could almost hear the Doctor's voice saying, 'No. Stay here, Jo.' And no doubt Mike would have agreed. But Jo was sure that something was the matter. They would have tried to save that man, if they could. She walked to the console, put her hand on the door control, hesitated. The creatures seemed to have gone, but they could be simply out of sight.

She moved her hand to the scanner controls, rotated the camera. As far as she could tell the TARDIS was standing on a crude wooden platform supported by several large branches of a tree. The corpse was on the opposite side of the platform. Beyond, one of the branches sloped upward towards a distant shadow, which Jo assumed was the trunk of the tree. It was massive, perhaps fifty yards across, far bigger than any tree trunk Jo had seen on Earth or anywhere else. Ridges stood out on the bark, and she could see a jumble of dark shapes beyond: other trunks, or perhaps other branches.

Rotating the camera further, she could see that the platform on which the TARDIS stood was fringed with thick, dark foliage on both sides. She couldn't tilt the camera up far enough to see the sky, but she had an idea that it must be at least partly covered by leaves from higher branches, because there were only a few tiny diamonds of sunlight on the scene, shifting a little as leaves moved in the wind.

Then, as she rotated the camera back to the main trunk of the tree, another movement caught her eye. Oddly enough, it wasn't near the point where the branch joined the trunk – that point was above her range of vision through the screen – but at the edge of the part of the trunk she could see. She glanced down at the console, wishing she'd had a chance to get the Doctor to explain in more detail how the scanner controls worked. Surely there had to be some way to zoom in.

The movement was repeated. It was almost as if something, or somebody, were climbing out of a hole in the trunk.

'Mike?' she wondered aloud. 'Doctor?'

It was possible. The distance, the poor light, the distorting effect of the screen, all made it difficult to decide on the size or shape of what she was looking at. It definitely wasn't one of the monkeylike things: their fur had been pale grey.

I've got to find out what's happening, she decided. If it is Mike or the Doctor they could need help – and if it's not it could be something that's going to attack them. She found the door control again, and activated it.

Outside, Jo at once felt curiously light, as if the ground was likely to fall away from under her. Low gravity, she realized. That's how these huge trees are able to support their own weight. She grinned to herself: it was nice to see that the Doctor's habit of thinking about everything as a problem in science had rubbed off to some extent.

It was very hot. She'd kept her jacket on in the TARDIS, not knowing what conditions on Karfel were going to be like. But this place was like a steam bath. Condensation had started to form in the air around her feet as the colder air drifted out of the TARDIS. She shrugged out of her jacket and slung it over her shoulder, then closed the TARDIS door behind her.

As the condensation cleared, Jo saw that she was standing near the edge of the wooden platform – too near for comfort, especially since there was a large hole in the fringe of leaves immediately in front of her. The edges of the hole were ragged and fibrous, as if recently broken. She peered cautiously over the edge, but couldn't see the ground, only a descending gloom of tangled trunks and branches. She moved around the TARDIS until she was standing safely in the middle of the branch, but still within range of the TARDIS door if she needed to make a run for it. The scavenged corpse wasn't far away from her. She winced at the sight, but made herself examine it – although there wasn't much left to see, apart from the insects and the ropelike worms.

No. She looked again. The white things weren't ropelike worms. They were just rope, moving a little as the insect bodies wriggled around it.

The man had been tied up.

She tried to remember if the monkey-faced animals had possessed hands. If not –

She jumped at a loud tapping sound from the direction of the tree trunk. She looked up, saw a small, dark figure, apparently humanoid, walking across the rough surface of the platform towards her. The tapping sound seemed to be caused by its walk, and was unnaturally loud, as if it were wearing hollow clogs.

After a moment she decided it wasn't human. It was too dark, too wide at the chest and shoulders. As it got closer, she could detect a glossy polish on the surface of its body, as if it were made of wood. Its eyes were blue, and had the appearance of crystals or jewels.

A wooden robot?

It was less than fifty yards away now. Jo looked over her shoulder at the TARDIS, judging the distance in case she needed to run. She tried to work out what the Doctor would do in this situation.

Say hello, probably.

'Hello,' she said. 'I'm, umm, looking for my friends . . .'

The wooden figure stopped and bent down. With a shock, Jo noticed that there was a second corpse, also tied up, also crawling with flies, at its feet. She hadn't noticed it against the dark wood. She remembered the second man, the one who'd screamed for help, and shuddered.

The wooden figure pulled at the ropes that bound the corpse for a moment. The insects took off suddenly, with a shockingly loud roar.

'Can you help me?' asked Jo. Her voice sounded weak, wavering. She looked over her shoulder at the TARDIS again.

The wooden figure looked up. Its eyes glittered.

'Can you help me?' it echoed. Its voice sounded hollow and breathy, like a man speaking through a long tube.

Jo took a cautious step forward, then pointed to herself. 'I'm Jo.'

The wooden figure stood up. Its eyes glittered again. Then it too took a step forward.

'Yes,' it said. 'Good. You are Jo.' It pointed to its own chest. 'Can you help me? I am Dead.'

Four

Confessor-Senior Aapurian waited, more because he had nothing else to do than in any real expectation that his visitor would arrive. The weather was surely too bad for the man to have made the voyage up from the ground. The clouds were usually well below the Temple of Iujeemii, but today they were all around it, a grey ice storm rattling against the chiming panes of the windows, sending faint discordant melodies through the rooms and galleries of the building. The wind was powerful enough to set the Temple swaying against the ancient cables that anchored it to the Sky, and the deep bass groan of the wooden walls flexing added itself to the music of the ice. Again and again, Aapurian let his eyes trace the grey-green slivers of light that danced in the water of the Community Pool below his high perch. In following the light there is peace, he told himself. In following the light we bring harmony to ourselves and thus to all things.

But he didn't really believe that any more. He was fairly sure he hadn't even believed it when he had been a man.

He stretched his wings, felt the cold seep into the old, creaking joints. He'd heard the talk in the corridors and flyways of the Temple, the hushed saddened tones of the younger naieen: 'I hear he can barely fly any more'; 'They say his stomach is so weak he can only eat soup'. Sound carried a long way in the Temple. Aapurian often felt like snapping back – as another oldster was said to have done before him – 'Yes, and I hear he's growing very deaf as well.' But he felt that such a riposte would be beneath his dignity. Besides, he wasn't as feeble as the others thought. He could still fly against the wind, if he put a mind to it. But he thought it best to conceal some of his remaining strength, in order that he should be under-estimated when the time came.

The time was very near now. The End, as the Flight called it. The Judgement of the Company Beyond the Sky. Aapurian wasn't so sure about the theology of it, but there was a core of truth in the old legends. Either the darkness would win or the light – or, as the Flight put it, either men or naieen.

Except that it wasn't so simple. Nothing was ever simple. There were good men, men who still did the bidding of the Sky. But more and more of them followed Epreto, the ways of steam and false power. And, at another level of truth, even that wasn't quite accurate: not everything Epreto did was bad. Nor were his motives bad. And then there were the Dead. Nobody understood them at all, though the philosopher Xaaleeni had claimed that –

A sound recalled Aapurian's wandering mind: the distant groan and rumble of the temple's groundward door opening. He felt the air stirring around him. At once he let go of his perch and let himself glide slowly to the ground. The chill air slid under his body wrap as he flew, making him shiver. His landing was barely controlled, and the impact on the hard tiles jarred the joints of his legs painfully.

He shuffled towards the archway that led from the rest room to the main gallery. Here, everything was noise and movement. In the air around the wooden catwalk where Aapurian was standing, young naieen performed acrobatic manoeuvres, gliding, swooping from the bright mosaics of the roof to the long windows in the floor, all the while talking and laughing. Small dirigible stalls were tethered to the wooden rails that ran the length of the room's carved walls. Merchants, both men and naieen, sold bright metals, dried spices, glass pots and other Land-made wares. At the far end of the gallery, perhaps a quarter of a mile away, mist billowed through the open groundward doors. Aapurian could already see the steamwing hauling itself inside with long, creaking strokes of its mechanical wings, breathing steam from its iron snout. It was a loathsome perversion, he thought, like an Unpromoted naieen, if such a thing could be. He wondered why the Flight had ever let such things into the temple.

Because they are weak, he thought. Because they are old souls, waiting to die. Because they don't care any more.

But of course none of that was exactly true either. Everything was a half-truth, a grey shadow, an absence of light that was nonetheless not quite dark.

Now who had said that?

Aapurian waited, leaning against the rail of the catwalk, trying to remember the ancient philosopher's name, until the doors were shut and the huge machine had settled itself on the specially braced landing platform at the far end of the gallery. He saw the small bipedal figures emerge from the cabin, saw the characteristic blue coat flapping amongst them, the head of golden hair.

Yes. Karilee was here.

Aapurian took a few more steps in the direction of the craft, then saw that Karilee had already caught sight of him and was shouting something from the far end of the catwalk. Aapurian stopped again, and waited, watching Karilee's figure grow steadily as he jogged along the catwalk. Best to appear weak, even in front of your friends. Perhaps especially in front of your friends, when those friends were men.

Karilee trotted up and greeted Aapurian with a man-style hug. 'Aapurian! You old wonder – it's a pleasure to see you looking so well!'

'I pass,' said Aapurian with a smile. 'It's a pleasure to see you at all. I'd thought the storm would have stopped you flying up.'

Karilee laughed. 'Nothing stops one of Epreto's steam boats. The old devil has his uses, you know.' The man looked around him, perhaps checking for spies, then went on more quietly. 'You say the Flight are ready to authorize my research?'

'Possibly,' said Aapurian. 'There are questions of course.' It was a lie, as everything seemed to be, now that the end was so near. The Flight had heard nothing of Karilee's research, because Aapurian hadn't told them. And they never would hear of it, because it would never happen.

But Karilee nodded eagerly, obviously believing it. The movement of his head was gross and ungraceful by naieen standards.

Aapurian leant forward, feeling the bones of his back creak. He spoke quietly. 'They want to know what the purpose of the research is.'

Karilee frowned, then launched into a speech that sounded as automatic as one of Epreto's steam-powered machines. 'To provide an extract of the heartmeat that facilitates Promotion. To circumvent the awful waste and unfairness of the fights, for those who feel –'

'I know all that,' interrupted Aapurian softly. 'And so do the Flight. It's the moral purpose we wish to under-stand.'

Karilee seemed to think for a moment. Behind him, one of the merchants' dirigibles had come loose from its moorings and was drifting across the gallery, trailing ropes and spilling brightly coloured flowers. People were shouting.

'To give people a choice,' said Karilee eventually, raising his voice over the hubbub. 'Becoming naieen or Dead will no longer depend on chance, on our bodies, on our luck and fortune in life. Surely that's better than fighting to the death for the privilege of wings?'

'It isn't the natural way.'

'It is an *improvement*.'

'Like Epreto's "improvements"?' Aapurian gestured at the steamwing.

Karilee didn't fall into the trap. 'Like those, yes, but without the side effects. Without the smoke, the poison, the depletion of the Land. This is a purely beneficial change.'

47

'You can argue the case for that if the research is successful,' said Aapurian quietly. 'In the meantime, you may carry out the research without interference from us.' He let the relief form on the man's face before adding, 'But there is a condition. We have a commission for you.'

Karilee laughed. 'You mean another one of your little spying missions? Who do you want watched this time? Some fringeland priest who might be having treasonable thoughts of becoming a hermit?'

Aapurian raised a wing to silence his friend. 'We should go to my room,' he said, gesturing behind them where the merchant's stall was still drifting in mid-gallery, now attended by a disordered flock of naieen trying to push it back into place. It wouldn't be long before agents of the Flight turned up. And perhaps others, even less desirable.

Karilee glanced at the scene, sobered at once, nodded. He picked Aapurian up, carried him easily back along the catwalk, past the Community Pool, and through the brick archway that led to the living quarters. Twice Karilee had to ask Aapurian which way to turn in the labyrinth of plain brick walls beyond, even though he had made the journey several times before. By the time they arrived at his room, Aapurian was a little dizzy and more than a little sick, and his belly hurt where the young man's strong arms were holding it. Still, it had been easier than walking or flying.

The room was small, with a single, round floor-window of petalled glass. To Aapurian's surprise, a line of bright sunlight was shining up through the window, making an ellipse in patchwork colours, low on the tapestried walls. When Karilee put him down, he shuffled over to the window and opened it. Meltwater from the cloud's bullets of ice still dripped from the frame, and he could hear it chattering from the gutters, but the storm was past. Through the marvellous clarity of the rain-washed air below, he could see all the way to the ground: the city of Kaygat gleaming in the sun, the newly developed factories of Neef Island, the glittering water in between, all of it seeming beautiful from the height of the temple, as if it were a dream.

Which it was, of course. Epreto's dream. The power of steam, the noise of machinery, the perfect, ordered world of logic and reason. And, just like the factories, that dream looked beautiful from far enough away, in the right sort of light, but get close and all you could hear were the grinding of gears, the hissing of steam, the breaking of souls to a pattern alien to their nature.

'This commission, then,' said Karilee suddenly from behind Aapurian. There was the clink of glass as the young man poured himself a drink of water from the condenser. 'You don't want the Flight to hear about it.'

Aapurian felt a stab of worry as he realized that Karilee had seen through his deception, then decided it didn't matter. Obviously Karilee was assuming that Aapurian alone could authorize his research. Feeling a renewed sense of guilt, Aapurian said nothing for a while, just stared at Epreto's beautiful city, at the world from far above, the world as a dream. He wondered if his own dreams, his own deceptions, were really any different from Epreto's.

Slowly, the world below disappeared behind a new white barrier of cloud. Aapurian shut the window, cutting off the draught that suddenly seemed chill.

'Confessor?' said Karilee. His voice was tight, and Aapurian realized how afraid the man was. He knew that he was being deceived, but he didn't know by how much or why.

'It's not the Flight,' said Aapurian, calculating the lie carefully, so that it contained a proportion of truth. 'There are men who have spies, as well as naieen.'

'Who?' Karilee didn't sound surprised. Aapurian himself was constantly surprised by the new boldness of men, their open opposition to the power of the Flight; but to Karilee it was just a fact, a fact that he lived with. Like steam power.

'Juliu Epreto,' he said.

Karilee's glass clinked. 'Yes. I've had cause to approach him in the course of my researches. I wouldn't be surprised if he has spies, even here.'

'Epreto has gone to the childlands with some companions,' said Aapurian. 'I have reason to believe he is trying to contact the Dead. We think he has ambitions.'

'If he has, I doubt that anything you can do can stop them. He has steam engines. You can't deny the power of steam, Confessor.'

Aapurian sighed again. Even Karilee didn't understand. None of the men did. He supposed he wouldn't have done, had he been a man – short-lived and childish – in this time of change.

He turned and met the man's eyes, then hesitated, aware of how strange what he was going to say would seem to Karilee. Educated and intelligent though the man was, he did not know the secrets of the naieen. Aapurian looked out of the window again, at the white mist where a moment ago there had been a view of Epreto's golden island, and wondered whether he could risk telling him.

He would have to, he decided. There was no other way. Whatever other lies he had been told, Karilee had to know this much of the truth.

He turned back to the man and said slowly, 'We think that Epreto plans to move the sun.'

'I can't do it,' said Jo.

'Please. You must. The bodies must be returned to the ground soon, or they will be lost.' The wooden figure's face was twisted into a strange grimace, which might have been intended to be pleading, but only frightened Jo even more. She looked at the corpses, at the heaving mass of flies, the glimpses of blood and internal organs beneath.

'I can't promise you any reward, but the Land will be grateful,' said the figure.

'The Land . . .?'

The strange crystal eyes looked into hers. 'You don't understand, do you? Are you from . . . another Land?'

50

The eyes were glittering with internal light: Jo wondered if the thing was trying to read her mind.

'I'm from Earth,' she said.

The eyes glittered some more, then suddenly went dark.

'Then let me explain. On this world the bodies of the dead must be buried in order to safeguard their lives. Does that make sense?'

Jo shook her head. 'No.' Then she thought about it for a moment, remembered the importance many people still attached to a 'decent Christian burial', and quickly added, 'But we have similar customs.'

The eyes of the figure glittered again. 'In our case this must happen quickly, or else the essence of being is lost. I was sent to release these two, but my hands . . .' It stretched the fingers, and Jo could see that, whatever they were made of, they weren't mobile enough to undo knots. 'Please.'

Jo looked at the bodies again. Suddenly she remembered Catriona Talliser, the reporter she'd met in Kebiria. She remembered her saying that courage was doing things when you were afraid, because you knew that they had to be done. She remembered Catriona sacrificing her life so that she, Jo, could get away, and wondered how afraid Catriona had been then.

So. She was going to do it. Now.

She stepped forward to the first corpse. The flies, which had returned to the feast whilst they had been talking, burst into the air, the sound so loud that Jo jumped back in shock. But she made herself go on, made herself kneel down by the grisly mess and undo the bloodstained knots.

The wooden creature that had called itself Dead looked on. When she'd finished, it stepped forward and gently lifted the remains over the side of the branch. It didn't say a word, just let the body drop.

'Is that all?' asked Jo.

'The Land will prepare a place for the body. Please help with the second man.'

Jo nodded, moved to the second corpse. This one was more intact: his face was whole, with glossy black hair and a short beard. His eyes were open, bulging from their sockets, his features contorted in terror. Again, she made herself untie the knots. When the last one was done, her body began to shake. She turned away, trembling, staring out through the gloom to the distant pillars of the other trees, now dimly visible through the haze.

'You're sure you haven't seen my friends?' she said after a while.

'The Land hasn't touched them. They may have been taken by the Sky.'

Jo turned round, aware that there were tears in her eyes. Aware that she was frightened and angry. Aware that she'd gone out on a blind date and ended up alone on an alien and incomprehensible world. Again. Would this sort of thing ever stop?

'I don't know what you're talking about,' she said to the alien. 'Can you help me look for them? Please?'

To her surprise, the figure advanced and took her hands, a gesture that immediately reminded her of the Doctor. Its hands were unexpectedly warm, and slippery, the substance more like wet clay than wood.

'I was a man once,' it said. 'I remember it well. It is so difficult to be alone.'

Jo just stared.

'I will be your friend, for the time being. Call me Jobanu: that was my name as a man.'

'But you're not a man now?' asked Jo.

The wood-coloured face twisted into something that might have been a smile.

'Of course not. But you can trust me. Come with me, and I will help you find your friends.' Jobanu let go of her hands and began walking slowly up the branch.

Jo hesitated, then set off after him.

Climbing in the forest wasn't as easy as the Doctor had said it would be. The branches and trunks were all slippery, and Mike fell over more times than he could count. The low gravity made it easier to control the falls and avoid injury, but even so his left ankle was hurting, he'd cut his hand on the razor edge of a trailing vine, and his jacket was ruined, the material plastered in mud, moss and the grey spores.

There goes another ten guineas, he thought, looking at the mess. I really ought to ask the Brig for a pay rise.

The Doctor was well ahead of him. He was walking lightly up a forty-five-degree slope in the near darkness as if he knew exactly what he was doing, but Mike was beginning to doubt that this was really the case. On every side, all he could see were more of the rambling, intertwined branches, covered in the ropelike vines and sharp-leafed epiphytes, everything dripping water. In every hollow in the wood, pools of water accumulated, covered in greyish froth.

It had been getting darker for some time.

'Doctor,' he called. 'Are you sure we can get back to the clearing from here?'

'Of course,' said the Doctor, holding up something with a flashing green light on it. 'We've had to make a few diversions, but the locator here will find the TAR-DIS wherever –' He broke off suddenly, raised a hand. 'Listen.'

Mike listened. After a while he heard it. A steady thudding noise, accompanied by a rhythmic hiss. Metallic creaks and groans. He looked around, but couldn't see anything moving. But then he couldn't see more than fifty feet in any direction.

The sounds got louder.

The Doctor was suddenly running back the way they came, jumping from branch to branch in a strange, slow-motion way that was almost, but not quite, like an action sequence in a movie. Mike followed as well as he could. He saw a patch of brighter light ahead, then realized that they were approaching a clearing – no, a wooden plat-form, surrounded by thick trunks and roofed with thin branches and blue sky.

The Doctor was standing on a projecting branch, waving his arms as if signalling to someone.

'Doctor, are you sure about this?' yelled Mike. The last thing they needed was to get mixed up with the locals. They needed to get back to the TARDIS, make sure Jo was all right, then get the hell out of here.

But the Doctor only went on waving. Mike caught up with him, saw through the fine branches of the forest canopy a thing that looked like a huge beetle made of wood and brass, with a pointed head and several sets of wheels. It was flying, long canvas wings slowly rising and falling on either side of it, the boiler jetting steam. As Mike watched, it stopped climbing and started back down towards them.

'A flying steam engine!'

'Yes, of course,' said the Doctor, beaming brightly.

The steam engine fell through the canopy, its huge body clattering against the thin branches. As Mike watched, the wings folded inwards and upwards and the body lurched clumsily to a bumpy landing on the platform. He wondered why it didn't fall through the flimsy-looking wood, then saw the gaudy balloon floating above the machine, attached by a thick rope. Presumably that was taking some of the weight.

There was a loud thud from the machine, then the sound of a manual winch. Mike looked down, saw that a wooden platform was being lowered from the side. When it was fully extended, three men stepped out. Two of them were dressed in rough clothes of stitched leather, like American frontiersmen. The third was a tall, striking person with a bushy head of black hair and a long, carefully trimmed beard, in which were mounted several large golden rings. He was wearing an elaborate jacket in white and green that almost seemed like a uniform. He stared at Mike, and then the Doctor, with deep-set black eyes, then nodded to himself. All three held weapons, long-barrelled guns that looked similar to hunting rifles. They weren't pointing them at Mike or at the Doctor, but their expressions told him that they wouldn't hesitate to do so if they felt it had become necessary.

The Doctor took a couple of steps towards them, so

that he was standing right on the tip of the branch, and smiled broadly. 'A very good day to you. I'm so glad you stopped. My companion and I have inadvertently become separated from our vehicle, I'm afraid. I wonder if you could possibly give us a lift.'

The two shorter men each gave a glance at the third, which confirmed Mike's impression that he was their leader. He in turn gave a curious glance at the Doctor, then after a moment he spoke quietly.

'Certainly. We will be pleased to help in any way we can. My name is Juliu Epreto.'

The Doctor extended a hand. 'I'm the Doctor, and this is Captain Mike Yates.'

'Captain?' Again the curious expression. 'Yes. I see.' A pause. 'Where did you leave your vehicle?'

The Doctor was looking around as Epreto spoke, a puzzled expression on his face. 'Well, actually, I rather thought we'd left it here. You haven't seen it by any chance? Or is there another platform very like this in the forest?'

'This is the only landing platform. And it belongs to me. I very much regret it, but, if you landed your vehicle here, it has probably been confiscated.'

'Confiscated? Well, I'll have to ask you to give it back, then. Sorry for the inconvenience and all that –'

'I fear that you don't understand me,' said Epreto. 'It will have been taken, not by me, but by the Dead.' He shook his head, looking from one to the other of them. 'And I regret to say that nothing ever comes back from the Dead.'

Jo was getting worried. The forest was dark, and it appeared to be endless. She had no idea where she was. Did Jobanu really think the Doctor and Mike had gone this way? She'd asked him, several times, but all he would say was that he was taking her to a place where everything that happened in the forest was 'known'. He hadn't explained how this was done, and Jo was finding it increasingly hard to believe that such a place existed.

There was no sign of a village or anything like that. There weren't even any clearings as such. The tangle of branches, vines and foliage just seemed to go on forever. They had skirted the main trunks of the trees, instead clambering along the wide surfaces of the branches, sometimes sloping up, sometimes down again. But Jo had the impression that, overall, they were descending. Not only was it getting darker, it was getting wetter, every branch covered in trickling water and slime. Jo was getting steadily more tired: several times she'd lost her balance and only been prevented from falling by Jobanu, who for all his apparent robotic clumsiness could move surprisingly fast when he wanted to.

'We are almost there,' he said suddenly. He was standing several yards ahead, up to his knees in the water of a pool trapped in a wide, low branch. The pool was covered in grey froth. 'You should stay very close to me now.'

Jo caught up with him, but skirted the pool.

Jobanu went on. Jo noticed brightly coloured leechlike things clinging to his legs where they had been under the water, but he didn't seem to notice. Ahead was a grey tree trunk, so massive it seemed almost like a wall. Jobanu walked up to it, then abruptly turned and leant back against the bark. He gestured for her to do the same.

'What do we do now?' she asked.

'We wait.'

'What for?'

'The forest.'

'That doesn't make any sense.'

'You will understand soon.'

'How?' asked Jo. But, as soon as she sat down, she realized that it didn't really matter. She needed a rest, whatever was going on. And there was something comforting about this place, about leaning against the living wood, low in the darkness of the forest. The bark was soft and spongy, almost warm, like the wood-clay body of her new friend. The heat, which had seemed oppressive when she was moving, now seemed relaxing. She felt the

56

muscles in her legs, in her back, in her neck, slowly loosen, felt the easy circulation of blood through them. She became aware of sounds: the slight creaking of the wood behind her, a grumbling sound like water running in a pipe, a faint hollow booming. A sort of mist was forming over the forest, a brown blanket that she could almost touch.

'This is so peaceful,' she said.

Jobanu didn't reply. Jo turned to look at him, but he wasn't there.

Funny. She would have heard him move away, wouldn't she? She tried to lean forward, so that she could see more, but found she couldn't. A gelatinous blanket had formed in front of her. She struggled against it, but it had glued itself to her arms, her legs, her body, her face.

'Help!' she shouted. 'Jobanu! Help!' But her voice sounded muffled, far away from her ears, as if she were standing outside her own body. She felt, too, as if she were only going through the motions of panic and protest: her body still felt easy, warm, infinitely relaxed. The light from outside had almost faded away now, and Jo couldn't move at all. She tried to call for help again but her lips wouldn't move. She felt as if she were falling, sinking through the tree into the roots of the world. Which was all right, she suddenly realized. There wasn't anything to be afraid of. She would understand everything soon.

The forest had come to her, as Jobanu had promised it would.

Five

There was a Promotion going on in the factory, in the main hall between the weaving machines. Aaviar Omonu looked out through the leaded windows of his office at the two heavy, big-muscled men, who were already circling each other slowly, bare-chested, fists clenched. Around them a crowd of hands and hustlers shouted, cursed, jeered, the noise clearly audible through the thick glass.

Most of the machinery was shut down, though the steam engine that powered it was still turning, wheels creaking and pistons thudding, clouds of steam venting from the seals in the chimney. Light from the windows made solid bars of silver through the vapour. The priest was there in his wooden box, taking bets through the grille. Two naieen were perched on the iron arch at the entrance to the hall, silhouetted against the daylight, watching.

Waiting.

Omonu too watched, with all the fascination of utter terror. He had always been weak, easily tired, his bones light. In a Promotion he would have no chance of winning – unless he fought a cripple. And he couldn't quite bring himself to the dishonour of doing that.

He watched the two men snarling at each other, the crowd cheering. Yes, he thought, I will die this way. I will stand there, all too soon. Some stranger – or some friend – will rip my heart out and eat it.

He raised his hand, superimposing it on the scene through the window, feeling the bulging muscles of his arm. But there was not enough muscle. He knew it wasn't enough.

Again he felt the raw rush of panic. He had an absurd impulse to hurry out to the main hall and try to put a stop to the fight. But he knew that it was impossible. These men wanted to fight: their Holy Biology dictated that they should fight. Even Epreto would have admitted the truth of this, and would not have tried to stop them had he been here. His plans were of a longer kind than that.

Too long, thought Omonu, looking again at his arm, at the muscles almost visibly swelling under the shirt.

Suddenly, there was a snarl from the hall. One of the two circling fighters dived at the other, hands extended like claws. He made contact, but the other slipped away. Omonu stared with a sick fascination for another moment, his heart hammering, then turned away from the window and hurried across the shadowy space of his office. He had to go away from here. He had to get out of sight and sound of this fight. Every stimulation, every sight or sound or smell of violence, shortened the time remaining to him now. He took his green factory manager's coat with its gold buttons and pushed it on. His right arm became stuck in the sleeve, and though he heaved and turned he couldn't get it through. He began to panic, his heart speeding, his muscles tightening.

As if for the fight.

Near to screaming aloud, Omonu threw the coat on to the floor and walked out on to the gallery in his under-jacket. He could hear the animal breathing of the two men now, carrying to his ears somehow over the noise of the crowd and the big steam engine. He twisted his head away and hurried up the steps, almost running. There were shouts from below, but he ignored them.

There was only one place where he would be safe from the fight: Duboli's office. The factory treasurer had no need to oversee the operations directly, and Epreto had given him an office high in the factory tower, braced against the chimneys, so that he could see the sun.

The climb was a long one, partly outside, and the effort of it took some of the panic out of Omonu's body. There was a storm building, a great hammerhead of cloud drifting in over the water beyond Neef Island, hiding the Sky around the Temple of Iujeemii. Lightning flickered below the cloud inside dark curtains of rain. Omonu stared at it for a moment. He could remember times when such storms had been rare: now they seemed to happen almost every day. He wondered if it was true what Epreto said: that the other, frozen, Lands were jealous of their own and were sending the storms and earthquakes to destroy it and everything that lived there. That there would one day be a War of the Continents, and that their own Land might not be the winner.

Omonu realized that it really didn't matter to him. He had more immediate concerns.

The fire in his belly. The desire to fight – not now, maybe, but someday soon. Omonu could try to deny it, but he knew it was there.

The door to Duboli's office was open, but the man wasn't behind his desk. Omonu hesitated, staring at the streaks of sunlight across the mottled wood and wondering if he should just wait outside. But the wind was already beginning to lift with the approach of the storm. It would be easy to be swept off the narrow stair and die in the uncontrolled fall that would result. He went in.

'Sir?' he asked, just in case Duboli was in the shadows, invisible to his sun-dazzled eyes. But there was no response. Omonu walked to the window behind Duboli's desk, wishing that there was someone here to talk to. Anyone would suffice, even the dusty, money-minded treasurer.

A sound from behind him made him jump round, every muscle tense once more. It was a noise like that made by the weaving machines in the factory, but much quieter and clearer. It seemed to be coming from a white box on Duboli's desk, an object that Omonu had noticed before but never really thought about.

Now he could see a tiny lamp flickering on the white surface. He stared at it, wondering if the machine was somehow keeping watch, if it had seen him come in and was now trying to signal to Duboli. He'd heard that Epreto had found such devices in his travels to the other Lands.

60

There was a faint crackling sound, and a piece of paper began to emerge from the device. The paper seemed unnaturally smooth and glossy, and was inked in odd, old-fashioned formal-hand characters, the sort you might see in a naieen proclamation. For a moment Omonu found them impossible to read, then, slowly, the message made sense to him.

Duboli – I have found two men from another Land. They are different – weaker than us, but more mindful. They may know of the powers of the sun. I believe they can help us, so prepare accommodations. All else goes as planned – Epreto.

Omonu stared, frowning. What did it mean? Two men from another Land? But weren't all the other Lands long dead? And how could men be 'different'? Surely they were men, or they were Dead, or they were not-men, such as the naieen?

The War of the Continents, thought Omonu suddenly. That's the answer. It's real. And this is the evidence for it.

He backed away from the piece of paper, almost hoping that it wasn't real. But it remained, glossy and solid, on Duboli's desk beside the strange device that had produced it.

Rain pattered on the shadowside window, and Omonu looked up at the black cloud that now filled the Sky. The sun was still shining behind him, and, as he watched, a rainbow began to form across the darkness of the cloud. Omonu watched it for a while, then saw Duboli pass in front of it. He hastily shuffled around the desk, sat down in the visitor's chair.

Duboli came in. He was a small man, hardly out of childhood, with the bright clothing and slightly arrogant air of one whose talents have allowed him to be promoted beyond his worth in years.

'Curse that Kayolo!' he snapped, shaking water from his hat and stamping it from his boots. 'I put a gold coin – one whole coin! – on the man, and he lost almost at once. I'd half a mind to burn his body and deny him to the Dead!'

61

Duboli's gambling habits were well known around the factory. Omonu managed a weak smile. 'Ill fortune, Mr Duboli.' He hesitated. 'There is a message on your desk from Mr Epreto. It came from the machine while I was waiting for you.'

'Epreto? The machine? But he said he wouldn't send –' Duboli stepped forward, dripping water over Omonu's silk underjacket as he picked up the shiny paper. He looked at the message, then at Omonu. 'Did you read this?'

Omonu felt his face colouring. 'I didn't intend any impropriety, but I couldn't help but notice –'

Duboli slowly, carefully, ripped the message to pieces, then put the pieces in a small tray on his desk. He set light to them with a lamplighter, then watched until they'd burnt to ash.

Then he pointed at the ash. 'Don't tell anyone what you have read, Mr Omonu. Or we may have to do this to you. Understand?'

Omonu stared, swallowed. 'Of course, sir.' But, in fact, he didn't understand at all. The threat seemed greatly in excess of necessity. Like the paper itself, it seemed almost unreal.

'Now, why have you come to see me?' asked Duboli briskly.

'The receipts – there was an imbalance.' It was true, but then it was usually true. A few coins always seemed to go astray. Duboli nonetheless seemed happy with the excuse, and they discussed the figures for a few moments with no further mention of the curious mechanical message. But later, when Omonu retreated down the rain-puddled steps to the main hall and his own office, when he saw the men at their work and the priest quietly cleaning the bloodstains from the floor, he thought about the message again. About something he hadn't fully absorbed at first: the way Epreto had described the men he had found.

'They are different – weaker than us . . .'

And Epreto was bringing them here. He had asked Duboli to prepare accommodation.

Perhaps they would be ready to fight. If they were weaker than men of this Land, but not actually crippled, then Omonu might stand a chance. More than a chance: he might win.

Omonu shook his head. The idea was madness. How would he get to the strangers if they were in Epreto's care? What if something went wrong? But the phrase wouldn't leave Omonu's head. *They are weaker than us.* It was like a nail, being driven through his skull by the hammer of his desperation.

And there is a War between the Continents, he thought. So I could kill one of them. It would help in the War. Epreto would forgive me for it.

He might even thank me.

For the first time in many weeks, Omonu felt something like hope.

The cabin of the steamwing was dark, hot and humid, and it stank of smoke and sweat. There was no furniture, only a brass rail around the walls and leather straps hanging from the low ceiling. The walls were made of wood panelling with wide ribs of brass, and they boomed with the rhythm of the steam engine, underneath which Mike could just hear the faint counterpoint groan of the wings. Epreto's two companions were leaning against the wall, their rifles still casually held in their hands, not quite pointing at Mike and the Doctor. Epreto had introduced them as Jitil and Hanu, and called them his assistants, but to Mike they looked more like guards. Epreto himself had disappeared through a wood-panelled door at the front of the cabin shortly after they'd left and hadn't yet returned.

The Doctor was next to Mike at the cabin's single porthole, his face pressed close to the thick glass, peering down. Every so often, he looked at the locating device in his hand and gave it a shake, but nothing happened. No green light. The TARDIS had well and truly vanished, and Jo with it.

Mike was beginning to wish he'd obeyed standing orders and told the Brigadier where they were going. Not that it would have done any good, since as far as he could make out they weren't in the right place – not even on the right planet – and if they had been the Brig would have had no way of reaching them. But it would have made Mike feel better to know that he would probably try.

'What happens if we can't find the TARDIS?' he asked the Doctor. 'Is there any other way of getting back?'

'Oh, we'll find her all right. The old girl rarely goes missing for long. It's Jo I'm worried about.'

'Surely she can't come to any harm inside the TARDIS?'

The Doctor fixed Mike with a direct stare. 'Always assuming she stayed there.'

They looked at each other. Mike began to realize that he'd made a number of bad judgements this evening, which had already cost one life – and now they might have cost Jo's. Until now he'd always thought of the Doctor's adventures in the TARDIS as a sort of joke, a distraction from the real business of UNIT HQ.

Now, too late, he realized that they were just as real, just as dangerous.

'You know, I think this place could be artificial,' said the Doctor suddenly. He was squinting up through the small porthole, sunlight on his face.

Mike looked at him. 'What? The whole planet? But that's impossible!'

'My dear Captain Yates, lots of people build planets. And the only way that the gravity could be so low is if the sky is solid, to keep the atmosphere in. I thought I saw a building of some sort up there, but it's hard to tell through this haze. Unless they're using a force field, in which case it would be one of the anchor stations.' He appeared to think for a moment. 'But that wouldn't explain the sun. The angle of elevation has altered considerably since we first travelled out of the forest. That implies that the sun isn't far above the cloud tops – which means it isn't a sun at all. It has to be artificial.'

'It's the sun,' said Jitil suddenly from the other side of the cabin. 'It lights up the Land. That's all we need to know about it.'

The Doctor ignored him. 'It could be light from a real sun, of course — diverted by a system of mirrors. Or it could be a local light source.' He turned to Jitil. 'Tell me, does this sun of yours grow dim at night, but remain visible, or does it just switch off?'

'It fades away and dies. What else would it do?'

Hanu spoke up. 'If you could see it at night, it wouldn't be the sun, would it?'

'Hmm. Yes.' The Doctor resumed squinting out of the window. 'Now if I had the spectroscope from the TARDIS . . .' He trailed off and shook his head.

Jitil got up and without a word of explanation left the room. Mike heard his footsteps retreating up what sounded like a metal stairway. He glanced at the Doctor, got up to follow the man; but Hanu made a gesture with the gun, slipped his finger over the trigger.

Mike sat down again, angry and confused. Why couldn't the Doctor have kept his mouth shut? They hadn't been doing too badly until he had started babbling about the sun.

He waited. Nothing happened. The Doctor continued to stare out of the porthole, occasionally muttering what sounded like trigonometric measurements. Mike glanced at his watch: ten o'clock. It occurred to him that he was hungry. Once, in another world, he had been about to go out for a meal. His stomach still remembered that, whatever had happened since. He wondered how long it would be before Epreto got around to giving them something to eat. There didn't seem to be any eating facilities on the steamwing, so presumably it would have to wait until they got to wherever it was they were going.

At last the door opened and Epreto appeared, his huge body filling the frame. 'Where are you from, that you don't know about the sun and talk about building the Sky?' he asked, without any attempt at preamble. 'Are you from another Land?'

The Doctor turned to face Epreto. 'You could say that.'

'Earth,' said Mike at the same time, then immediately wished he hadn't.

'Earth? Which Land is that?'

'It's very far away,' said the Doctor.

'Then you admit you are Dead.'

'I'm sorry, but I really don't see how that follows.'

A pause. 'No, I suppose it doesn't.' Another pause. 'Tell me, does the sun in your Land live? Does it shine?' Mike noticed that Epreto's voice was trembling with excitement. The man's eyes were fixed on the Doctor.

'Of course it does. It shines constantly, but it moves. That's why I was so curious about yours which appears not to move.'

Epreto stepped inside the cabin, gestured to Hanu. 'Leave us, please, Mr Hanu.'

The man obeyed. Mike heard his footsteps retreating up the wooden stairway outside. Epreto waited until they had faded away, then shut the door carefully.

'If you are telling the truth,' he said quietly, 'this will be extremely important to me. Where is your Land? How can I navigate to reach it?'

'The navigational instruments on the TARDIS aren't fully calibrated yet, you understand. I really can't tell you.'

Epreto frowned. 'So how does this . . . TARDIS travel?'

The Doctor shook his head. 'I could explain, but you wouldn't understand. Suffice to say she doesn't use steam power.'

'Something more advanced?' Epreto left the question open, clearly expecting an explanation.

He was sharp, thought Mike. You had to grant him that. And it was the first time he'd seen the Doctor put in the position of having to answer all the questions.

'The TARDIS utilizes the power of space–time itself.'

Mike could see that the Doctor expected that statement to be the end of the discussion: but Epreto wasn't letting go.

'How far can you travel?'

'Oh, a very long way. Tell me, how fast can this steam-wing of yours travel?'

66

'Thirty miles per hour in a good wind. But it's your machine I'm interested in. I need an answer. How far can you travel, Doctor?' The last words were spoken with a cold emphasis that reminded Mike rather too much of the Master. Whatever Epreto was so excited about, it didn't seem as though it was going to be good news.

The Doctor seemed oblivious of all this. 'Well, anywhere in the Universe, really,' he said easily. 'If I can get the navigational systems sorted out.'

Epreto appeared to consider this.

'Then your Land – it is above the Sky?'

The Doctor nodded.

Epreto smiled. 'I need to travel above the Sky. We will be able to work together.'

The Doctor stroked his chin. 'Perhaps.'

The cold emphasis returned to Epreto's voice. 'You are my guest, Doctor. It is customary here for guests to offer some trade to their hosts in return for their hospitality. I say this only to advise you, in case the custom may be different in your Land.' He turned and left, closing the door behind him. After a moment, Jitil and Hanu returned and resumed their station against the wall of the cabin.

This time the guns were openly trained on Mike and the Doctor.

'Looks like we're prisoners, Doctor,' muttered Mike.

The Doctor was looking out of the window. 'Oh, I shouldn't worry about it,' he said. 'Happens all the time. You'll get used to it after a while.'

– soft –
  – soft dark –
  – soft dark warm –
  – soft dark warm comforting –
  – softwarmcomfortdarknesssoftwarmcomfortdarknesssoftwarm-
comfortdarkness –
I am Dead.
  – yes –
I am Jo.

67

— yes —
I am Dead. And I'm alive.
— yes —
That doesn't make any sense.
— you will remain alive —
— should be alive —
— until you choose to be Dead —
You want —
— yes —
— something —
— there is something —
— something I can give you, that's why you want to talk to me —
— there is a person —
— a person who is known to you —
— a traveller from another Land —
— the one who knows the most —
The Doctor!
— the Doctor will know —
— you must bring him —
— we need him —
— need him to tell us —
Tell you? What do you want him to tell you?
— bring him —
— bring him and we will find —
— find out what he knows —
But I can't do that. He won't just agree, you know —
— you know the Doctor —
— you will be made alive again —
— then he will not know —
I don't want to be alive. It's nicer being Dead. And I don't want to betray the Doctor
— then you will bring him because you want to be Dead —
— because it is nicer to be Dead —
— because you want him to be Dead —
— because the Doctor is your friend and you cannot betray him —
— for this reason you will bring him —
— when you bring him —

68

– you will choose to be Dead –
– he will choose to be Dead –
– you will both know softwarmcomfortdarkness –
And I'll have done something for him, I'll have –
– when you join with us –
– he will tell us what he knows –
– he will give us the knowledge we need –

I've done something for the Doctor at last. I'll have given him something back for all the things he's done for me.

– you will have done more for your friend than you could ever have done on your own –

Thank you. Yes. I will bring him to you –

– we will join him to the Dead –

– and he'll understand why I did it. He'll even thank me for it, when he sees how nice it is.

Won't you, Doctor?

Six

Xaai was not one of those permitted to fly. That was what they told her.

Sometimes her cage swayed in the darkness, and Xaai felt the wind across the skin of her wings. Then she wanted to fly. She yearned for the freedom to soar, to glide. Her wings would stretch out – but she would only feel the iron bars of the cage, rough metal scraping against the skin like a cold poison. She would scream then, frustration and fear and anger tearing at her throat until it was raw. Sometimes a guard would come, a wing-less slave-man with thick, ugly arms and pillar-like legs, wearing dull blue cloth around his body. She could see the jumping flame of his hand-torch reflected the damp bricks of the walls around the cage.

'Shut up,' he would say. 'Shut up or I'll cut your wings off and hang them up to dry.'

And Xaai would retreat into herself, wrapping wings and arms and legs about her body, burying her face in the loose skin of her wings, her whole body shaking.

I only want to fly, she would think. To fly. Please. Let me fly.

But Xaai was not one of those permitted to fly.

'You must remember first,' the grey-faced priest told her, his huge eyes staring into hers through the metal bars. He was balancing precariously on the rail around the outside of her cage, wings spread wide, his red–gold robes of office trailing to the stone floor below. 'We need you to remember.'

He pushed the metal bowl across with its burden of fruit and coloured water. Xaai picked it up, found that it was slightly warm in her hands. She cradled the warmth for a moment, then put it to her lips and sucked greedily. It was sweet – so sweet!

'We need you to remember,' said the old priest again. His face was almost bald, with only tufts of grey fur still adhering around wizened cheeks. Xaai unconsciously smoothed her own face, the thick mat of fur there. She must be younger than the priest, she supposed. Perhaps quite young. She'd never really thought about her age before. She'd never really thought about anything, except flying. Except wanting to fly.

'What do you need me to remember?' she asked. 'I don't remember anything before here.' That hadn't seemed unusual until now, but suddenly it did.

'Do you remember my last visit?' asked the old priest.

'Last visit?' She hadn't seen him before. She was sure of that. 'No.'

She saw from his face – the lowering of his eyes, the sadness there – that she'd given the wrong answer. But all he said was, 'Finish your food, Xaai. One day you will remember.'

Trembling, Xaai asked, 'Will they let me fly then? Will I be permitted to fly?'

But the priest only sank away through the air, his wings spread, his robe rising like a fan. She heard his feet clatter on the stone as he landed, far below.

And she knew then that he would not set her free, that he *could* not set her free. Not ever. Even remembering wouldn't be enough. Xaai buried her face in her wings again and tried to cry. But she couldn't.

'Let me fly,' she moaned. 'Please let me fly. Then I'd remember everything.'

But the only reply was the long echo of her voice from the stone walls.

Johannas Karilee stepped cautiously past the lowest of the gaslit corridors and on to the last staircase, the one that led to the ground. He had forgotten that it was so

71

far down. The stairs seemed to go on for ever in the near-darkness, always the same spongy, blood-red clay. It was difficult to walk on, shifting oddly under his weight as if it were breathing. He supposed that at this level it was indeed half alive, still part of the Land. There was a rail, but it too was slippery, like the stiffened entrails of some huge cold animal. It was actually easier for Karilee to keep his balance if he didn't rely on it.

The stink of the ground rose up to meet him. Rancid water. Rotten meat. A sickly sweet smell which might have been a man's corpse, but was probably just a dead wallrat. There were sounds, too: the scratchings and scrabblings of live rats, and bigger noises, distant thuds, echoes of shouts. There was no way of telling whether they came from above or below. Karilee hoped it was above, behind him, known.

A faint phosphor light glowed ahead. Karilee froze on the steps, breathing lightly. Something moved, and Karilee saw a puffy white face, blotched with grey pustules.

Only a beggar. He relaxed.

The man looked up, and made a weak croaking sound. Wood scraped on stone, and Karilee saw a bowl, with a single rusted copper coin in it. He took another step forward, allowing the light from the hallway above to fall on the beggar. He saw that the man had no arms, and wore nothing but a ragged cloak. His body was huge, almost obscenely bloated. Karilee had seen that before: it was the effect of near starvation at a time when his body was trying to build itself up for the fight. The beggar would have been more than ready if only he'd been whole – or even if he'd been wealthy. Now he was merely huge and agonized, his body filling itself with fluid in a useless imitation of the muscles he should have grown. Karilee supposed that someone – some weak pervert desperate for an easy Promotion – would come and kill him soon.

The thought of that, more than the sight of the poor

72

man in front of him, made Karilee feel sick; not for the first time, he wondered why the world had to be like this. The naieen might talk about the Holy Biology, but had they ever, since the long-forgotten groundling part of their lives, seen suffering like this? Karilee felt like running back up the steps, catching the next 'wing up to Iujeemii, and physically carrying Aapurian down here to see this beggar.

No doubt the old skinflap would put a gold coin in the bowl and tell Karilee that it was survival of the fittest; it was the way the world had always been, and there was nothing more that could be done about it.

'Well, I don't agree,' muttered Karilee. He squatted down by the beggar, trying to ignore the soapy stink of the man's deformed flesh, and said gently, 'I'm going to help you. I'm going to help you right now.'

The man stared at him with eyes almost blind behind watery folds of skin. 'Mon—ey,' he grunted. 'Mon—ey.' He pushed at the wooden bowl again, knocking it against Karilee's foot.

'I'm going to do something for the naieen, and they're going to let me do something that will help you,' said Karilee, aware even as he spoke that it was a lie, that nothing could help this man now, nor any beggar. Only later generations might be saved.

'Mon—ey,' repeated the man, tapping at the bowl with his foot.

Karilee realized that he was talking to the air. The man's intelligence was gone. He put a silver coin in the man's bowl. 'I *will* help you,' he said fiercely.

'Mon—ey,' said the man, tapping the bowl.

Feeling sicker than ever, Karilee walked on.

The stairway ended perhaps a hundred feet lower, in a pool of stinking water and a stone floor covered in filth. It was almost completely dark here, and the only sounds were the crawlings and chitterings of rats and faint shouts echoing from far above.

'Anyone here?' he asked, feeling rather stupid. If anyone *was* here, it would almost certainly be best not to attract their attention. But he had to know. He had to have privacy for the next stage of the plan.

Once he was satisfied that there was no one watching him, Karilee took off his blue cloak and folded it carefully until it was small enough to slip into the small pack he was carrying on his back. He shrugged off the pack, took off his silk underjacket. From the pack he took out a cheap, coarsecloth robe, then put the underjacket and his own cloak in its place. Then he put the pack on, and the robe on top of it, so that he looked hunchbacked, deformed. As an afterthought, he shrugged off the robe and replaced it with one sleeve hanging loose, folding the other arm against his body. At a casual glance, he would look like a deformed, one-armed beggar – and therefore should attract no more than that casual glance.

He hoped.

He walked across the floor, practising a halting gait, treading the muck into his shoes. There was no door as such to the outside, only a low archway through which filtered a dim hint of outer light. He went through, followed a twisting corridor that was in places little more than a sewer. Gradually the light improved, though it retained the blood-red cast of the polluted city clay.

Eventually the pathway became open to the air. Karilee could see the steep red walls of High Dock Tower behind him, the curved buttresses and roses-grotesque sculpted by the architects who had grown the building from bud so many centuries ago. Around the higher parts of the building, the clear air was full of moving specks: row-wings, clock-copters, and the new pedithopters, winking red or gold or green as their carapaces caught the sun. Beyond the tower, on its sunside, Karilee could just see the top of the sculpted white dome that was the High Temple, surrounded by the thin, elegant spire blocks of the wealthy, their red living clay disguised with festoons of many-coloured ivies. On the darkside, in the ancient, endless shade of the city where Karilee walked, the factories rose like dark skeletal trees, factory-baked bricks laid by men's hands, braced with steel of men's making. Clouds of steam and filth rose from the chimneys, and the workers' tenements clung around them like the tattered remnants of flesh to bones.

The contrast between the two parts couldn't have been greater, and Karilee wondered why it wasn't obvious to his fellow men that Epreto's way was wrong, that the factories and workshops, the dead clay, were destroying the Land. But he knew the answer: because Epreto gave them what they wanted. Material comforts, yes, but, more importantly, power. Power over their own lives instead of having to beg for everything from the naieen.

Karilee wondered whether there was really any difference between what Epreto was doing and what he wanted to do. Did he have the right to interfere with the natural life cycle of children, men and naieen?

The only way to find out was to try, thought Karilee. He followed the path, which now showed the remnants of tiling beneath a coating of dirt and smuts. It skirted the factories, occasionally becoming hemmed in by high walls of dead brick. It crossed a Deadland, and the air was suddenly sweet with the smell of decaying corpses. Karilee stopped there for a while, looked at the tumbled soil between the tall reeds and head-high mushrooms, listened to the thick sucking of clay as the Land slowly ate the Dead men's brains and made them one with itself.

If his research was successful, would all this stop? Given a free choice, would everyone become naieen? He knew they wouldn't. Many would still choose to fight, to live the natural way. Others might even choose to become Dead. But it would give men a choice in the manner of their lives. It would no longer depend only on their luck and their strength. Surely that was better than fighting to the death for the privilege of wings.

'Hello?'

Karilee jumped, then realized that the voice had come from the side of the track. He looked across, saw a dark figure crouching in the deep shade of a clump of mushrooms.

'Hello?' repeated the man. 'I think I'm lost.'

There was something odd about the voice: it was curiously high and even in tone, almost like a naieen. He wondered if the man was a singer. He was dressed in dark clothing, so dark that for a moment Karilee thought he might be of the Dead.

No, his eyes were alive. And his face was pale, unusually so.

'You're in the Old Deadland in the Factory Quarter. Where do you need to be?' Karilee asked.

'I need to find the Doctor.'

'Are you ill?'

'No. *The* Doctor. He's a friend.'

'Oh, I see,' said Karilee, although he didn't. 'Where does he live?'

'In the TARDIS.'

Karilee struggled to think of a district or building in Kaygat that had that name. He knew most places, but he simply couldn't think of it. He became aware of the ridiculousness of the situation: here he was, on a secret mission to spy for the naieen, and he was stopping to give someone directions.

'It's in the forest,' said the young man.

'The forest? Which forest?' Karilee was gradually becoming aware that this was a very strange conversation. Was the man mad, perhaps? Or was he trying to tempt him down, to rob him? Was he a spy, Epreto's man, sent to follow him?

'The one with the very big trees,' the man was explaining. 'I was there with the Doctor and Mike. I – I don't know how I got here. I don't remember.' He didn't sound like a criminal or a spy. He sounded confused, and a little bit afraid.

'Very big trees?' Karilee thought for a moment. 'Do you mean the childlands?' But that didn't make any sense:

the childlands were at least four days' walk away. How could the man have got here from there and not know where he was? Had he lost his memory?

'Please!' The man took a cautious step forward. Out of the shadows, Karilee could see that he was deformed. He had two large swellings on his chest, and there was something wrong with the shape of his hips. He seemed to be standing awkwardly; Karilee noticed that he had specially built-up shoes, so probably his feet and legs were deformed too.

Karilee felt an immediate wave of sympathy. He remembered the beggar on the steps. To live in such a condition, knowing there was no chance of Promotion, must be torture. No wonder the man was so desperate to find his way back to this Doctor.

'Are you sure the Doctor lives in the childlands?' he asked the man, speaking slowly and carefully, as if to a man newly from the childforest. 'That's a long way away, you know.'

'The child . . . lands?' The man said it as if he'd never heard the word before. 'No, he lives in the TARDIS. I left the TARDIS in the forest. I was —' He broke off and shook his head. 'I'm not sure. I think I've forgotten.' He stared at his shoes, evidently puzzled by his situation.

Poor man, thought Karilee. He must be mentally deficient as well.

He became aware of a change in the light, away in the sunlit part of the world. The sun was fading: it would be night soon.

He couldn't wait here any longer.

'I'm really sorry,' he said to the man. 'I really can't do any more for you here. There's something very important I have to do.' He started walking slowly towards the grey-green reeds that fringed the sunside of the Deadland. He could see the gate, and beyond it the grey wall around Epreto's private estate. The sunlight on the stones there was visibly dimming now. If he didn't move quickly now he wouldn't be able to see the lie of the land before dark. And Epreto might return at any time.

'*Please!*' said the crippled man. 'This is really important too! People have been killed!'

Karilee stopped. 'Killed? Where?'

'In the forest. They were tied to the branches. I −' he broke off, shook his head again. 'I don't remember. I wish I could *remember*.'

Shock, thought Karilee. He's not mentally deficient: he's suffering from shock.

'These people, were they men or naieen?' he asked quickly.

The man frowned, then said, 'Men, I think. At least they looked like you and me. And there was another man − no −'

Karilee considered. If something was happening in the childlands − something that shouldn't be happening − then he needed to know about it. Hadn't Aapurian said that Epreto was visiting the childlands?

He looked at the man again. 'How long ago was this?'

The man only shook his head. 'I don't *know*. It was light. I suppose it was today.' He looked around him, seemed to notice the gathering darkness for the first time. 'If I come with you, perhaps I'll remember.'

Karilee came to a decision. It was possible that the man was raving, deluded; but he didn't seem that way. There was a possibility that he might know something relevant to Karilee's mission. It was even possible that he had travelled back with Epreto and somehow escaped the man's custody. In which case, any information Karilee could extract would be vitally important.

'Come with me,' he said, when he had thought all this through. 'But you must do exactly as I say. If you remember anything, anything at all, you must tell me at once.'

'Thanks,' said the man, walking forward, clumsily but with surprising swiftness, and extending a hand. 'My name's Jo.'

'I'm Karilee.' Karilee took the man's wrist and clasped it, but there was no returning clasp, just a feeble pawing with the fingers.

The light was almost gone now: a factory siren wailed in the distance and gaslights flared up in the shadows of the city, filling the sky with a dim yellow haze. Karilee realized there was no more time to lose.

He took Jo's arm. 'We have to hurry,' he said, and began to walk swiftly out of the Deadland, pulling the cripple after him.

Seven

Epreto had taken Mike and the Doctor up to the
observation platform for the final approach to the city
called Kaygat. It was almost dark, and the air was cold,
except for occasional gusts of sulphury heat from the
boiler. Epreto stood at the rail with the Doctor, talking in
a low voice, pointing outward from time to time. Standing on the other side, guarded by Jitil, Mike caught only
the occasional word over the noises of the machine, the
hiss of steam and the steady thudding of the engine.

At first glance the city was almost normal, Earthlike.
There were towers, lighted windows, long straight roads
glittering with traffic. True, there were far more flying
things than you would expect on Earth: it was impossible
to tell in the darkness exactly what the moving lights
were, but Mike caught glimpses of coloured wings, half-
shadowed balloons, and distant, fire-misted steamwings.
In addition, the buildings were unusually slender and
the roads seemed as though they didn't quite touch the
ground – but the Doctor had assured him that all this was
due to the local gravity being so much lower than the
Earth gravity Mike was used to.

As the 'buildings' drew closer, however, and the details
of their surfaces became apparent, Mike saw that they
were irregular, almost spiny, more like a coral reef than
anything of human construction. A fine web of ropes
connected the buildings at various levels, glowing slightly
in the dark. The glow rippled steadily back and forth
along the webs, reinforcing the impression of something
organic. As the steamwing descended it had to thread its
way between these, and Mike saw that they were covered

80

with what looked like butterfly wings. The wings flapped constantly.

'Filter feeders,' commented the Doctor, his voice carried across the platform by some random movement of wind. Epreto said something in reply, but Mike didn't catch it.

The steamwing banked sharply, and Mike gripped the rail hard. He saw that what he'd taken to be a road was in fact an airway, defined by the lighted ropes, streaming with a constant winged traffic. He was close enough now to see that there were men in wings, small steamwings, and things that looked like pterodactyls but appeared to fulfil the role of horses. There was a net below the road, glowing a soft salmon pink. The ground below was dark.

The steamwing ignored the road, sailed above the traffic and then descended past it. Mike noticed some of the pterodactyl-like creatures shying away; one of the drivers shook a fist at the steamwing. Then the towers were falling away behind them: ahead were harsher shapes, coloured a cold grey and blue. They appeared to be headed for the largest, a jagged projection as big as the Houses of Parliament, pitted with bright square windows with no apparent pattern.

A rattle of metal from below made Mike jump. He looked down, saw figures moving around the bulky shadow of the boiler. A moment later the top of the boiler seemed to unfold, propelled by a cloud of flame and steam. Mike heard fabric billowing, the roar of gas being released. He jumped back from the rail as the dark shape rose, surrounded by whirling red sparks.

'Doctor!' he yelled. 'It's going to explode!'

But his voice was lost in the roar of gas and steam. The Doctor didn't even look round. Mike could see Jitil waving the gun at him, shouting.

He jumped, intending to push past Jitil and get to the Doctor, somehow get them away from the danger, but in the low gravity he misjudged the jump and found himself flying over the rail of the platform. He tried to catch hold of the wood, missed, fell towards the boiler. Flames were roaring out of the firebox. A crewman stared at him, open-mouthed. There was the sound of a rifle shot behind him, the whistle of a bullet far too close to his ear. The craft lurched to one side, and Mike saw the ground, long green grass perhaps fifty feet below. He was falling past the boiler, in front of the wings, into empty space. For a moment he felt sheer panic, then he remembered: this place had only one-sixth of normal gravity. Fifty feet was the same as . . . about eight feet on Earth. Parachute training ensured that he could land from a jump that high without getting hurt at all.

Assuming he could compensate for the gravity correctly.

He saw a huge wing moving above him, felt a hot wet breath of steam on his face. Then he was clear, falling freely in the cool air. He caught a glimpse of the Doctor struggling with Jitil on the platform, and then the steamwing righted itself. He looked down, saw the tall grass rushing up to meet him, grey-green in the dim light from the windows of the house. He braced himself. His shoes jolted into soft earth, soft enough that he almost sank into it. He let himself fall sideways, rolled with the impact.

There was another gunshot from above, then a roar of venting steam. Mike looked up through the grass, saw a balloon filling out above the steamwing. The billowing flames and steam from the boiler had almost stopped. He grinned ruefully to himself as he realized his mistake. The steamwing hadn't been about to explode at all: it was simply preparing to land. The Doctor was safe.

No matter. He had, however inadvertently, escaped from Epreto. Now he could do something. Perhaps help the Doctor to escape. Perhaps find the TARDIS – and Jo.

He picked himself up, ran through the wet, head-high foliage until he was satisfied that he was out of range of Jitil's and Hanu's clumsy rifles. Then he looked back at the clear trail he had left, shook his head and ran on. Gradually the grass grew thicker and more tangled, and Mike found that he was struggling to make progress. It was almost entirely dark: his only guide was the noise of the steamwing. He tried to keep it behind him.

Suddenly he came out on to a wide stone path lit by tall lamps. Looking to his left, he saw the steamwing settling in front of the house, wreathed in sparks and vapour. It was barely fifty yards away. Mike realized that he must have been forced into something close to a circle. He turned to the right and ran as fast as he could, keeping low and checking over his shoulder every few seconds for signs of pursuit.

After a few hundred yards the path came to an end at a sheer wall of grey stone. Mike stopped and leant against it, breathing hard. The surface of the wall was smooth, almost polished. There was no gate, and no way to climb over it. Experimentally, Mike jumped, but he got only about halfway up the sheer surface. He fell back slowly, the sensation seeming almost unreal in the low gravity. Just before he hit the ground he heard footsteps approaching. He bent his knees to cushion his fall as well as he could, but he knew that whoever it was must have heard the impact.

Sure enough, there was a sharp intake of breath and the footsteps stopped. Mike slipped to one side of the stone path, then crouched down in the grass and waited, breathing as lightly as he could. After a moment the footsteps resumed. Someone walked past in the grass no more than a couple of metres away.

Then stopped again.

A voice whispered urgently, '. . . someone *here*.'

Another person whispered a reply, but Mike couldn't hear the words over the pounding of blood in his ears. He forced himself to keep breathing, to keep his blood oxygenated, and tensed himself to jump and run if the need arose.

There was a sudden movement in the grass behind him. Mike dropped to the ground, heard something whistle through the air near the back of his neck. He saw the shadow of a man against the dim light from the path, saw the glint of metal in his hands.

'No!' A very familiar voice. 'Karilee! He's a friend!'

The figure above Mike froze. 'Are you sure?' asked a low voice.

And then Jo's face appeared. She crouched down beside Mike, then frowned at him. A curious, searching expression appeared on her face, as if she was looking at him for the first time in her life, and found him rather strange. 'At least, I think –' she began, then broke off and looked away abruptly.

Mike stared at her. 'Are you OK, Jo?'

Jo reached out and touched something on the front of his jacket. The vacant expression was slowly replaced by a smile. 'Absolutely certain,' she said, winking at him. 'I'd recognize that carnation anywhere.'

The priest was carrying a key.

It was impossible, thought Xaai. It couldn't be true. It must be a dream.

But no. The brassy metal of the key gleamed in the priest's hand. It was getting closer, passing into shade as the priest's body cut out the light from his lamp. Then he jumped up on to the rail around Xaai's cage and the key clattered against his belt, metallic, real. The prison walls seemed to vanish, stone melting into a darkness defined only by the light shining on that key.

Xaai was staring so hard at it that she didn't even notice that the priest himself was a different person – in fact not a male at all but a woman – until she spoke.

'My name is Acolyte-Ordinary Iikeelu,' said the priest. Her voice was rich, fluting, almost melodious after the croaking of the old man and the animal grunts of the slave-man guards. 'We are going to try something new today.'

Xaai looked at her properly for the first time. She was younger, much younger than the other priest: her face bore the black-and-white markings of a young woman and her eyes were bright. Her robes, too, had a new, bright lustre, as if she had only just been ordained.

'Did you hear me?' asked the fluting voice.

Xaai looked at the key, looked at the lock of her cage. Said nothing. Emotion gummed up her voice.

Iikeelu held up the key. 'We have decided to let you fly, in an enclosed space. We think it may help you to remember.'

'Yes,' said Xaai, because she had to say something. 'Yes. Yes. Yes. Yes.'

The priest looked at her then, and she noticed that there was no sympathy in her eyes. 'We must take certain precautions,' she said. 'You must return to your cage on my word, without question. No matter what your feelings. Do you understand?'

'Yes,' said Xaai. 'Yes. Yes – I understand. Yes.' She was shaking from head to foot, her wings twitching. She could scarcely focus her eyes.

She would *fly*!

The priest put the key in the lock. The cage trembled. The lock clicked, sprang wide. The door opened.

'You can come out now,' said the priest, extending her thin hand to help her.

Xaai hesitated. The space outside between the cramped cage and the walls, which had always seemed so wonderful, so inviting, was suddenly terrifying, empty, dangerous. The bricks of the wall seemed too far away, the floor too far below.

'I don't think I can fly,' she said. Her voice was shaking.

'Don't worry. Everybody thinks that, at first.' The young voice was soft, reassuring. But the woman's eyes were still cold. 'Just jump, when you're ready.'

Trembling, Xaai took her hand and stepped forward into the dim light of the hallway. She wobbled on the perch: the priest put a wing across her body, stabilizing her. Xaai looked at the ground – bare, dirty bricks – and felt a surge of emotion that contained both panic and ecstasy.

I have to do it, she thought. I have to do it now or there may never be another chance. They might lock me in the cage forever.

She jumped.

She spread her wings.

She flew, half tumbling, barely controlled, inside the walls of her prison.

And, almost immediately, she began to remember.

His body trembling with a strange mixture of fear and excitement, Aaviar Omonu steered the pedithopter towards the cold blue-grey shape of Epreto's house. He was gliding now, his feet slack against the pedals, the night air cold on his face. The long, narrow wings of the 'thopter were invisible in the dark, detectable only by the feel of their lift and the faint hiss of the wind against their fabric.

Every nerve told Omonu that he was doing the wrong thing. Exposing himself to danger. Exerting himself when he could be sleeping. All this would only bring the inevitable day of his Promotion – or death – closer. But he tried to ignore his fear, to concentrate on his excitement. The day of Promotion had to be *now*. The otherlanders were in Epreto's house: he had watched the steamwing land from the factory. He had no idea how long they would stay. They might leave again in the morning. And Omonu knew that killing one of the otherlanders was his only chance of winning the fight, of becoming naieen.

'*They are different – weaker than us . . .*'

He could see the wall now, and the long straight runway between the formal arrangements of decorative grasses and fungi. Everything seemed unreal in the dim light, a shadowy echo of the familiar daytime shape of the gardens.

Omonu began pedalling gently. The wings of the 'thopter flapped slowly, creaking a little, and the wind lifted into his face, smelling of smoke and oiled metal. Looking down, Omonu could see the steamwing, its wings pale, the metal wheels and pistons glinting in the light from the windows of the house. He looked up at those windows and wondered if the otherlanders were somewhere behind them. His legs began to tremble again at the thought. He could hardly keep up the gentle rhythm of pedalling.

He wondered what would happen if he met Epreto's guards, or even Epreto himself. What would he say? He realized that he simply hadn't thought about it. What excuse could he make for visiting Epreto's house at night? The answer was simple: none. If they caught him, he would probably be disciplined. He would lose his job, certainly – and probably worse. He remembered Duboli's threat that afternoon. The strange message, burning in the pipe-tray on the desk, smoke coiling upwards.

Omonu shuddered. The 'thopter lurched to one side. Omonu struggled to correct it, pushing down with his whole weight on the steering bar. His clammy hands slipped on the cold metal, and the 'thopter lurched the other way. Omonu took the bar in both hands, wrenched it straight. The 'thopter steadied, but Omonu's whole body was shaking now. The view of the house, the speckled lights of the Sky beyond, blurred and trembled.

I should go back, he thought. Just go. Forget this episode. Forget that I ever saw the message.

'They are different – weaker than us . . .'

Omonu felt that surge of glandular excitement, that tightening of his muscles. No, he thought. I can't go back now.

I have no choice. I have to go on. I have to kill someone.

Eight

Mike Yates squatted on his heels in the earth-scented fungus grove where he'd taken cover with Jo and Karilee, and tried to make a list of his priorities.

One, evade Epreto and his men.

Two, get the Doctor back.

Three, find the TARDIS.

Four, get out of this place before anything else goes wrong.

And then − there was something the matter with Jo. She'd said she'd lost her memory, and Mike wondered if she'd hit her head on something in the forest. He added a fifth item to his list: to get Jo a medical check-up as soon as they got back to UNIT HQ.

If they got back.

One thing at a time, he thought, forcing himself to concentrate on the situation as it was. First he needed to find out what Karilee was doing and why.

His companions' faces were pale shadows in the dim light seeping between the head-high caps of the mushrooms. He looked at Jo and was reassured by a quick grin: very normal, very Jo-like. Perhaps she was feeling better.

He listened for a moment, but could hear no sounds of pursuit around them.

'Do you know where the TARDIS is?' he asked Jo quietly.

Jo shook her head. 'I don't know anything. I was in there and −' she shrugged '− then I was here. Karilee found me.'

Mike looked at Karilee. 'We need to get our friend back. The Doctor.'

'Jo told me about the Doctor,' said Karilee. He too seemed uneasy. He peered over Mike's head, his eyes scanning the silent garden for a moment, then went on. 'I can help you, if you need to get into the house. But you will have to help me in return.'

Mike nodded. 'What do you need us to do?'

'I need to find out what Epreto is doing. I need to inform the Flight about his activities.'

'The Flight? Is that some sort of police service?'

Karilee stared. 'It's the Flight!'

Mike remembered Jitil's words in the steamwing: 'It's the sun . . . That's all we need to know about it.' Perhaps, this time, it would be best not to appear too ignorant.

He thought for a moment, then asked cautiously, 'And is the Flight different from Mr Epreto's Flight?' He wanted to be sure just what he was getting into: international espionage, or a criminal investigation. Both might be equally dangerous, but there was a difference.

'There is only one Flight,' explained Karilee, shifting his weight slightly so that the fragments of dried fungus on the ground creaked under his feet. 'But Mr Epreto has chosen to fly in a different direction.'

Full marks for not answering the question, thought Mike. He glanced at Jo, who shrugged, the movement barely visible in the near darkness.

Mike decided that he would have to worry about local politics later. 'If we get the Doctor out, are you prepared to help us find the TARDIS – that is, our vehicle?' he asked Karilee.

Karilee hesitated. 'In the childlands? It would be better for you to return to the Sky with me. The Flight could help you.'

'I'm not sure the Doctor should meet the Flight,' said Jo suddenly. 'It's better that –' she frowned. 'It's better that he doesn't. Not just now.'

Mike stared at her. 'Why not?'

Jo shook her head. 'I'm not sure. I just know it isn't a good idea. We should just get him out,' she said. 'And then – well, see what happens. Don't you think that's sensible?'

No, thought Mike. It isn't. We don't know where the TARDIS is. Maybe the Doctor can get it back from whoever has taken it – and maybe not.

'Karilee's willing to help us, Jo,' he said aloud. 'I think we should let him.'

'No,' said Jo, her voice oddly wooden and hollow. 'No, we can't. Not once we've got the Doctor back.'

Mike wondered what had really happened to Jo in the forest. He remembered the moment in Kebiria when he'd thought she'd been taken over by the Xarax. Was something similar happening here? A cold feeling entered his gut. If he couldn't trust Jo . . .

'Why not, Jo?' he asked, trying to keep his voice level, normal. 'You've got to tell me what you know.'

'I don't know anything!' she said. Now she sounded wary, almost panicky.

Mike glanced at Karilee, who was looking from one to the other of them in evident confusion.

Best to change the subject, he decided.

'What do they think Epreto is planning to do?' he asked Karilee.

Karilee hesitated. 'If I tell you,' he said carefully, 'you must promise not to tell anyone else here. If word of Epreto's plans should spread, there would be panic. Chaos.'

Mike nodded. 'All we want to do is get the TARDIS back and get away as soon as we can. We won't tell anyone here. We don't know anyone here. I'd just like to know whose side I'm helping, that's all.'

Karilee nodded. 'And you, Jo?'

'I won't tell anyone either.' She sounded tired now, and frightened. And entirely herself, Mike noted with relief.

'Very well,' said Karilee. 'We think Epreto plans to move the sun. Perhaps closer to the Land, to the world of men, and leave the people of the Sky to freeze. Perhaps away from the Land altogether. We're not sure yet where, or why or even how. That's what I'm trying to find out.'

'But you can't *move* a sun!' protested Jo. 'It's impossible!'

'I don't think this is a real sun,' said Mike. 'The Doc said it was only about thirty miles up.'

Karilee glanced at him. 'We don't know how he intends to do it, either. That's part of what they're sending me to find out. All we know is that one of Epreto's friends spoke to a representative of the Flight four days ago, hinting that he had heard of such a plan. And for some time Epreto has been sending steamwings to investigate the sun at night. He claimed that it was for scientific purposes.' He looked at Mike again. 'You say it's not a "real" sun. What do you mean?'

Mike explained what a real sun was. Karilee nodded solemnly. 'If our sun were so big and so hot as that, none of us would be alive.'

That much was obvious, thought Mike. He wondered what this 'sun' really was, that Epreto thought he could fly it. Some kind of floating power station? Perhaps the Doctor had managed to find out. He was usually pretty good at getting information out of people, especially about scientific matters.

Suddenly, Karilee half rose, raising a hand for silence. Mike listened, heard the faint but unmistakable creaking of machinery. Something was flying overhead. Karilee pointed up, then, moving almost silently, took cover under the canopy of one of the mushrooms.

Mike glanced at Jo, and they both did the same. A shadow passed overhead, and Mike held his breath. There was silence for a moment, then Jo whispered something.

'. . . danger comes from above – only from above . . .'

Mike felt the cold sensation in his gut return.

He turned to look at Jo, but heard only her wooden, hollow voice. '. . . all danger is from the Sky.'

There were voices ahead.

Omonu heard them, quite suddenly, when he was only feet from the ground, with the wings of the pedithopter already raised in readiness for a landing. He froze in panic, and as a result the pedithopter sailed almost straight into a cluster of men standing on the

91

main pathway, near to the folded wings of the steam-wing. One of them looked like Epreto himself. In panic, Omonu banked to the left, pedalling as hard as he could to compensate for the folded state of the wings. He managed to avoid the men, but he landed hard, with a clatter of metal and fabric, only yards from where the men were standing.

The voices stopped.

Even if they didn't see me they must have heard me land, thought Omonu. They couldn't have helped hearing that noise. He couldn't see the men – something was in the way, perhaps the steamwing – but he was sure it wouldn't take them long to find him. Again he tried to think of a legitimate reason for visiting the grounds. Another discrepancy in wages? It seemed ridiculous. Perhaps he could say that one of the machines in the factory had broken down.

The voices had started again. He recognized Epreto, heard the words, 'Search the grounds. He must be some-where.'

They know I'm here, thought Omonu. They must have seen me. His heart began to thud with panic. He began to shuffle away from the pedithopter, but soon realized that in the dark he had no idea where he was going. He could hear someone walking along the path, and whispered voices, frighteningly close.

Shivering, Omonu crouched down, then slowly crept in the opposite direction to the sound of voices. He ran into something, and his whole body jolted with fear: then he realized that it was the sinewy stalk of one of the decorative mushrooms he had seen from the air. He slid around it, felt his way forward until his hands touched another stalk.

He heard more voices ahead.

Omonu froze.

Gradually he began to make out some of the words.

'. . . was a pedithopter landing. We should keep moving.'

'No, we could blunder straight into them. We'd better

keep still and wait for the fuss to die down. Don't move unless they get near us.'

Omonu frowned. These people didn't sound like they were looking for someone. They sounded like they were the ones who were being looked for.

With a flood of relief, he realized that he wasn't the target of Epreto's search. Something else was going on here. Perhaps he wasn't the only one seeking the other-landers. With luck, Epreto's men would assume that the sound of his landing had been to do with these people. He remembered the words he'd heard: '. . . better keep still and wait for the fuss to die down'.

Yes. That was sensible.

But his muscles were taut, his whole body singing with energy. He wanted to run, he realized. He wanted the physical exertion.

No. It was more specific than that. He wanted to hit something.

To hit somebody.

He wanted to *fight*. The time was now.

Omonu realized that the exertion and fear of the last half-hour had triggered his killing response. It had worked. Feeling something between exultation and panic, he closed his eyes.

But he knew he would have to wait a little while yet.

Suppressing the killing urge as much as he could, he sat down very slowly on the soft ground, and listened.

Juliu Epreto looked at the entity who called himself the Doctor and wondered how much he could trust him. The stranger was sitting on the ground by the steam-wing, with his knees drawn up to his chest and his chin balanced on his steepled hands, staring into a private distance. That distance seemed to Epreto further than any that he would personally care to think about. The marks of the Doctor's alienness – the deep cracks in his face, and his white, fungus-like hair – only served to emphasize the fact that his motives, his needs, his dreams, the things that Epreto could normally rely on to control people, were all unknown.

It's possible he already knows everything about me, thought Epreto. It's possible he's been sent to investigate my sins. But by whom? The Dead of some other Land? But the Doctor had claimed not to be Dead. And so far, though he had asked endless questions, they'd been the questions of a stranger to the Land, with no particular curiosity about the sun, much less Epreto's personal plans.

'What do you think your friend, Captain Yates, will do?' Epreto asked.

The Doctor didn't reply for a moment, but continued staring into whatever vast distance he had chosen.

'Doctor?' prompted Epreto.

'Oh, I expect he'll try to rescue me,' said the Doctor after a while. He looked up at Epreto and smiled. 'You know, he had this strange idea that we were being taken prisoner.' Despite the smile, the Doctor's eyes were hard, measuring.

Epreto looked away into the darkness of the grounds. 'That wasn't the intention, Doctor. I merely wanted to ask for your help.'

The Doctor nodded, then slowly stood up. 'Ask away, old chap. But don't expect me to do very much for you if Mike gets hurt.'

Epreto thought about it for a moment, then decided there was no point in unnecessarily antagonizing the Doctor. He clapped his hands, and Hanu materialized out of the shadows.

'Call Jitil and the others in,' Epreto said to the servant. 'Tell them –' He looked at the Doctor.

'Just tell them that Captain Yates can look after himself,' said the Doctor with a smile.

After the first thrill of liberation, Xaai had quickly found that flying wasn't as easy as she'd hoped. The actual mechanics seemed almost beyond her. She could clamber to the top of the bellshape of her cage, holding on precariously with her hands and feet; but when she let go

94

the rush of air over her wings terrified her. She could feel the lift, but she couldn't control it. Floor, wall and cage had swirled around her crazily, and she'd landed badly. The first time she'd scraped her knee and bruised a wing; the second time she'd hit her head, hard. It had hurt. All of it had hurt. After three or four attempts Xaai had given up and lain down on the cold stone, crying.

Iikeelu had watched, her eyes cold. 'You must learn,' she'd said. 'And quickly. We need you to remember soon, or it will be too late. Too late for all of us. Do you understand?' A thin desperation had crept into the priest's voice. A desperation that only frightened Xaai all the more.

Now, after what seemed an endless number of attempts at flight, Xaai was exhausted. But she could soar to the ground, and land correctly: she'd conquered the air to that extent.

'You must learn to take off.' Iikeelu spread her wings. 'Watch me.'

She pushed her wings down, down and back against the air, and jumped at the same time. At once she was gliding, swooping low beneath the hanging cage, then swerving to avoid the brick wall of the chamber.

It looked easy, but Xaai knew that it wouldn't be. 'Can't it wait?' she said when Iikeelu had landed.

The young priest shook her head. 'No. If you are to remember anything before –' she stopped, then said simply, 'You must remember now.'

Snow.

Snow boiling.

Snow boiling into mist into steam. And Tuy.

It came to Xaai quite suddenly as she stretched her wings once more. She wasn't sure it was a memory, because it didn't make much sense. But it had seemed important at the time – it was strange, frightening. A shiny surface, curved like a ball but the size of a hill, covered in snow and swirls of white vapour.

Had to fight. Had to kill. Fight Tuy. Kill Tuy.

Xaai shuddered. Kill? Had she killed someone? If so

95

she too would have to die – wouldn't she? Wasn't that the law, the Holy Biology?

But who was Tuy? The name didn't make any sense. It was a man's name, not a naieen's. Perhaps it had all been a nightmare – a transition dream. But a transition from what?

She recalled her first 'memory', the vision she'd seen in her first falling flight: the exploding room, the metal floor, the light. She hadn't told Iikeelu about that; it had been dreamlike, and all but forgotten again as soon as it was remembered. She wasn't really sure it was a memory at all.

But this . . .

'What is it?' Iikeelu hop–glided across the room, her wings half spread. 'Have you remembered?'

'There was steam. Steam in the snow.'

'Steam? Where?'

Xaai shook her head. 'It's gone.'

There was a banging sound behind her. Xaai jumped, was almost flying. Iikeelu snapped, 'Into the cage!' Then, as Xaai scrabbled desperately to get into the air, Iikeelu jumped over her, towards the steps, shouted, 'No! Wait!'

Xaai looked round. Was Iikeelu talking to her? She saw a very old man standing in the doorway, a bright lamp in his hand. His face was almost bare of fur, pouched and wrinkled. It took a moment for Xaai to recognize the old priest who had been her first visitor.

'Confessor-Senior Aapurian!' said Iikeelu. 'You must understand –'

'I understand very well,' said the old priest. His voice was tight, furious.

'She will remember more if she can fly. There's no more time –'

Aapurian looked at Xaai, asked softly, 'You have flown?'

Xaai sensed that there was something behind the question, something much more than the simple matter of whether she had used her wings. She glanced at Iikeelu, but her expression revealed nothing.

'Yes,' she breathed.

Aapurian looked at Iikeelu. 'Are you trying to get us damned?' he snapped.

'I'm trying to keep us alive. To keep the world alive.' Iikeelu too was angry. 'Killing this —' She broke off.

There was a silence.

Aapurian looked at Xaai, his eyes measuring, and suddenly Xaai felt cold. Even colder than this damp, dark stone room should make her feel. Even colder than she did after hours inactive in her cage.

'Killing this one . . .' That was what Iikeelu had been going to say. They were going to kill her. They were going to kill kill kill —

And suddenly she was flying. Flying over Aapurian and Iikeelu, towards the open door behind them. She heard Iikeelu shout, heard Aapurian's hoarse voice raised in some kind of protest. She struggled through the doorway, which was too narrow to accept her spread wings.

On the other side of the doorway was a dimly lit corridor, walled in brick. Xaai flew as fast as she could, ignoring the voices behind her. She heard footsteps ahead, metallic clatterings on stone. There was a turning and she took it, her bruised wings scraping painfully against the wall. Ahead she could see a wide doorway, with light on the other side. She flew through it, and found herself in a long, brightly lit gallery. The windows of the gallery showed that it was night outside, but it wasn't quite dark: a line of lights reached across the Sky, gaslights perhaps, and fainter glints around them which suggested metal, or perhaps some kind of crystal.

Inside the gallery, tethered skyboats twisted gently in the air currents, occasionally touching the carved walls with a dull thud. There was no one in sight. Xaai hesitated, confused, afraid of falling in the open space. But then she heard Iikeelu's voice from behind her: '. . . her and Epreto too . . . too dangerous . . . that way . . .'

Instinct took over. There was a skyboat ahead that seemed larger than the others, big enough for its high sides to conceal her body. A memory stirred in her of sails and knots and the pattern of winds. Her wings seemed to stretch of their own accord, and her tail steered her without her knowledge. The boat approached: without being aware of how she'd done it she found herself gripping the wooden rail that ran along the middle of the craft. There was a rope running along the rail, and Xaai began hauling on it.

The boat moved forward. There was a creaking sound from ahead of her. A winch. She was winching the boat out, which meant that the doors would be opening. She needed to get the doors open so that she could fly away.

But where were the doors? She shook her head in confusion, peered up cautiously over the rail of the boat. She saw rope stretching away, a glimpse of a dark gap in the floor.

There was a shout from behind her, the deep ugly shout of a man. If only she was still a man, thought Xaai. Then she would be able to fight them.

Something whistled past her head, and the frame of the boat shuddered. She heard Iikeelu's voice: 'Shoot to wound! Only to wound!'

Xaai peered forward again, keeping her head as low as she could. She could see two men, guards, heavy, ugly, holding long rifles. The rifles were aimed at her. Between the boat and the guards, the door gaped wide. Xaai could feel the cold night air swirling around her wings.

Instinct took over again. She jumped from the boat rail, into the darkness that was the doorway, keeping her wings furled so that she fell as fast as possible. She thought she heard a bullet whistle past her body, but it was impossible to be sure.

Then she was outside, and the night air had enfolded her body. She let herself fall, the sound and feel of the air assuring her that the ground was far away. When at last she opened her wings, and felt the air catch them, she could see the lights ahead.

They were the lights of an army.

An army of naieen, each one carrying a long-barrelled

gun close against his or her chest. Each one riding the wind, wings wide.

Helpless, terrified, Xaai was falling straight towards them.

I'll die now, she thought. I'll die, and I'll never know why it happened.

I'll never remember.

But at least I flew.

Nine

The back of Epreto's house was shadowed, window-less. There was some light from the city and from the temples in the Sky, but it was faint and diffuse, hardly more useful than starlight. Mike had to walk slowly for fear of running into something, guiding himself by the sounds of Jo's and Karilee's footsteps. Karilee had said this was the best way in — he'd claimed to have memorized a map — but Mike couldn't see any indication of an entrance.

Nonetheless he knew he had little choice but to trust Karilee. He only hoped that Jo's strange fears about evil coming from the Sky weren't in any way justified. If only he knew what had happened to her in the forest, he might have some chance of judging the reliability of her information. As it was, he didn't know what he could trust, and what he couldn't. It was an unsettling feeling.

A faint pale shape appeared ahead, then there was a flare of light. Karilee had lit a taper. In the unsteady glare of the flame, Mike saw the wall of the house, yellow-painted, scabby with brownish fungal creepers. Holding the taper low and keeping it close to the wall, Karilee paced slowly, obviously looking for something.

There was a faint sound behind Mike. Something moving on the soil. He whirled round, peered into the darkness, but his eyes were still dazzled by Karilee's flame.

'What is it?' hissed Jo.

'I thought I heard something.'

Jo stared for a moment, shook her head. 'Can't see anyone,' she said.

Ahead of them Karilee had stopped and crouched down. He beckoned them over. Mike could just see a darker patch on the ground where he was standing. Jo hurried over, and Karilee handed her the taper, then removed a wooden cover to reveal a deep pit.

Mike looked down, but saw only dry earth walls fading away into blackness.

'The deadspace,' breathed Karilee. 'Where the clay for the stone walls was removed.'

Jo winced, muttered, 'How could he *do* that?' Her voice shook with revulsion.

Mike wondered what a deadspace was, and why it was so shocking. What had *happened* to her? But there was no more time to worry about it now.

Karilee had picked up a small stone from the ground, and as Mike watched he dropped it into the pit. There was a long silence, then a faint clattering sound. Karilee looked at Mike. 'We can jump it, but I'm not sure about the cripple.'

'I'm not a cripple!' said Jo. 'If you can do it, I can do it.' Her voice held a stubborn tone that Mike recognized all too well. Again he felt a surge of relief: whatever had happened, she was still Jo.

'OK, Jo,' he said. 'But you jump last, and let us catch you.'

Karilee was already sliding over the lip of the pit. Jo gave him the taper as he let go of the ground and began to fall. After a moment Mike peered over the edge and saw Karilee about twenty feet down, still dropping with a majestic slowness. A muddy-looking floor seemed to form underneath him in the light from the taper, and he landed gracefully.

Karilee looked up and beckoned. Mike hesitated, instinctively. The total length of the drop was perhaps thirty feet.

Low gravity, he told himself. There's nothing to worry about.

He slid over the edge of the pit. As he fell, he became aware of a thick, animal odour in the air. Rats? he

101

thought. He landed, slipped in the mud and scrambled upright. Karilee took his arm. 'Step back, so that Jo can jump.'

Mike looked up, but couldn't see the top of the shaft. 'Come on, Jo!' he whispered, hoping his voice would carry to the surface.

There was a scrabbling sound, and Jo dropped into the light of the taper. Mike extended his arms to help her, but she landed without his aid. Then frowned. 'What's that smell?'

Mike shrugged. The musky odour was even stronger down here. It was like the inside of a zoo. He glanced at Karilee, who sniffed the air, then shook his head. 'I'm not sure. Some large animal, perhaps. It might be here to guard the house. We should be careful.'

'It should be all right if we stick together,' said Mike. 'Animals won't usually attack people if they're in groups.' Unless they're trained guard dogs, he added mentally.

Karilee had begun to walk, his boots squelching in the mud. Mike could see the bare stone that was the base of the wall of the house. It was broken by a crude archway. Karilee ducked through it without hesitation.

Mike glanced at Jo, who shrugged. They followed.

The ground was even wetter on the other side of the arch, and to the odour of musk was added the sour tang of sewage. Mike wondered momentarily what plumbing arrangements there were in Epreto's house. Karilee squelched forward for a few steps, then stopped and held up a hand.

'Listen.'

Mike listened. He heard a faint dripping of water, his own breathing, his heart thudding.

No.

Other breathing. Not his. And too harsh to be Jo's or Karilee's.

Jo whispered, 'I think we've just found the guard —'

She was interrupted by a hoarse, echoing scream. It

sounded almost human, but too deep, and too loud. A gorilla? Mike wondered. Did they have gorillas here?

Karilee was backing up, whispering something under his breath.

I should have brought a gun, thought Mike. I should never have agreed to go in the TARDIS without a full kit. But he knew it was far too late to worry about that now.

The scream was repeated. It seemed nearer this time, though Mike was aware that this could easily be illusion or imagination.

Jo caught Mike's arm. 'Let's go back. I don't want to wait to find out what that is.'

Mike stepped back, slipped in the mud, fell on his face. Heavy footsteps sounded behind him. He staggered upright, saw light ahead, saw Jo holding the taper on the other side of the crude stone arch.

Heard her sudden intake of breath.

He turned, saw something standing in the light. For a moment he thought it was a man, then realized that it couldn't be. A dark, puckered face, shaggy grey hair over the body, arms and legs almost deformed by the weight of muscles. The muscles seemed to move of their own accord, crawling and tensing under the skin like a nest of snakes. Long ropes of veins and tendons hung about them, some broken open and rotting. The stink was appalling.

The creature stopped and stared at Mike, points of reflected light from the taper flickering in its eyes. It drew back its lips and snarled.

No. Not quite a snarl.

A word. A word repeated, over and over, on each breath. 'Fight. Fight. Fight. *Fight*.'

Omonu pressed his body against the soil and peered down the long shaft below the trapdoor where he'd seen the other fugitives take cover. A glimmering light rose from the space below, and muttered voices.

And a smell.

Omonu's body knew that smell. The sick overripe musk of it.

Epreto keeps the Unpromoted under his house.

But he was sure that the other fugitives had gone down here. And he was almost sure — from the way they had talked — that at least one of them was an otherlander. He had followed them, hoping to find out more, but now he was wishing he hadn't.

Because it was true. He could smell it. He could *hear* it. The low, snarling breath.

Epreto keeps the Unpromoted under his house.

They had used to talk about that when Omonu had been a fineworker — one of the young men straight from the forest, employed by Epreto's predecessor to work those parts of the machines unsuitable for the clumsy hands of older men. The others, the ones who had been there longer, had teased him mercilessly, jumping above him, shrieking, eyes bulging, thin fingers flexing in imitation of the monsters' strangling hands. Omonu had believed it all to be literally true. But he'd long ago dismissed it as a lie, an excuse for the others to torment him. Epreto was an industrialist, an inventor, a man of state and substance — not a pervert and a criminal. Factory gossip was just that: gossip.

He hadn't even thought about it when he'd planned his break-in. Guards, yes. But not —

A series of thuds shook the ground beneath Omonu's feet, as if a giant were walking towards him. How big were the Unpromoted? Suddenly all those fineworkers' tales of monsters as tall as buildings no longer seemed like legends and gossip.

He breathed it again, the sick overripe musk. He was seized with a frenzied, stupid desire to jump down into the deadspace, to meet the Unpromoted. It would kill him, but at least it would be over. All the fear, all the longing.

The thought frightened him even more than the sounds and smells had done. No, he thought. Not now. Not when I'm so near to the otherlanders. Not when I have a chance to *win*. He backed away from the trap, slammed the door to shut out the smell, the sounds, the temptation.

Then, shaking, he slowly walked away.

'Oh *no*,' said Karilee. 'It isn't possible.' Mike could see the man standing in the scuffed clay where they'd jumped down the shaft, the light from his taper dancing on his face. 'The door's closed. Someone's closed the door.'

'Well, we'll have to open it,' said Mike. He moved slowly across to take a look, glancing over his shoulder at the beast. He looked up the shaft, saw no obvious handholds. But it shouldn't be too difficult in this gravity. He could probably jump most of the way, scramble the rest. Even if he couldn't get the door open, it should be possible to get enough of a grip on the frame to hold himself up there. In fact, with three of them up there they could probably hold each other up against the walls of the shaft and if necessary batter the door open.

He looked down again, and suddenly realized that Jo was no longer standing by his side.

'Jo!' he called.

But she was standing in the archway, twenty yards away. The beast was visible, in the shadows beyond, far too near to her.

'Jo! Over here! And walk slowly!'

Jo ignored him.

'Jo, you've got to move.' Mike kept his voice calm. 'If you move slowly, it won't attack you.'

'Yes it will.' Karilee's voice. 'They said Epreto kept them. I didn't believe it until now. I didn't believe it was possible – no wonder they wanted to know –'

'What is it?' asked Mike urgently.

'It is an Unpromoted.' Karilee's voice betrayed a dark contempt. 'Epreto hinted to me that he was experiment-ing with such things when I last spoke to him – before this business of the sun came up. I didn't believe he would do it. That poor devil is a man. A man who has been kept alone when he should have been Promoted, so that he has had no opportunity to fight or die. Now he will try to kill anyone.'

Mike felt a rising panic, a weakening of the knees that his training wasn't supposed to allow him to feel. The creature was still standing there, barely five yards from Jo, its fists clenched, its body stinking of fear and death and there was *no way out*.

'It's OK, Mike,' said Jo suddenly. Her voice had changed again, become wooden, remote. 'There's no need to be afraid. It won't attack me.' There was a curious emphasis on the last word, as if Jo thought that she was especially protected.

'I don't think we can take that chance,' said Mike. He took a step forward, but his feet slipped in the loose clay. He stumbled and almost fell.

The beast growled, advanced a step. Its eyes were strangely bright, like a cat's. 'Fight.' It seemed to be pleading. 'Fight. Fight.'

Behind them, the light of the taper faded. Looking over his shoulder, Mike saw that Karilee had retreated to a corner of the cellar. He had drawn a long knife and was holding it in front of his body.

Sensible chap, thought Mike.

'Come on, Jo,' he said. 'If we get through there with Karilee the three of us should stand a chance against it.'

'No, Mike,' said Jo. She was staring at the beast, her face twisted into an expression of agonized concern. 'That's not the right way. You have to fight it alone.'

She's gone mad, thought Mike. He took Jo's arm, tried to pull her away, but she dug her heels in. All his strength wouldn't move her.

'There's no way you can fight it,' he said. 'You need our help.'

'Mike! Don't you see?' Her voice was normal now, but her muscles were like iron, immovable. 'This poor thing has to be Promoted. You have to fight it. You. It wants you.'

She turned to him and smiled, a friendly, pleading, little-girl smile. A Jo smile.

'Please, Mike,' she said. 'You have to let it kill you.'

Ten

'Everything in this building,' said Epreto, 'is laid out to a strictly rational order. There is nothing of the muddy clay of the natural world here.' He gestured from the hallway where they stood towards the angular stairs, the clockwork regularity of doorways leading off. He pointed upward, watched the Doctor's bright, intelligent gaze following his direction. 'Observe the pattern of the stairwell as it rises,' he said. 'First a triangle, then a square, then a pentagon, finally a hexagon on the top floor. Each shape made by trigonometric methods from factory-polished stone. And the whole assembled in less than half a year! Do you know how long it took for the clay towers of Kaygat to grow?'

'Around a hundred years, I'd guess,' said the Doctor, examining the wall around the door with a slightly unnerving closeness, as if he were looking for flaws.

'More than five hundred! That's how slowly the "natural" world grows. And of course it isn't any more "natural" than this place – that clay is trained to grow by men. It's fertilized, it's shored up by metals and by wood. It's a building, just the same – just as artificial. The only difference is that it's a slow and inefficient way of building compared with this.'

The Doctor continued to examine the wall. 'You know, in five hundred years I doubt that this place will still be standing. This stone will rot, you know. It's not really stone anyway, just baked clay.'

Epreto felt his earlier nervousness returning. The Doctor was behaving like an examining judge, finding fault with every one of Epreto's designs. What would he think of his longer-term plans?

Epreto realized that he would have to be very careful about how he explained himself to the Doctor.

'Probably it won't last forever,' he conceded, of the stone. 'But, when it's so simple to build another, does that matter?'

The Doctor rapped his knuckles against the wall. 'Hmm. Possibly, and possibly not. You know, taking this much clay out of the ground isn't really a good idea. From what you're saying, it seems the stuff is alive, which implies —' He broke off. 'Now that's interesting.' He turned to face Epreto. 'Tell me, this Sky of yours. Is it the same substance as the ground?'

'The Sky?' Epreto considered. It was clear that the Doctor had little idea how the world really worked, for all his questions and intelligent guessing. He decided to risk a lie. 'No. The Sky is made of an inert substance. The Temples are alive, of course, like any other old-style building.'

'The Temples?'

'The naieen Temples grow downwards from the Sky in the same way that the buildings of men grow upwards from the ground,' Epreto explained.

'Naieen being . . .?'

Epreto stared at the Doctor, then realized that he really didn't know.

'Men become naieen, Doctor. That is the Holy Biology. Every simpleton knows that. It is unfortunate, of course, especially when an intelligent, rational and civilized man has to be sacrificed to base instinct, but —' He broke off, realizing that he was giving too much away, saying too much of what he truly felt.

But the Doctor didn't seem to be listening anyway. He stroked his chin, muttered, 'So that's what happens to the imago stage.' He turned to Epreto again. 'And the children leave the forest to become men?'

'Yes. The forest makes the children, children become men, and the fittest men become naieen, with the right to fly. We men are the central stage of the metamorphic process.' He clenched his fists, unable to restrain the force of emotion. 'Do you understand now, Doctor? Do you understand why I have had to do all this? *We* are the superior beings. Men have all the rationality – it is men who make everything new in the world. But because we don't have the power of flight – because we are caught in this perverted trap they call Holy Biology – we are preyed on by children and ruled by naieen.'

Epreto swallowed, realized that his body was shaking with emotion. But the Doctor still seemed unimpressed, almost distracted. 'Have you any idea who – that is, have you any history which explains how this situation came about?' he asked.

'History is the naieen's story,' said Epreto disgustedly. 'And according to them nothing ever changes.'

The Doctor nodded, as if he had expected this reply. 'What about legends?' he asked.

'Legends?' Epreto was puzzled. 'Doctor, I took you for a rational man! Of course there are legends – both men and naieen make legends. There are a whole basketful of them. But they don't make any sense, and they all contradict each other. What I'm interested in is how you can help me to –'

'I can't help you at all unless I fully understand your situation. Now, do you have copies of these legends?'

'There's Reekaa's *Compendium* in the library, but I don't see what –'

'Good.' The Doctor looked around the stairway again. 'Now, perhaps you could tell me which of these trigonometrically arranged doors I must go through to get there.'

Omonu hadn't gone far before he realized the mistake he'd made.

The otherlanders were in the deadspace with the Unpromoted. Which meant that the Unpromoted was going to kill them before he, Omonu, got a chance to do it.

He had to go down there, however afraid he was. There was simply no choice.

He hesitated, shifting from foot to foot on the cold ground, then turned and slowly made his way back towards the trapdoor. It took him some time to find it in the darkness, then it seemed to take forever to get it open. At last the wooden panel lifted. Without giving himself time to think about it, Omonu jumped down into the darkness.

He fell. Below him, there was a high, unearthly shriek – not that of a man, not even an Unpromoted or a naieen. It sounded like something not even of this Land. Something *alien*. Something he couldn't possibly fight. In panic, Omonu scrabbled at the edges of the shaft, trying to stop himself, but his hands could find no purchase in the bare dry earth and he carried on falling.

The unearthly shriek was repeated. Omonu landed, crumpled to the ground. Before him was a scene worse than any fineworkers' gossip, worse than anything Omonu could have believed he would live to see. A man was backing slowly across a floor of wet, blood-coloured clay, holding a taper in one hand and a large piece of white stone in the other. The stone had a sharp edge, and that edge was dark with blood. A vast, shambling beast approached him, covered in grey fur matted with the red clay, or perhaps more blood. Another man, smaller and seemingly deformed, was shrieking in that high-pitched, other-worldly voice. A third man, older and bigger, was visible in the shadows, his back against a wall, terror on his face. The air was full of the musky smell of Promotion – Omonu felt his own body react, his fists clenching, his heart pummelling into overdrive.

'No! Mike!' shrieked the smaller man, as Omonu stood up. 'You can't use a weapon!' He caught hold of the hand holding the rock, tried to drag it away. The beast advanced towards them.

Omonu knew that it would kill them both in these circumstances. And they were the otherlanders – he was sure of it. There was something about the way they were dressed, the shape of their bodies. Particularly the smaller one.

'Just kill it!' Omonu shouted. 'Kill it now!'

At the sound of his voice the beast stopped, an arm's length short of the struggling couple. They too froze, and stared at Omonu.

The beast growled.

And then it turned.

Its eyes fixed on Omonu.

He realized at once. He was bigger than any of the men in the deadspace. He smelt right.

The beast had recognized that.

Omonu scrambled to his feet, looked up at the shaft he had fallen through. He was sure it was too far to jump, but he had to try. It was the only way out.

The beast advanced another step. Then, amazingly, it spoke.

'You,' it said. 'You fight. Please.'

'No,' whispered Omonu. 'I'm not ready.'

The beast took no notice, but began advancing on Omonu.

'Must fight,' it said. 'Fight. Please. Fight.' It seemed to be weeping.

Omonu felt sweat trickling down his back, treacherous sweat that probably smelt of his readiness to fight. He crouched down, getting ready for a desperate jump, perhaps over the top of the beast.

There was a sudden, very fast movement.

'No!' The high-voiced one again.

But the other small man was behind the beast, and then the creature was falling, at first slowly, then too quickly, its limbs flailing. There was a splash of clay as it hit the ground, and Omonu felt the cold stuff splattering his face and body.

The small man stood. The Unpromoted's breathing, Omonu realized abruptly, had stopped, though its muscles were still writhing under the skin of its arms and legs.

'You shouldn't have done that!' said the high-voiced one again.

'Jo, there wasn't any choice. It was going to kill all of us.'

'It would only have killed – have killed –' The small man collapsed on to the ground. 'Oh *no*.' He began sobbing.

The other man looked at his companion for a moment, then stepped forward and leant over Omonu. 'Are you all right, sir?'

Omonu stood. 'Yes. I –' He stopped. He had to know who these people were, whether they were really otherlanders.

The high-voiced one, still sobbing, was crouching over the body of the Unpromoted, his hand gently stroking its forehead. 'You were playing by the rules, weren't you?' he said. 'Despite everything that's been done to you. And we cheated. I'm sorry. I'm really sorry.'

'I'm sorry,' said Omonu quickly. 'I came here by accident. I didn't mean to cause . . .' He gestured at the dead creature.

'Don't worry, you were just in time!' said the small man cheerfully. 'I'm Mike Yates, by the way, and this is Jo Grant. We're from – from –'

'A long way away,' said the one called Jo Grant.

Omonu frowned, then felt his fear and confusion drain away in a sudden giddy rush of excitement. 'You mean you're from another Land?' he asked carefully.

Jo nodded. 'Yes, that's right.'

Omonu felt his muscles tensing again, this time in anticipation. It was true. These people were the otherlanders. And, yes, they were smaller than ordinary men.

He would be able to kill after all. He would be Promoted.

He only hoped that he could control his reactions long enough to get one of them alone. He forced himself to relax, to attempt a smile. 'I'm very glad to meet you,' he said. 'You have saved my life, and I'm grateful.'

Xaai had almost glided right through the flying army before she realized they weren't going to kill her. In fact, they barely took any notice of her, though one shouted at her, something about noncombatants. At first she was too

113

relieved to think at all, but as the last ranks of armed flyers drifted past she thought to pull herself up, staying level with the nearest of them in the air, and shout at him, 'What are you doing here?'

The flyer laughed. 'Best you don't know.' A pause. 'What are *you* doing here? Don't you know the Temple's been cleared?'

Confused, Xaai dipped her wings, dropped below the flyer, then recovered herself in a confused flurry. 'Should I go, then?' she asked.

The flyer looked at her properly for the first time. 'You're a neophyte, aren't you?'

Not sure what a neophyte was, Xaai didn't reply.

'You should go to the commander's gondola.' The flyer gestured upwards, at a pale, boatlike shape floating above them, held up by several dimly patterned balloons. 'She'll get you an escort out of here.'

Xaai thanked the flyer and soared on, flapping her wings to gain altitude towards the gondola. She was confused. Who were these people? Were they Aapurian's people, or were they fighting against them?

But naieen didn't fight. Did they?

. . . wingers don't fight: they're sneaking cowards . . .

Who had said that? The voice in her head was strange, but the words felt like her own. Her own from a long time ago, before she'd understood, before she'd even dreamt. She had been a man.

But who? Why was she so special? What was it that they needed her to remember?

Xaai looked over her shoulder, breaking the steady stream of cold air tumbling over her wing. She could still see the lights of the army, dropping steadily away from her. Ahead, the gondola was closer, but the wind had pushed her to one side of it. With an effort she corrected her course, watched as the pale shape resolved itself into an elaborate crenellated hull with fixed masts for sails and balloons.

Not a very good design for a boat, she found herself thinking.

As she drew level with the deck, a naieen woman hailed her and asked her business.

'I need to see the commander,' said Xaai. 'I'm a –' she paused, remembering the word '– neophyte. I'm from the Temple.' She gestured above and behind them, though the Temple lights were no longer distinct from all the others in the Sky, and she wasn't even sure she was gesturing in the right direction.

She became aware that she was falling behind the gondola as it drifted. She struggled to correct the drift, but her wings seemed to become entangled with the currents of the air and she started to fall. Desperately she scrabbled her way sideways towards the crenellated wall of the gondola, grabbed at the wood with her arms.

Strong hands took her wrists, hauled her aboard. Her wings bruised on to the hard deck, sending stabs of pain through her body.

Gasping, she slowly righted herself and looked up at her rescuer.

Iikeelu was staring down at her. There was ice in her eyes. 'You wanted to see the commander,' she said. 'I am acting for the commander.'

Xaai slumped to the deck, felt the hard rough wood against her skin. 'Don't,' she said. 'Please don't kill me.'

Iikeelu raised a hand. Xaai flinched, thinking the older naieen was going to hit her, but she was only beckoning two guardsmen. Their heavy bodies clumped across the deck.

Then Xaai saw that they were carrying whips.

Iikeelu smiled coldly.

'The pain should help you remember.' Iikeelu smiled. 'I'm sorry. It's the only way.'

But Xaai was looking into her ice-cold eyes, and knew that she wasn't sorry. She wasn't sorry at all.

Eleven

'Your plan is quite insane, and it can't possibly work. Even assuming this "fallen sun" that you've found actually was, at one time, capable of travelling between the stars — that it was a true starship — it's quite obvious that it's now severely damaged. And you simply haven't got the technology to repair it.'

The Doctor was pacing to and fro between the brightly coloured shelves of the library, as if the place were his own. In the strong gaslight the lines etched into the flesh of his face were even more evident. To Epreto they seemed almost like symptoms of the cracks, the alien rifts, in the Doctor's mind. Why couldn't he *understand*? He was a rational being, wasn't he?

'Doctor, we have to escape this world. The sun of our Land will die, just as all the others have done. Just like the one we found. I have more foresight, more ability to make rational plans, than the others of my species. I am merely preparing for the future as best I can.'

The Doctor stopped pacing and glared at Epreto, seemingly angry. 'Don't you listen? Whatever means you use to "escape" — these old starships or whatever they are, or the TARDIS — it can't possibly work. It's quite clear from what you've told me — Promotions, the naieen, the children in the forest — that the entire life cycle of your species is tied to this place. You *can't* escape — if you leave, you'll die. Can't you see that?'

Epreto turned away from the alien, looked at the ranked shelves of books in their painted, colour-coded bindings. He could feel his whole body trembling, and hoped the Doctor couldn't see it. Trembling was not the

116

act of a rational man, and Epreto knew it. 'We have to be able to escape from our biology, Doctor. It's part of the trap. It's part of the deliberate cruelty of our destiny. And I firmly believe that if we can escape the Land – if we can pilot the sun beyond the Sky – we will escape the biology too.' He paused, made himself turn and face the Doctor. 'But I am not a fool. I know that men cannot live on the air. I know that they need a means to reproduce. We will be taking samples of all the stages of men, including some naieen. And of farm animals, crop species. I even have seeds from the childforest.'

The Doctor walked between Epreto and the shelving, sat down at one of the five reading desks – the one where he had left Reekaa's *Compendium* open – and examined the book. 'It still won't work,' he said after a while. 'You only have to look in this book, this *Compendium* you have here, to see that you have been genetically engineered to exist only on this world. Even the length of your year is an arbitrary number of days designed to fit the reproductive cycle of your species!'

Epreto jumped across the floor, slapped the book closed. 'Those are legends! No more than lies! They were invented by naieen, and naieen sympathizers amongst men, to make it seem inevitable that the world should carry on this way! Don't you understand that? Do you think everything you read is the truth?'

'No,' said the Doctor mildly, still examining the book. 'But even the lies have a way of telling you things you need to know.' A pause. 'Look, there are things I can do which will help you. If I can get at the living sun, there may be a way to stabilize it, make it last longer, so that it won't be a problem in your lifetime.'

Epreto felt the breath leave his body. Had the Doctor somehow guessed that it was the living sun he planned to take, and not the Dead one? It was, after all, a far more rational plan. And, even if the alien didn't seem to approve of rationality, he certainly understood the principles.

Epreto looked into the alien eyes, tried to read them. If

the Doctor for one moment guessed his true intentions, then everything would be lost.

'I don't have access to the living sun,' he said at last. 'Some naieen say they have been there . . .' He trailed off, sharply aware that it would have been better to say that no one could go there.

'Well, if the naieen can go, then we can go.' The Doctor got up, resumed his pacing. 'If only we could find the TARDIS.'

Epreto shrugged. 'The Dead have that.'

The Doctor appeared to consider this for a moment. Then his face brightened with a smile. 'We could use the steamwing! You said that it could make thirty miles in an hour, didn't you? So, provided we leave the sun an hour before dawn, we should be clear in good time.'

'The naieen will stop us ever getting there.'

The Doctor continued pacing. 'It rather depends upon the speed of flight. Your steamwing can do thirty miles per hour. The naieen . . .?' He looked up.

Epreto shrugged again. 'Perhaps fifteen.' It was amazing, to see the Doctor following the exact line of thought he himself had developed so many years ago.

'So they must leave before we do,' concluded the Doctor. He stood up. 'We should have long enough. How many hours until dawn?'

Jo looked at Mike's face and tried to understand what he was saying. She could see his lips moving, could see his eyes studying her own face, but she couldn't quite make sense of the words.

'. . . were you telling me . . . Unpromoted?'

The Unpromoted? The Unpromoted was Dead. Destroyed. Permanently lost.

Destroyed. And Mike had done it.

'I don't understand,' she said aloud. 'I don't understand how you could have cheated like that. You're not a cheat, Mike.'

'You were telling me to lie down and die!'

'No! Why don't you *understand*? I was telling you to

118

fight!' There was a reason why Mike didn't understand, Jo was sure of it. Mike wasn't stupid, after all. But Jo couldn't quite grasp what that reason might be. Was there something else that she should have told him?

'We really should get on. The longer we stay here, the more dangerous it gets,' said Karilee. He was pacing impatiently along the deadspace wall, the taper sputtering in his hands. The other man, Omonu, was sitting under the stone arch staring at Jo with an expression that made her a little bit afraid.

Karilee spoke again. 'May I suggest something?' Mike glanced at him, nodded. 'I will go with Jo and find the things I need to find. If you, Mike, and Mr Omonu could distract Mr Epreto whilst we do that, then my mission will be accomplished. After that we can find your friend the Doctor. If the Doctor wishes to accompany me later when I report to the Flight, he can. If he has other business, I will not detain him. I am not like Mr Epreto.'

'That seems reasonable,' said Mike.

But Jo shook her head. 'The Doctor has to come with me.'

Mike looked at her with that odd searching expression. 'What do you mean, Jo?'

Jo stamped a foot on the ground. It was all so frustrating. 'I don't *know*,' she said fiercely. 'You just have to trust me.'

There was a long silence. Jo wondered why Mike didn't automatically trust her any more. He usually did. What had she done wrong?

She became aware that Karilee was speaking again. 'If Jo will follow me, then we will find the Doctor.'

Karilee was already walking deeper into the deadspace. They all followed him, since there was no other way out. At Karilee's suggestion, however, Mike took another taper and left with Omonu to examine the sunward side of the deadspace. Jo watched the little flame moving, the two half-lit faces. Something about Omonu worried her. Something about leaving Mike with Omonu. If only she could have a minute to think, perhaps she would be able to remember why. It was something to do with the Unpromoted – and the Dead . . .

Who were the Dead?

'I think there's a way up to the house here,' called Karilee from a few paces ahead, breaking into her thoughts. He had the taper raised in one hand, illuminating a narrow gap in the ceiling. Peering up, Jo saw that there were steps built into the shaft above.

'This must be where they fed the Unpromoted,' said Karilee. 'But it would have been too narrow for him to climb.'

Jo nodded, examined the space for a moment. She glanced at Karilee, measuring him up against the available room. 'We should be able to make it,' she said judiciously. Karilee nodded.

Jo called to Mike and Omonu, but there was no response. She frowned, looked across, saw the flickering light of the taper emerging from a gap in the far wall.

'Leave a taper burning here,' said Karilee. 'They'll find the place soon enough.' He jumped up from the ground, sailed into the passageway. Jo heard a grunt, then a clattering sound. Bits of dried clay fell around her.

'There's a door,' announced Karilee. 'And it's locked.'

'What kind of lock?' asked Jo. 'Is there a keyhole?'

Scraping sounds.

'Yes. I think so. I don't see how –'

Jo smiled. At least this was something familiar, something she understood. 'Don't worry,' she said. 'Let me get up there. I'll see to it.'

The gap in the wall had led to stairs, but the stairs led nowhere. Blank, hard, Dead stone. Mike lodged the taper in the soft clay of the ground and felt around on the stone for a while, wondering if there was a concealed doorway, but could find nothing. If this had ever been a way out, it had been thoroughly blocked off.

He turned to Omonu. 'We'd better go back.'

Omonu frowned, his big face puckering until it looked almost like that of the gorilla-like creature Mike had

120

killed below. The Unpromoted, or whatever Karilee had called it.

'We have . . .' Omonu's eyes were darting around nervously. 'That is, we should . . .'

'We're never going to get through that wall, if that's what you mean,' said Mike.

Omonu pushed past him, almost crushing him against the side of the passage, then stood below him, facing him. The taper again accentuated the deep wrinkles on his face. 'I never had a chance to explain my business,' he said.

Mike felt a faint stirring of fear. Was Omonu, too, Unpromoted?

'I think we should get back to the others,' he said quickly, hoping his nervousness didn't show. 'There's probably only one way out of this cellar and I expect they've found it by now.'

Omonu shook his head. Then shook his whole body.

Like an animal.

The muscles bulged on his arms.

'I am ready,' said Omonu. His voice was shaking, and beads of perspiration were glinting on his skin. 'I am ready to fight you now.'

'Are you . . .' Mike broke off, swallowed. He looked at the narrow gaps between Omonu's body and the sides of the passage, and knew he wouldn't make it past the man. He felt a cold terror in his gut, as he realized that this time there really was no way out. He was going to have to fight Omonu, and if he couldn't kill him, he would die.

Omonu growled again, and stepped forward.

Twelve

Xaai could feel Iikeelu's eyes still on her, through all the pain.

She wasn't sure where she was any longer: she supposed she was still on the gondola. The room was dimly lit, wood-walled, and that only seemed to make the pain stand out more, in lines of fire along her body. She could almost see the blood-coloured glow of it.

And there was sickness. Deep, poisonous sickness in her stomach and her veins and her mind.

'What do you remember?'

Iikeelu's voice. Icy.

'You *must* remember.'

'I killed Tuy,' said Xaai desperately. 'My name as a man was Xa. There was a fallen sun. There was a priest, a priest you couldn't see. That's all I can remember now. Please, if you just let me rest, I might remember more.'

The silence that followed her words seemed to go on forever. Xaai became aware of two slave-man guards standing by the door, watching the scene with their ugly, furless faces. The whips were still in their hands.

'Where was the priest?' asked Iikeelu.

Xaai struggled with the images in her pain-sodden mind. 'Inside. Inside the sun. There was a chamber –'

'So the sun was hollow?'

Snow. Steam in the snow.

'Hollow. Yes. And cold inside. Even when –'

'*The sun is alive!*'

'– it was cold even when the sun was hot. It was shining.'

Iikeelu sighed. 'Thank you. You've told me what I

122

need to know. Jaxei! Call the squad commanders to my cabin!'

Xaai struggled upright. Pain danced around her body, and bile rose in her throat.

'Please . . .' But she wasn't sure what to ask for. Perhaps she should ask Iikeelu to kill her. Even death would be better than this.

'I suggest you get some rest,' said Iikeelu briskly, half stepping, half flying, over Xaai. 'I'm sorry for the pain, but we had to know.'

Then she was gone, and Xaai was alone in the darkened cabin.

Slowly, painfully, she dragged herself across the rough wood to the door and tried to open it.

It was locked.

'Please let me die,' she whispered. 'This isn't what I wanted when I was a man. This isn't what I dreamt about. Please let me die.'

But her heart kept beating, obstinately, despite the pain and sickness.

Eventually she started to cry.

The hallway was dark, but it was not quiet. Jo could hear the steady thudding of machinery, and a distant roar of steam. She looked around at the panelled stone, the geometrically arranged doors.

'Does Epreto keep machines in his house?' she asked Karilee.

'Not as far as I know. I think –' Karilee broke off, and Jo heard his steps echoing off hard stone as he walked across the hallway. There was a faint flicker of red light. 'Quickly! They're leaving!'

Jo ran after him. 'The Doctor too?' There was another flicker of light. Jo realized that she was looking through a window, a big picture window that reached almost to ground level. Outside, a huge, cumbersome-looking machine was throwing out clouds of steam and red sparks. She caught a glimpse of the Doctor standing on a railed platform, his hair flying, and next to him a big man who might be Epreto. Above them was the billowing canvas of a balloon.

'Doctor!' she yelled, though she knew it was hopeless. 'Doctor! You can't leave! I need you!' She beat her fists on the window frame. 'I need you so that I can take you to the Dead!'

But the steamwing was already rising into the air. The Doctor disappeared behind a wall of steam.

Jo sagged back to the ground, then saw Karilee staring at her. Too late, she realized what she'd said.

'The Dead,' said Karilee quietly. 'I should have realized.' He reached down, lifted her up and slung her over his shoulder. Jo struggled, but it was no use: Karilee's grip was as firm as steel. 'I think you'd better come with me,' he said.

'Put me down!' Jo protested. 'I can explain!'

But she knew that she couldn't. That was the really frightening thing: she couldn't explain what she'd said at all.

Mike knew there was no chance of surviving a fight with Omonu for long. His only hope was to try to talk the man out of it.

'I'm not even from the same world as you,' he said, desperately dodging the hands that had become bony, almost clawlike. One caught him on the shoulder, ripping his jacket, slamming him against the wall. Mike tried to wriggle past Omonu's body, but it was impossible in the confined space of the stairway. Instead he lost his footing, tripped sideways up the stairs, fell hard against the wall at the end.

'This is wrong,' he said, gulping for breath. He was remembering what Jo had said to the Dead Unpromoted, about playing by the rules. Remembering how the creature had *asked* to fight, despite its obvious desperation. 'You shouldn't be doing this. It's not honourable.'

But Omonu only growled, a gut-wrenching echo of the growl of the Unpromoted earlier on. Mike took a step backward, then, as Omonu jumped forward. He

124

dropped on to one knee and made a dive at the bigger man's leg.

He might as well have tried to demolish a concrete pillar. A hand grabbed his collar, and Mike heard and felt material tearing. Pain shot down his back.

'Jo!' he shouted. 'Karilee!'

Omonu growled again. Mike felt hands gripping his shoulders, pushing him back. He kicked out with his legs, hit something, heard a grunt of pain. Then his head jolted back, and a hand closed round his throat. He tried to move his arms to grip it, to push it away, but Omonu's other hand was holding them above his head.

He could feel the bones of his wrists being crushed. The pain was unbelievable.

A knee landed in his stomach, and Mike felt a tearing pain which rapidly spread to his chest. He kicked out again, writhed desperately, but the pain only got worse. His lungs strained for air.

Then the hand was removed from his throat and he was breathing again, gasping, almost screaming, his vision hazed with pain. He saw Omonu's hand hovering above his eyes, saw the claws bursting through the skin, felt the blood dribbling on to his skin. Then the hand moved away, revealing Omonu's triumphant face.

'Weaker than us,' he said. 'Weaker, weaker, weaker.'

Then he growled, and the clawed hand reached down towards Mike's chest.

Jo heard the scream through the open trapdoor. She struggled in Karilee's grip. 'Let me go! That was Mike!'

Rather to her surprise, Karilee did let her go, dropping her clumsily to the floor before jumping down through the trapdoor. Jo got up quickly and followed him. As she fell, she heard a faint, but ominous, gurgling sound from below.

A sick feeling rose in her stomach. Why had she left Mike with Omonu? She realized, too late, what had worried her about the look on Omonu's face.

He had been ready to fight.

She hit the ground, ran after Karilee, who was already headed for the dim shaft of light on the far side of the deadspace. When he reached the light he stopped, pulling a gun from his belt.

'You are no more than an animal!' he yelled. 'You don't deserve Promotion – you don't deserve to live!'

'No!' shouted Jo. 'Mike didn't mean it!'

But Karilee was out of sight. There was a flash, and the sound of a shot echoed around the deadspace. The light from within the tunnel went out, leaving the deadspace in darkness.

Jo ran forward. She thought she could hear heavy, gasping breaths, but she wasn't sure. The blood was pounding in her ears. She sensed movement ahead, saw the flare of a taper.

Karilee. Shadows danced on his face. He was aiming the gun, one-handed.

'Don't shoot Mike!' she begged. 'Please!'

'I'm not going to.' Karilee's voice was even, calm.

Jo became aware that the gasping breaths were getting louder. She looked ahead, saw Omonu, blood streaming down his face, staggering forward blindly.

Karilee fired, and Omonu tumbled backward, landing awkwardly on the floor. He was still breathing, great heaving shuddering movements, but as Jo watched they subsided.

She stepped forward. 'Mike?'

Silence.

'I think it may be too late for your friend,' said Karilee solemnly.

'Nonsense. That can't –' Jo broke off, as she noticed Mike's legs trailing over the top of the stairs behind the carcass of Omonu.

The trousers were drenched in blood.

'Mike?' She climbed the stairs quickly, stopped when she saw the blood-filled pit in Mike's chest, the cold, glazed-over eyes.

'Mike!' she shrieked. The stairs seemed to drift up towards her, and her vision blurred. 'No,' she moaned.

'You can't die. This is impossible.'

She crumpled on to the clay. Cold, dead clay. Clay filled with Mike's blood.

After a while, she noticed that Karilee's arms were around her shoulders. 'It has happened,' he said gently. 'Your friend is Dead.'

And Jo screamed.

Book Two

The Sky

Thirteen

Acolyte-Ordinary Iikeelu flew steadily in the near darkness, her body tense with expectation, the night air cold under her wings. Ahead, the dark mass that was the sun already eclipsed Kaygat, the city of men, and the Temples of the Edge: she could see the curved line that marked its rim steadily advancing against the dim flightways of the Sky as she flew closer. Every time she made this journey, Iikeelu realized afresh how huge the sun was, and how great the mystery that held it in the air between Land and Sky.

It was hard to believe that the Sky could just be destroyed. And by a man – a primitive, wingless, childish man. She wondered if Xaai's story was true, whether they might have misinterpreted the story of the fallen sun in the alien Land.

The inside of the sun is hollow.

The inside stays cold when the outside is hot.

The sun can fly where it wants – but only if the Sky is broken.

Those were the implications of Xaai's story. They might not be true. Xaai's jumbled memories of her last hours as a man were certain to be confused. But her information tied in with what was already known about Epreto's activities.

Iikeelu could see the guards' lights now, forming a misty necklace around the dark body of the sun. The gondola was there ahead of her, its lights doused, visible only as a shadow in the middle of the army. Iikeelu tacked, pushing her body into the wind, feeling the turbulence, the dancing of the air, racing across her body.

131

She folded her wings, dropped, let it buffet her freely for a few moments. The tension in her muscles eased slightly, but the sensation of expectation remained. The gun in her belly pouch was still there, heavy, uncomfortable, undeniable.

The necklace of lights jolted closer. Soon she could make out the spread wings of the individual flyers, tiny double arcs of light against the huge darkness of the sun behind them. Iikeelu spread her own wings and glided again, looking directly below her, where the childlands lay hidden in the night. She saw a faint spark of red mist.

Instantly she felt a tremor of alarm and excitement. A steamwing? At night?

It could only be Epreto. She struggled to follow the spark, to get a bearing, but it was gone. There must be clouds down there. No doubt Epreto was hiding within them. She peered downward again, but there was no sign of light. Ahead, the army were still some way distant. Iikeelu knew she had to reach them quickly, give them the news of her sighting. She dived to pick up speed. The rush of air made her hands, her eyes, the undersides of her wings sparkle with energy. It's good to be alive, she found herself thinking. Even now, when the world is in such danger. Perhaps especially now.

As she pulled up out of the dive, a shadow moved ahead of her. In an almost automatic response, her mind full of Epreto and his evil machines, her hands moved down to the gun pouch on her stomach.

But it was a naieen voice that spoke. 'Acolyte Iikeelu! Is it you?' The voice belonged to Priest–Senior Eeneeri, commander of the guard.

'I have sighted a steamwing!' she called back. 'Epreto!'

'I know,' said Eeneeri briskly. 'I saw it too.' He drew up below her, then climbed the rippling air until he was alongside. He was beautiful, she thought: the shape of his wings, the glint of his eyes in the guards' dim lights. She felt a tremor of arousal, and suddenly wished the sun, the guards, Epreto's steamwing, would all just go away, so that she could fly in the night and make love with Eeneeri, watch their seed drop on to the distant forest.

But there was no time for any of that. There wasn't even time to think about it. Not now.

'There are new instructions,' she told Eeneeri, keeping her voice brisk.

'From Aapurian?'

'Of course from Aapurian.' She risked a slight flirtation, a flicker of her eyelids. 'Who else would be instructing the guard of the sun?' She expected Eeneeri to laugh, but he said nothing. She knew then that he guessed what Aapurian's instructions would be.

'We are to kill Epreto.' She spoke slowly, clearly. For some reason she remembered Xaai's tears, her screams of pain, her bloodied body, crawling away from them slowly after telling her story. 'At any cost,' she said.

There was a moment's silence, then Eeneeri said, 'He is asking us to place our souls in jeopardy.'

'I know,' said Iikeelu softly.

Their wingtips brushed, just once. Iikeelu wondered if it was an accident, decided it probably wasn't. She felt another rush of sexual excitement, but suppressed it. There would be time for that later.

If they were still alive.

She could see the lead troopers of the guard now, their tattooed skins showing dull red and blue in the light from their search lamps on their breastbones. Their wings beat steadily, slowly, matching the wind, holding their positions. Some were scanning the Land below with binoculars. All of them had long-snouted guns slung under their bellies, and the small dull spheres of bombs. Despite her own mission, Iikeelu shuddered at the sight of this multiplicity of killing machines.

She flicked her wings, cleared herself of the emotion. There was no time for emotion now, either.

'It's all very well Aapurian telling us to kill Epreto,' Eeneeri said suddenly.

Iikeelu looked at him. Her heart began to thump

133

rapidly. Was Eeneeri about to defy Aapurian? The old priest had said it was possible. He had also given her instructions for that eventuality.

The gun seemed even heavier in her pouch, as if it were trying to drag her down to the Land, where the souls of murderers go.

'The trouble is,' Eeneeri went on, 'we have to catch him first.'

Iikeelu realized that the commander was only thinking aloud about strategy. She relaxed.

Eeneeri was still speaking. 'Aapurian doesn't seem to understand the consequences of the fact that the steamwing could fly twice as fast as any naieen. Nor does he understand the size and weight of the craft, and the degree of its defences.'

Iikeelu nodded. She asked Eeneeri if they'd got an accurate record of the steamwing's position.

It was Eeneeri's turn to flick his wings. 'The flyers on watch only got one brief sighting. One sighting is no good. By the time we've got to the spot, the machine could easily be ten or fifteen miles away – or more likely halfway up to the sun.'

Iikeelu scanned the darkness below, but saw no repeat of the misty glow. Had she and the guards both imagined it? It would be easy to see what you were expecting to see in the tension of the night.

But no. It had been real enough, she was sure of that. And Eeneeri had seen it too. Most likely Epreto was taking cover in the mist above the forest, waiting for the time when the army would have to leave the sun unguarded.

'Someone could wait for him here,' said Iikeelu quietly. 'A single assassin. He wouldn't be ready for that.'

Eeneeri looked at her, eyes suddenly bright. He wasn't stupid. He knew what she was thinking.

'You?'

Iikeelu said nothing, quietly checked the gun in her stomach pouch.

They had almost reached the surface of the sun now.

It was completely dark, but Iikeelu could feel it ahead of her, a wall of shadow, a trace of heat. She knew, without consulting any timepiece, that it was barely more than an hour until the sun would start to glow. By then the entire guard force had to be at least twenty miles away – which meant they needed to start within a few minutes.

Eeneeri was obviously thinking along the same lines. 'If we dive, it will give us some extra time,' he said. 'We'll spread out. One of us should come close enough.'

'No,' said Iikeelu. 'I will take the blame. You will merely provide the diversion.' She didn't dare look at Eeneeri. 'Those are Aapurian's instructions.'

She remembered Aapurian's last words to her, the old eyes heavy with sorrow: 'The action is blessed, Iikeelu – but remember, it is you who must kill Epreto. You who must live with that killing, take the responsibility. Are you prepared to do it?'

And she had said yes. Without hesitation. The ancients of the Flight might be afraid to act – even Aapurian might be afraid of the consequences – but Iikeelu wasn't. She would gladly sacrifice her soul for her world.

Eeneeri was looking at her steadily, his head turned against the slow wind of their flight. 'You don't have to do this,' he said quietly.

'Aapurian said that,' she replied.

A silence. Eeneeri began treading air, hovering, his wings making perfect rotations in the faint light. Iikeelu thought again how beautiful he was. And how clever, moral and wise. That such a person should be employed as a commander of a squad of killers showed what Epreto had done to the world. Why he had to die.

Yes. That was the way to think of it: he *had* to die. She, Iikeelu, was only an instrument of that inevitability.

'If he doesn't come here?' said Eeneeri at last.

'I will leave at the last possible moment. If I don't survive, there are others to take my place.'

'What has Epreto done to the world?' asked Eeneeri suddenly, his voice full of pain. 'When I first flew, most naieen didn't even know what a gun was. Now we have spies, flying armies and assassins. When did the world change?'

Iikeelu didn't reply. She stared ahead of her. She still couldn't see the sun, though it must be almost close enough for her to brush it with her wings. She knew it was there – she could feel it, the faint ionizing tension of power – but it remained invisible, a wall of darkness.

Like the future, she thought. The future that none of us know.

'Maybe it would be better to do nothing,' said Eeneeri. He sounded resigned, weary. He didn't seem like a commander any more.

'Would you let Epreto destroy the world?' asked Iikeelu fiercely.

'Are you sure he's really going to do that?'

'Yes!'

Another silence. Iikeelu realized with something bordering on horror that it was she who had lowered Eeneeri's spirits. It was her sacrifice. The fact that she was actually looking forward to shooting Epreto. To destroying him. That she had been looking forward to it from the moment of Aapurian's blessing.

'I think the action I have been given is proper,' she said.

It was Eeneeri's turn not to reply. He just hung there, like a judgement.

Iikeelu let herself drift forward and, yes, the surface of the sun did brush her wings. It was warm, and vibrated a little.

'We will dive,' said Eeneeri suddenly.

Iikeelu nodded, and said formally, 'The Confessor-Senior authorized me to approve such a plan. It is blessed.'

Eeneeri dipped his wings in formal acknowledgement, then soared away, whistling instructions to his people.

He didn't say goodbye.

Iikeelu looked below, at the dark mist where Epreto was hovering, waiting.

I'll kill him, she thought. I'll kill him and all those who are flying with him. And the world will be made new by my actions. Cleansed. Purified. It will be a world fit for people like Eeneeri to live in.

Iikeelu smiled at the thought, and balanced on the slight updraught created by the warmth of the sun, waiting for her moment.

Karilee did all the work: undressing the body and wrapping it in a winding-sheet stolen from Epreto's house, digging into the red clay, lowering the body into the pit. Jo couldn't even bear to look. This was *Mike*. Not an alien. Not even a stranger. *Mike Yates*. Surely he had been special? Why did he have to die? Why couldn't she have died instead? She sat on the cold stairs above the cellar floor, her face buried in her hands, trying not to listen to the scraping, shovelling sounds, and somehow unable to cry.

She had told him to die. She could remember that now. 'You have to let it kill you,' she'd said.

Why had she said that? Was it something to do with her loss of memory? It had to be. With hindsight, it seemed insane. Mike had thought it was insane at the time. He had wondered what on earth she was doing. Of course he had. So would she have done, if she'd been sane.

She remembered his puzzled concern for her, his total lack of concern for himself, and shuddered miserably. If only she hadn't left him in the cellar. She'd known what that expression on Omonu's face meant, hadn't she? So why hadn't she said something, or done something? Had that been another part of the insanity?

Had she deliberately left Mike in the cellar to die?

If only the Doctor was here. If only she could cry. But Jo knew that crying wouldn't bring Mike back.

And neither could the Doctor.

'Are there any words?'

Jo looked up, saw Karilee's kind face looking down at her. A single oil lamp, taken from Epreto's house, stood

137

on the cellar floor, beside a pile of broken clay.

He put a hand on her shoulder. 'Are there any words that should be said? From your Land?'

Words, thought Jo. Words. She looked at Mike's white, dead face projecting from the top of the winding-sheet. All she could think of was 'May God have mercy on his soul', but she supposed she should say more than that. She stared at the heap of clay for a while, made herself stand up. *Then* she started to cry, uncontrollable tears streaming down her face, sobs almost choking her. Karilee touched her shoulder again, left his hand there, giving silent comfort until the fit was over.

'He always tried to protect me,' she said at last. 'He tried to protect everyone. And not just because it was his duty – because ... because he wanted to.' Jo stopped, unable to think of anything else to say. It seemed ridiculous, that there was so little after nearly three years of friendship, but it was true.

'May the Dead take him,' said Karilee after a while.

'The Dead?' said Jo uneasily. She remembered something then: a robot. A robot made of wood.

Karilee shrugged. 'It's possible. The clay of the Land takes the bodies and souls of men. Maybe it takes their minds, too. Sometimes they are said to come back.'

Yes, thought Jo. *Yes.* That's what I want. She flung herself on the broken clay, hammered at it with her fists. She picked up fistfuls of the wet stuff, threw it down at the body so that it splattered over the dead face like some obscene half-mask. 'Bring him back!' she yelled. 'Bring him back! He was a *good* person!'

Eventually, exhausted, she sank into the clay, willing it to be warm, willing it to be alive.

But it was only cold and dead.

After a while she stood up, muddy, bedraggled. Karilee was standing at the bottom of the steps, watching her quietly. She took a step towards him and made a halfhearted attempt to wipe the mud off her jacket. He reached out and took her hand.

138

'I think I should take you to the Sky,' he said. 'Things are better there.'

He began shovelling the broken clay into the pit, finishing the job that Jo had started.

The Doctor had decided to stand on the observation platform of the steamwing, despite Epreto's protests. He was still standing there when Epreto pulled the control lever that would start the climb to the sun. It was dark around them: the city was already far below. The only light came from the open door of the firebox, a dull red glow which glinted off the wooden rails and the brass controls. The dimness of the light, or perhaps its red quality, also had the effect of smoothing out the strange furrows on the Doctor's face, making him look almost like a normal man.

Epreto decided to make a last attempt at getting the Doctor out of his way. 'We might meet the naieen on the way up,' he said. 'I'd rather face that encounter from inside the cabin.'

The Doctor didn't so much as glance round, but continued to gaze silently into the mist.

'As you wish, Doctor,' said Epreto eventually. He turned to check the controls.

'I know someone else who thinks like you do,' said the Doctor after a while. 'It's always for your own good, isn't it? The direct approach. The simplest solution. The only difference is, Lethbridge-Stewart does care about the consequences.' A pause. 'You're planning to take the live sun, aren't you? The one that still works?'

Epreto hesitated, decided to avoid the main question. 'Perhaps your friend doesn't live in the same kind of world as I do, Doctor. Here, only those who are intelligent, strong and virtuous are Promoted. They become naieen. The stupid, the weak and the unworthy will die.'

'And you think that's the best way?'

Epreto thought for a moment. 'Possibly not, but how

else could it be done? How else is it possible for the world to make progress?'

The Doctor appeared to think about this in his turn: at any rate, he remained silent for some time. Epreto watched the controls, lit by a small lamp with a downward-facing mirror. The needle on the pressure gauge climbed steadily.

'There are other methods,' said the Doctor at length. 'They take a bit longer, that's all.'

The steam pressure reached the trip point, and anything more the Doctor had been going to say was drowned in a thunder of gas as the buoyancy balloon was inflated to its maximum extent for the climb. Epreto watched the swelling fabric, thought with pride of the intricate machinery of valves and regulators that controlled it, that made it possible to govern the climb with a single hand on a single lever.

'We haven't got "longer",' said Epreto when the din had subsided. 'We've got as long as this sun lasts. When it dies, we all die anyway.' He turned away from the controls, faced the Doctor.

'I didn't choose this way, Doctor. I found the fallen suns by accident. I drew my conclusions because there were no others to be drawn. Do you know how many people in this world believe that the suns are built? The naieen certainly don't. I showed them drawings; I invited them to fly out and look for themselves, but they wouldn't go. Not one of them. When I tried to convince the Flight that something had to be done before the sun fails and we all perish, they accused me of blasphemy. I told them about the clay of the other continents eating away at our own, out in the fringelands, and they said it was "natural" and "the will of the Company Beyond the Sky". In the end they tried to have me restrained – and they only failed because my friends stood up for me. They sit up there, flying round and round the sun every night because they're frightened I'll steal it, but they've got no idea how I plan to do it. They've no notion of science – they think everything's done by magic. It's impossible to reason with them.'

'Are you sure of that?' The Doctor looked at Epreto, that bright searching gaze again. 'Have you ever really tried?'

Epreto remembered the flat eyes of the naieen priests watching him, struggling to understand, failing utterly. He nodded. 'They can't understand. They're incapable of it.' The steamwing was perceptibly climbing now. Epreto could feel the deck pressing against the soles of his feet. He told the crewmen to shut the boiler door, so that the naieen wouldn't be able to see them too easily. The instruction was only just in time: as the door shut, the faint lights of the Sky became visible through the clouds.

The Doctor was looking up at them. 'In my experience facts are easy to understand if you present them in the right way. But what you were offering the naieen was the early destruction of their world and an escape ark controlled by you. Now that was never likely to win them over, was it?'

Epreto shrugged. 'I've told you. They won't even go inside the sun. If they would just look – if they would just think about it – then perhaps some accommodation could be reached.'

The Doctor was still looking up, his face no more than a vague pale shape in the new darkness. He was silent for a few moments, then he said quietly, 'Well, it looks as if we might get another chance to persuade them.'

Epreto too looked up, and quickly saw what the Doctor meant. Some of the lights in the Sky were moving. Getting brighter. Getting closer.

The naieen were diving towards them.

The banging sounds from the kitchen made Jo jump at first, but Karilee only smiled and said that Epreto had left a couple of people to guard the house.

'I had to tie them up somewhere,' he said. 'At least there was plenty of rope in the kitchen.'

Jo tried a smile, but it wouldn't fit. Her face didn't seem capable of smiles at the moment. She kept seeing

141

Mike's face, the dead eyes, the blood-filled hole in his chest.

Karilee was saying something: '. . . the library, so we'll try the study.'

'Sorry?'

He looked back at her, smiled. A quick, glancing smile that instantly reminded her of Mike. 'I still need the evidence that the Confessor-Senior asked for. I think we ought to look in Epreto's study.'

'Oh – yes, OK.' Jo just wanted to follow. Follow and not have to think. She brushed at the drying clay on her coat. It was brown, shiny, almost like polished wood, and reminded her of something, though she wasn't sure what it was.

Karilee set off, following what appeared to be a sketched map. His lamp cast long shadows across a geometric floor. Jo was aware that at another time she would have been interested in the unique geometry of Epreto's house, the interlocking triangles and hexagons and squares. Now she didn't care. They were just shapes, that was all.

Inside the study, everything was decorated in subdued greens and yellows. The lamp, which had been good enough outside, barely seemed enough in here. There was a gas mantle on the desk, glowing softly. Karilee turned it up, began looking through the neat piles of paper. Then he tried some of the drawers.

'Locked.' He glanced up at Jo. 'Can you help?'

'Probably.' She fished her skeleton keys out of her jacket, circled the desk and began prodding at the lock. It opened at the third try.

Karilee quickly rifled through what was inside.

'There's a map of the Sky,' he said after a while. Then his eyes widened.

'What is it?' asked Jo.

Karilee didn't reply. He sat down slowly in the dark, upholstered chair behind the desk, and muttered, 'I don't believe this.'

Jo looked over his shoulder, saw a circular diagram covered in arrows and scribbles.

142

'What does it mean?'

Karilee was silent for a while, and when he spoke his voice was different. Jo recognized it: the quiet, toneless voice of extreme shock.

'He's going to poison the Sky.' Karilee looked up at Jo. 'Epreto's obtained a poison from the Dead and he's going to use it to kill the Sky. He's going to destroy the world.'

Fourteen

The naieen altered course, but they were too late. Epreto watched with satisfaction as the lamps of the guards fell below, still several miles behind the steamwing.

'You see, Doctor,' he said, 'they are inferior to men. They lack any capacity for planning. And to think that the best that might happen to me – to any intelligent man – is to become one of the naieen! Do you see now why things must change?'

'I don't think it'll be as easy as you think,' said the Doctor.

Epreto frowned at him. 'I'm not expecting it to be easy, Doctor. I just think it should be possible.'

'I wasn't referring to your long-term plans. I'm talking about the naieen guards.' The Doctor gestured at the blank space between the steamwing and the sun. 'I shouldn't think they'd be using lights if they wanted to sneak up on us. I imagine that the ones we saw were just a decoy party. The real attack is still to come.'

As the Doctor finished speaking, Epreto became aware of a change in the air. A faint whispering in the stillness. A sense, almost, of something breathing.

Wings.

The wings of naieen.

'You're right, Doctor,' he muttered. 'I suggest that we –'

There was a flare of light, followed by a rushing wall of hot, sulphurous air. Epreto dived behind the control panel, lay flat against the smooth wood of the observation platform. The Doctor, he noticed, didn't bother.

Reaching up with one arm, Epreto pulled the vent

lever. Clouds of steam roared out of the boiler. The observation platform began to tremble, then pitched as the steamwing lost balance and began to fall. Epreto pulled a second lever, which lit the flare lamps. He caught a glimpse of wild naieen eyes, furling wings, the white, crenellated wall of some sort of naieen craft, all tipping crazily in the night air. Then everything was obscured by the venting steam, as he'd intended.

'Gunners!' he bawled. He heard the clatter of metal from below, and felt a glow of pride. The crew were well trained in these situations, and must already have been at their posts.

The machine guns opened up, the vibration of their fire shaking the platform. Epreto got to his knees. He thought he heard the Doctor shouting, 'No!'

'What choice do we have, Doctor?' asked Epreto, though he doubted that the otherlander heard him over the racket of the guns. A bloodied naieen corpse tumbled in front of them, wearing some kind of crest on his uniform. A commander of the guards? thought Epreto.

Good.

The Doctor was still shouting: '. . . can't do this! This is no way to –'

The guns roared again.

Suddenly the Doctor leapt over the rail of the platform. Epreto stood up, saw him falling towards one of the crewmen at the guns. But he'd misjudged the jump: Epreto watched helplessly as he fell further, below the level of the boiler, and vanished into the swirling cloud of steam.

Epreto went back to the controls, and pulled back on the venting lever. Slowly the steam cleared, and the steamwing righted itself. After a few moments Epreto adjusted the trim of the wings and they began climbing again. There was no sign of the naieen or their craft in the air around them, either above or below.

And no sign of the Doctor, either.

Kimji Duboli knew there was something wrong as soon as the wings of his pedithopter passed over the wall around Epreto's estate. The house was too well lit – yellow light streaming from every window – and at the same time too quiet. The steamwing had been and gone: he could tell that from the smell of smoke lingering in the air. Epreto wouldn't have left all the lights burning, and he would have left a servant behind, at least one, someone who would have challenged Duboli by now.

Or at least waved to him.

Duboli banked cautiously around to the back of the house, let the 'thopter glide, and listened.

'Prepare accommodation', Epreto's message had told him, and he had done so. He'd moved the jumble of stores and pilgrimage mementos out of the spare room in his apartment overlooking the factory, and had a couple of beds flown in from the Old City. Then he had farwritten Epreto from the machine in his office, telling him all was ready, but had received no response. That had been odd in itself. If Epreto didn't reply, then one of the servants should have done so.

Add to that the fact that Omonu wasn't in his office, where he should have been, supervising the night shift, and that Omonu's 'thopter was missing . . . Duboli had thought that Omonu had been too calm, too unsurprised, when he'd found the farwritten message. He'd also thought that Omonu's reasons for being in Duboli's office at all had seemed more than a little specious. It had occurred to Duboli then that Omonu might be spying for the naieen; but he'd decided to keep his suspicions until he saw Epreto.

Now it was beginning to look as if he'd left it too late.

He saw the downed 'thopter as he rounded the corner of the house. The polished hardwood of the frame caught the light from the windows. It was right in the middle of the fungal gardens, not far from the wide stone apron that Epreto used to land the steamwing. It was impossible to tell from a distance whether it was in fact Omonu's, but Duboli had little doubt left now. Something was wrong. Very wrong.

He realized that he was going to have to do something about it.

He let the 'thopter glide down softly, landing it not on the long runway bisecting the gardens but on a shorter runway, one deliberately concealed behind a stand of high grasses. From there he approached the house on foot by an indirect route, periodically checking through the screening vegetation to see if there was any movement.

None.

Yet his landing on the concealed runway should have triggered several bells – in Epreto's library, in his dining room, in the servants' quarters. A whole posse of guards should be out looking for him by now. But no one had stirred.

Duboli put his ear to the elaborately carved coral-wood of the front door, and listened. After a moment he made out voices. They weren't speaking loudly enough for him to hear the words, and he couldn't be sure who they were, but one was very unusual – high-pitched, a little breathless, almost like a naieen. Duboli was sure he'd never heard that voice before. He wondered briefly if it was one of the otherlanders. But, if so, where was Epreto? Why was nobody answering the alarms?

The voices faded away, and there was the faint thud of a closing door. Duboli hesitated, then drew out his pass key. He turned it carefully in the lock, letting the tumblers fall one by one, so that no one inside would know he was there. Then he crossed the hall, very slowly, keeping the noise of his boots on the stone to a minimum. He hesitated again at the bottom of the stairs, wondering which way to go.

Then there was a sound from the kitchen. A muffled thud.

Duboli soft-stepped his way to the kitchen door, his heart thumping so hard that he wasn't sure he would be able to hear any more sounds above it. He drew his pistol, touched the door handle, flung the door wide.

The familiar faces of Jitil and Hanu stared up at him. They were tied to the great stone table in the centre of the room, gags across their mouths. Duboli hurried across

147

to them, ungagged Jitil, at the same time putting a finger to his lips.

'Someone is still here,' he whispered.

'I know,' said Jitil sourly. 'Let us get at him, that's all I ask.'

'Who is he?' whispered Duboli, as he began working on the knots binding Hanu.

'The one that attacked us was a big man, well armed.'

'An otherlander?'

'It's possible. One of the otherlanders got away earlier.'

'But that one was only a small man,' added Hanu, standing up awkwardly and massaging his limbs.

'There were some strange noises from the cellar, too,' said Jitil. 'We think they might have killed the Unpromoted.'

Duboli thought about this last piece of information for a moment. About the implications of it. If word about the Unpromoted got out, then Epreto's work was finished. The factory workers would lynch him for doing such a thing – or the city people would have him hanged by due process of law.

There was no time for messing about, Duboli decided. He turned to Jitil and Hanu, spoke quietly but clearly. 'We approach him with care. And we don't take any chances. As soon as we get close enough, we kill him and anyone who is with him.'

Jitil and Hanu nodded almost in unison, like the good servants they were. Duboli looked around the kitchen, searching the long racks of wooden and metal implements for those that would be the most use as weapons.

Iikeelu had seen the whole battle, from her solitary post by the quiescent sun. She had seen the false dive of the guards carrying their lights; she had seen the sparks of gunfire around the faint orange smudge of the steamwing as it attacked Eeneeri and his people. She had expected Eeneeri's pride to force him to attempt the kill, despite the odds and Aapurian's orders. Aapurian had told her to expect it. She was only surprised that she didn't feel any sorrow, and very little curiosity about whether Eeneeri had lived or died.

Everything in her mind was focused on the moment when the steamwing, and Epreto, would arrive.

She watched the orange blur approaching. It was easy for her to track it now: it could only be minutes away. She retreated against the dark surface of the sun, felt the warm pulse of energy ripple through her body.

No wonder Epreto had been tempted, she thought. No wonder he had wanted this power for himself.

But it wasn't his. It was the power of the Sky, and of Beyond the Sky. Iikeelu repeated that catechism aloud, holding on to it, holding on to the notion that she was defending the power of Beyond the Sky from misuse, and that this – and Aapurian's blessing – would justify her actions.

But, as the steamwing drew closer, the gun weighed heavier in her belly pouch, and she grew less and less sure whether anything could justify deliberate killing.

She dragged her mind away from the subject, concentrated on what she had to do. Surprise was everything: she would have only one chance. At last she drew out the gun.

'Activate,' she murmured.

Blue light flickered along the long, thin barrel of the strange machine.

'Active,' confirmed the weapon's tiny, strange voice. 'Remaining charge, thirty-seven; last active, present minus four hours; last program change, present minus three thousand, four hundred and seventy years and –'

'Stop list,' said Iikeelu. Once, she had let the machine go on: the numbers had never seemed to reach an end.

'Ready for instructions,' confirmed the gun. Remembering the formulaic language she had been taught, she said, 'Target humanoid, located quadrant four near strongest temperature gradient.' That description should find the steamwing, with its hot boiler.

'Power rating?'

Iikeelu took a breath, then said the necessary words. 'Fatal effect desired.'

* * *

Eeneeri folded his bloodied wing, gasping with pain. The nurse folded the bandage around it, as gently as he could, but nonetheless Eeneeri's vision blurred and his heart hammered in something close to panic.

He had watched the evil light of the steamwing slowly fade from the bullet-pocked timbers of the gondola's deck: now there were only flickering lamps, glassed-in tapers. Around him, dead or dying naieen lay in heaps, like broken puppets. But these puppets cried out and twitched and screamed and bled purple blood, enough blood to stain the timbers and drip down through the hatches to the interior of the gondola.

Eeneeri knew that it was his fault.

If he'd stayed within the permission given by Aapurian in his blessing – if he'd left it all to Iikeelu – then none of this would have happened. But he'd had to *try*. He'd had to try to save the world, to make Iikeelu's sacrifice unnecessary. Perhaps because he had liked her. Perhaps because their wingtips had brushed. It was a stupid reason for a military decision, and Eeneeri's people had paid the price for it with their lives.

And Iikeelu was still going to have to play the assassin.

'Sir!' The shout from the port side had the kind of urgency in it that made Eeneeri whirl around at once, all thoughts of regret forgotten. If Epreto was coming back for another try, they were all as good as dead.

But no. There was a brightly coloured, square-winged shape drifting towards the gondola, far too small to be a steamwing.

The surviving guards on deck had aimed their guns. 'Wait!' cautioned Eeneeri. 'Do not take a life in vain!'

The shape came closer, and Eeneeri could see that there was a man strapped to the flyer, though his wings had to be lighter and better made than any manmade type that Eeneeri knew. All the anger, the fury at his own mistake and Epreto's ruthlessness, suddenly boiled to the surface of Eeneeri's mind, and before he could prevent it he had struggled free of the nurse and, in a mist of pain, was aiming his own gun at the stranger. He remembered his own caution to the guards — *do not take a life in vain* — but it was no use. Whoever this was, it was a man. And men had become the enemy of the naieen. That had happened in the last few minutes: finally, irrevocably.

He watched the man drift closer, saw him smiling down at them from his harness. He felt his finger tightening on the trigger of the gun as the man came into range. Then the stranger's eyes took in the carnage on the deck around Eeneeri, and the smile faded, to be replaced by a look of shocked sympathy.

Eeneeri loosened his grip on the gun, and at the same time the man seemed to realize his danger. 'I'm not from Epreto,' he said. 'I've just got away from Epreto.' He landed on the deck, his wings collapsing gracelessly around him. Eeneeri stared in amazement as the brightly coloured material began to shrink, as if evaporating.

The man was looking around, his face solemn. 'I'm truly sorry,' he said. 'I should have prevented this. I didn't realize just how . . .' He broke off, his eyes scanning the deck again. Clearly he was lost for words. The wings had almost disappeared now, changed to a small sphere of material cradled in the stranger's hands. That alone told Eeneeri that this person was more than a man. And the stranger's face was . . . odd. Crumpled. Diseased, almost, except that he didn't look ill.

Eeneeri kept the gun aimed at him. 'Who are you?' he asked.

'I'm . . . a traveller. Call me the Doctor. I need to speak to the Flight.'

Eeneeri looked at the man, trying to judge him, trying to understand through the haze of shock and fear.

'What do you know about the Flight?' he asked.

'Well, so far, only what Mr Epreto has chosen to tell me.' The man smiled. 'I'd like to hear their side of the story.'

Eeneeri felt a sense of relief, almost of warmth, spreading through his body. This, at least, seemed to be a reasonable man.

But that was no reason to trust him.

'We will take you to the Temple,' he said carefully, 'but we will have to keep you under guard.'

The Doctor looked around the deck once more, and nodded. 'My dear fellow, I quite understand.'

Eeneeri took in the sympathy in the stranger's eyes, and said, 'I'm sorry, Doctor, but I feel I have no choice but to confine you in one of the cabins for the flight. I can't take any risk, however slight.' He took a breath, realized that he was afraid to acknowledge the reason for that, afraid to admit that the world had changed enough for the next words to be spoken. 'The Land and the Sky are now at war.'

Fifteen

Karilee sat at one of the library desks, looking through the papers they'd taken from the study and comparing them with the open pages of a huge leather-bound atlas. 'The points where Epreto wants to poison the Sky are above each of the Seven Hills,' he said. 'Look: Kaygat, Mirador . . .'

Jo peered over his shoulder at the brilliant colours of the map. She saw that the Land was roughly circular, like a decorated plate, with stippled hills at regular intervals approximately two-thirds of the way to the rim. Beyond them ran a wide strip of water, weaving in and out of the hills. Around the rim itself were grey-black mountains. It was hard to judge the scale of the place, and Jo had never had the chance to get a clear look at it in daylight, but she felt from the scale of things on the map, from the separation of cities and villages, that the entire Land probably wasn't all that big – no more than a hundred miles or so from rim to rim.

It was, quite literally, a small world.

Jo realized now the full implications of what Mike had told her about the sun. This place was artificial. Not just the sun – the whole place. The geography of the Land. The shape of the Sky. Everything. The shape was too regular, too contrived to be natural. And, if someone had built the world, then it was more than likely that they had also –

There was a sound. It was the faintest of scraping sounds, so faint that Jo thought for a moment she'd imagined it. Karilee didn't notice: he was scribbling notes on the back of his sketch map of the house.

Then the sound was repeated. Jo looked around Epreto's library, at the leather-bound books on their thick wooden shelves, the twin reading desks, the soft carpet with its design of leaves and flowers, trying to find something that could be a source of the noise.

Then she realized that the door handle was moving, the reflection of the lamplight shifting on the polished brass.

Karilee said, 'That's the list done. We should get this to –'

Jo shushed him, gestured at the door.

'There's someone out there,' she mouthed.

As she spoke, the door began to swing open, very very slowly.

'Get back!' snapped Karilee, pulling out his gun. Jo retreated behind him, towards the window. She searched the library for a weapon, but could see nothing but books.

The door slammed open. Jo saw two men wielding long knives and a third, smaller man with a gun. There was a pistol shot – another – and Karilee was falling from his chair, holding the atlas up in front of him as a shield. The paper he'd been writing on fluttered down to the floor, slid towards Jo. She picked it up and, at the same time, saw one of the knife-wielders crumple to the floor with a gasp of pain, hands pressed to his stomach. Jo dropped behind the reading table by the window, clutching Karilee's paper.

There was a third shot, another groan. Jo heard the splattering of a fluid on to the wooden boards, and guessed that it was blood.

'This one's dead. Kill the other one, quickly.'

Jo felt her skin prickle as a wave of sheer terror passed over her. Karilee was dead. And these people were going to kill her. Nothing else. They weren't going to interrogate her. They weren't going to imprison her. They were just going to kill her.

In desperation she put her shoulders under the heavy table, levered it forward. On Earth she couldn't have lifted it, but here her strength was just enough to get it moving.

There was a pistol shot, and wood splintered.

'Get her!' roared the voice. There was a thud of footsteps, and a series of metallic clicks.

Reloading the gun, thought Jo. She realized she had one chance. Now, and only now.

She got up slowly, let the heavy figure approaching see her, then, still slowly, started to dodge out of the way to the left. His eyes followed her movements, he jumped over the still-tumbling desk – and Jo darted to the right.

The man didn't dive straight through the window as she'd hoped he would, but he did become entangled with the desk. Jo jumped over him making for the door. The small man – the one carrying the gun – was still trying to reload. He left it just too long to stop doing that and try to get in Jo's way: she was past him, jumping over the prone form of the injured man.

The blood reminded her. Karilee.

But there was nothing she could do about him now. She half ran, half flew down the stairs, her feet barely making contact with the treads. The front door was open: she dived through it, heard a shot behind her and the thud of the bullet hitting wood, presumably the door.

Outside, everything was dark.

She ran. Ran *fast*, knowing she had to get away from the light shining through the door, had to be invisible before –

Another shot.

Four bullets last time, she remembered.

Run.

Another shot. Another. Jo couldn't hear the bullets, guessed they were going wild.

Good.

She kept running, but could hear footsteps on the path behind her now. She steered off the path, into the thick grass and bushes. The going was difficult and Jo quickly realized that she was not only making a lot of noise but was also leaving a trail that was easy to follow.

Her eyes were adjusting to the darkness now. The light from the windows was enough for her to see a cliff of stone not far ahead.

The wall. How was she going to get over the wall? Karilee had used a rope and grapple, but Jo had no idea where that was now. He had folded it up, left it concealed in the grounds somewhere. Had it been by the field of mushrooms? If only Mike –

Mike. Was dead.

She stopped running for a moment, felt an uncontrollable sob rising in her throat. At the same moment she seemed to hear Mike saying, '*Run*, Jo!'

So she ran again. She could hear her pursuers behind her; they too were in the undergrowth. It could only be a matter of time. She felt a sudden, sharp pain in her knee, and her leg crumpled under her. For a moment she didn't realize what had happened, but then she heard the echoing gunshot and thought, I've been shot.

Then she saw the wooden frame next to her, the folded wings, and realized she hadn't been shot at all. She'd banged her knee on this thing – this . . .

Jo stared at it, taking in the pedals, the complicated arrangements of chains and gears and the big pale wings.

This thing was designed to fly. To fly by pedal power. She'd seen a few of them over the city when she and Karilee had been walking to Epreto's. She had no idea how to work it, but there was no time to worry about that. She jumped on to what was clearly a saddle, reached her feet down to the pedals, and started pedalling. At once, the thing began moving. At the same time, Jo saw lights ahead, saw the face of the small man with the gun, his teeth bared in something that looked like a snarl. Jo leant to one side, riding the ungainly contraption like a bike, steering it around with the metal bar at the front that wasn't quite a handlebar, because it pointed towards her, like the tiller of a small boat. Somehow she made the turn, stayed upright.

She found herself cycling down a concealed concrete path, gathering speed. Suddenly, with a metallic snick, the wings dropped down, the front wheel rose – and she was flying.

There was one last gunshot behind her, and the vehicle vibrated from the impact of a bullet. Then she was rising into clear cold air, the light from the windows glimmering across the fabric of the wings. For a moment Jo thought she'd got away. Then she heard shouts below, and realized that it wouldn't be long before they found some way of following her. She also realized that she had nowhere to go. Mike was dead. Karilee was dead. She didn't know where the TARDIS was. She didn't know where the Doctor was. She didn't even know how she'd got here.

She thought for a moment. Who had Karilee said he was working for? The Flight?

So the Flight were against Epreto. It was Epreto's people who were after her. Therefore, with luck, the Flight ought to protect her from her pursuers. They might even help her find the Doctor. The only trouble was going to be finding them.

She turned the tiller, and the flying bike tilted to the left and began to pick up speed towards the wall. Ahead, she could see the tall towers of the city, sparkling with pinkish light.

Behind her, there was the faint but distinct sound of wood scraping on wood. Jo looked over her shoulder and saw something that looked like a racing yacht with wings sliding along the main runway of Epreto's house. She realized there was no more time for thinking about what she was going to do. She bent her body forward, pushed down on the pedals as hard as she could.

Slowly, too slowly it seemed, the city came closer.

Xaai woke up and, just for a moment, she thought she was still a man. The creaking of the gondola around her, the cold night air, the sound of sails filling in the wind – everything seemed familiar, perfect.

Then she felt the pain, and she remembered.

Tuy. Killing Tuy.

Metamorphosis.

Capture.

Imprisonment.

Torture.

She raised a wing, cried out at the livid pain. Now, she *couldn't* fly.

Blurry-eyed, Xaai tried to establish where she was. She could see the deck of the gondola, dimly lit by lamps. She could see other naieen, bodies, dark stains of blood. She crawled forward, trying to ignore the pain. But all she saw were dead eyes, limp wings, broken limbs. Is this my fault? she wondered. Did this happen because of what I told Iikeelu?

Xaai knew how urgent Iikeelu had said it was for her to remember. Perhaps this had happened because she hadn't remembered quickly enough. 'I'm sorry,' she said aloud. 'I did try. I tried as hard as I could.'

The dead eyes stared at her. A piece of torn skin flapped in the slow wind.

Xaai crawled a little further into the midst of the carnage, her muscles burning with every movement. She could see the crenellated wall of the gondola now, and above it the shining beehive windows of a Temple. Faint lights from the Sky gleamed beyond. She struggled towards the wall, pushing against bodies rigidified in broken, tortured positions.

'I'm sorry,' she whispered. 'I'm sorry I'm sorry I'm sorry.'

There was a clear space beside the wall, where some sort of gun was mounted. By using the cold metal of the gun barrel, Xaai was able to pull herself upright. Her back and wings a solid mass of agony, she scrabbled with wings and arms at the thick wooden blocks of the low wall, and managed to heave herself up on to the top of it.

She expected to fall, but she didn't: the wall was several feet thick, and she could balance on it. She looked, not across at the dim lights of the Sky, but down, down at the infinite blackness of the ground.

No. Not quite black. She could see a faint light there, perhaps a farm, perhaps some low-sailing flyboat crewed by men. She imagined that boat and its crew. She imagined the dry night wind, the smell of soil, the faint lowing of herdbeasts from below. That had been flying. She had been flying all along, when she had been Xa, when she had been a man looking with envy at the Sky. She had always been flying, and had never known it.

I can't fly any more, she thought. But I will taste the air again. One more time before I die.

Crying with the pain, Xaai hauled herself the last few feet and tumbled over the edge of the gondola, gathering speed through the cold air, helplessly falling towards the Land where she had once been happy.

Epreto saw the crewman die.

The light came from nowhere, a blue-white glow, as if lightning had struck on the boiler plate. The crewman dropped back, cried out, convulsed. Then the light faded. Epreto gripped the rail, stared, ready to jump down and take hold of one of the machine guns. But then he thought better of it. Whatever had killed the man was of the sun, and if it was targeting his craft then the naieen must be controlling it in some way.

Epreto thought for a moment, then roared, 'Loose the balloon!' If the naieen had truly taken over the sun, this manoeuvre would do no good. But he didn't think that they could have done that: this was probably an isolated weapon, something stored in the Temples for years, its uses known but its principles never understood.

The four remaining crewmen were running to the ropes. Epreto watched as they loosed the knots, admiring their discipline. Then the light struck again, the glow surrounding two men at once. The others staggered back from the dead bodies in terror. Somewhere in the back of Epreto's mind he was aware that he too was supposed to be afraid.

But all he could think was: above. They've got to be above me. He looked up. As the killing light reached its brightest, Epreto saw the faint image of a naieen, high above.

159

Out of range of the guns.

Epreto jumped down from the platform, landing on the narrow rail that was the balloon anchor ring before the dying men had stopped their convulsions. The other two men backed away, their faces blank with terror.

'Help me loose the ropes!' Epreto yelled at them. He was already struggling with the knots. 'Before they fire at us again! Quickly!'

The men came forward, but Epreto could see that they were barely able to control the movements of their bodies. He moved around the ring, taking the last two knots with one hand each, pulling at the loosing points.

'Now! Hold on to the ropes!'

One of the men understood, gripped a rope. The other seemed confused, hesitated, then desperately jumped up as his fellow, Epreto and the balloon rose clear of the steamwing.

The pale light bloomed around him. He screamed as he died.

Gripping the rope one-handed, Epreto pulled out his hand pistol and tried to find the naieen he'd seen above. As the light reached its brightest, he saw the faint movement of wings against the darkness of the sun.

Just in range.

He waited an instant, then fired. There was no way of telling if the shot had been effective: the light faded too quickly for that. All Epreto could do was wait.

The steamwing, her controls locked, ploughed on upwards. Epreto imagined the alarms chiming inside the sun, the strange chants of 'Proximity Alert!' He remembered what had happened when Wutil had brought a skyboat in at the wrong gate, many years ago. How the sun had defended itself from what it had deemed an intruder. He waited.

Light flared around the steamwing, light far brighter than that which had destroyed Epreto's men. It exploded at once, a ball of blue-white flame and roaring steam. In the light from the fireball, Epreto could see the naieen clearly, a female in grey uniform. She was diving triumphantly away from the sun, obviously assuming she'd achieved her objective.

And then she saw him.

Her wings spread, and she pulled up, turning in the air. Epreto saw the glint of metal in her hand, only feet above him.

He aimed the pistol and fired. Her hand shattered, and the metal dropped. Epreto recognized a sun-made hand-gun, but it was too far away for him to recover it. He aimed his own gun again, and fired, this time at the naieen's heart.

He watched her die, the light fading from her eyes as she fell slowly past him, to join the burning fragments of the steamwing on the long fall to the childforest below.

Then, judging his moment, Epreto began swinging on the rope below the balloon, building up momentum, swing by swing, until he had enough to make the leap towards the waiting surface of the sun.

He seemed to fall for longer than was possible. He was almost convinced that he'd misjudged it, that he would fall to his death, when his outstretched hands scraped on the warm, live surface.

'Aapex,' he said, wondering if he'd left the code word too late.

The surface softened, gripped his hands. He felt the material reach out, cloak him, draw him inside the skin of the sun.

He knew then that he had won the battle.

The world would end when he wanted it to.

Sixteen

Aapurian dreamt of the Sky falling. For some reason, it fell upward and outward: breaking, perhaps, rather than falling, just as the philosopher Kuujeeni had predicted. In the dream, Kuujeeni, wearing ancient robes like those on the Temple woodcuts, was doing a little dance, swinging from wingtip to wingtip in the impossibly still air underneath the falling-upwards Sky, saying, 'I told you so – I told you so', over and over again.

It should have been funny, but Aapurian woke with his heart hammering and pain reaching from his gut into his chest.

'Confessor-Senior.' One of the acolytes. Iikeelu? No. Not an acolyte at all. A black uniform. A commander. Eeneeri.

Aapurian sat up slowly, took in the guard commander's damaged wing, and the strange man with the crumpled face standing next to him. The room was still lit only by lamplight, gleaming off the polished walls: at least it wasn't daylight yet. The battle was yet to be decided. Probably.

'I'm sorry to have woken you,' said Eeneeri.

'I shouldn't have fallen asleep,' said Aapurian. Wondering why he was old. Now. When he needed to be young and strong. 'What happened?' he asked.

It was the man who spoke in response. 'Epreto opened fire with machine guns. The naieen were massacred.'

Aapurian remembered his dream. 'I told you so,' said the ancient philosopher inside his head. Aapurian just managed to stop himself from repeating the words aloud.

'And Iikeelu?' he asked instead.

'We don't know yet,' said Eeneeri. 'Epreto will reach the sun about now.'

Poor Iikeelu, thought Aapurian.

But he didn't say anything aloud. He didn't dare. Instead he slowly got up, his stiff limbs creaking. He felt sick and thirsty at the same time: a bad sign, he knew.

Eeneeri poured a glass of water from the condenser and silently gave it to Aapurian, who drank it slowly. When he had finished, the man stepped forward and extended a hand. 'Allow me to introduce myself. I'm the Doctor.'

Aapurian extended a hand in turn. The Doctor gripped it in a strange way, palm to palm instead of palm to wrist. 'Aapurian. Confessor-Senior.' He paused. 'You're not of this Land, are you?'

The Doctor shook his head.

Aapurian nodded. He felt his heart speed up again, felt a dull ache spread along his arteries. Could it be true after all?

'Then is this the end?' he asked quietly. 'Are you here to judge us?'

The Doctor frowned. 'Oh, no, my dear chap. I think you're under a terrible misapprehension. It's not like that at all.'

Jo was lost. The city was somewhere behind her, and it was utterly dark above and below. She had no idea whether Epreto's men were still chasing her. Occasional spots of water hit her face, so she supposed it was cloudy: for all she knew, she might be flying through clouds. Once, she'd seen what she thought was another pedithopter, but she hadn't been sure. It might have been a naieen. It might have been one of Epreto's men. She couldn't seem to think clearly any longer: the simple effort of keeping the pedithopter flying was tiring her out. Her back ached, her feet hurt, and every push at the pedals sent a stab of pain through her right knee. She was constantly afraid that she would somehow lose her balance and start to fall.

But Jo wasn't sure she dared land, either. The ground

was dark. She had no way of telling whether she was flying over a flat surface, safe for landing, or trees, or rocks. There could even be water down there. She had a vague idea that there was a narrow sea near Kaygat, and canals – more accurately open sewers – running into it from the city. But she wasn't sure how she knew that, and didn't particularly want to think about how she might know it. She didn't want to think about how she knew anything. It only made her more dizzy, and more afraid of falling.

If only she could find the Doctor. Everything would be all right then.

Suddenly there was a movement above her, a dark shadow in the periphery of her vision. She flinched, turned the tiller of the pedithopter, saw too late the bulky body falling towards the machine's own port wing.

'Look out!' she shrieked.

The falling thing stirred. She saw a wing extend, an eye glint in the dim light. Then, with a sickening crack, its body connected with the wing. The tiller was wrenched out of Jo's hands, the pedals kicked against her feet.

Then the body was gone, and she was falling, a slow, spiral descent. She pushed at the pedals, but heard only the clatter of disconnected machinery. An attempt at pulling the tiller over only made the machine lurch even further over to the left. Suddenly realizing that, despite the slowness of her fall, she was in real danger, Jo leant the other way, in an attempt to physically rebalance the craft. It appeared to have little effect.

She could see the damage to the wing now, in the light from a nearby window: a tear in the fabric, a broken wooden strut pointing upward. Then, with an awful shock, she saw a wall of stone beyond, illuminated by dull lamplight. A building, perhaps, or a cliff face. It was getting closer fast – she was being carried towards it by the wind. She pulled the tiller bar over again, and the 'thopter lurched. But the stone wall kept getting closer.

What a stupid way to die, she thought.

A voice called from below. 'Jump! I will catch you! I will cushion your fall!'

The wall got closer. Jo stared at it, mesmerised.

'Jump!'

The voice was naieen. Jo was sure of it.

– all danger is from the Sky –

She could see the fibres in the body of the wall now, the dried clay –

– you are clay you will join the living clay –

'Please jump!'

And Jo jumped, just as the pedithopter ploughed into the wall. She fell slowly into the shadow of the crumpling wings, through the cold air, past the clay walls, accelerating downward.

There was a crack of wings, and warm arms caught hold of her. Her face was pressed against fur, damp fur that smelt of sweat and fear. The world seemed to spin around, and Jo heard a grunt of pain.

'Please,' said a muffled voice. 'Please, I want this one to live.'

So do I, thought Jo.

Then there was an impact, a bone-jarring, breath-taking impact. When Jo had recovered her senses, she became aware of someone screaming. A long, pitiful, painful scream, tearing into her nerves and her brain. The arms holding her flailed.

Jo rolled clear, saw the naieen at last, a young woman with bloodied fur, rolling on her back in agony. The dim light was just enough to reveal soft muddy ground pooled with water and broken by swathes of long grass. She could hear the faint, regular scrunch of surf against a beach, not far away.

She leant forward, stroked the crumpled face of the naieen woman. 'Where does it hurt?'

The screaming stopped, and the woman looked at her. 'It isn't the pain,' she said. 'I'm still alive.' She began to wail again. 'I'm still alive, and I wanted to be dead. Please, please, I wanted to be dead.'

Jo looked around her nervously, feeling at the same

165

time vaguely irritated with her rescuer. Did nobody on this world do anything that actually made sense? 'Be quiet or we'll both be in danger,' she said briskly.

The woman blinked, stared at Jo with her large, dark naieen eyes. 'I . . .' She struggled upright.

Jo decided to take a chance. 'Are Epreto's people after you as well?'

'Epreto?' The woman didn't seem to have heard the name. She swayed, her wings and body shaking. 'I don't know. They were killed because of me. At least I think so.'

Jo looked up, but couldn't see anything moving in the air above them. 'Who were killed?' she asked.

'The naieen. All the naieen.' The woman leant forward, coughed. Black phlegm covered her lips, and her voice was reduced to a choked whisper. 'Everyone in the Sky is dead.'

Aapurian rested against the cushions of his bed. His breath was short, and the sense of sickness in his stomach had worsened. Eeneeri had given him a glass of sweet tea, but he wasn't able to drink more than the occasional sip.

The alien, the one called the Doctor, watched him from the other side of the room, sipping his own tea from time to time. He was sitting cross-legged just above the window in the floor. The first red, shadowy sunlight was just beginning to shine through the glass there, making strange, soft shadows in the folds of the Doctor's face. Aapurian wondered what had happened to Iikeelu. Whether she had got away in time. Whether she had killed Epreto. Whether it would make any difference, in the long run, when there were other men who would simply take Epreto's place.

'I don't understand why you didn't just wipe out Epreto a long time ago,' said the Doctor. 'You knew roughly what he was up to.'

'You don't understand, Doctor.'

'Yes, well, that's what *he* told me.'

Aapurian closed his eyes. How could he explain to this

stranger the way his world worked? Did it matter as much as stopping Epreto?

'You know that we and the men are of the same people? Part of the same species?'

The Doctor nodded. 'I gathered as much. Correct me if I'm wrong: children are born in the forest, probably from budding plants. They grow into men, leave the forest. The men grow huge, fight, and the winners become naieen, who breed. Survival of the fittest, Epreto called it.' The Doctor put his glass down next to the condenser and slowly stood up, staring at the walls. The frame of the Temple creaked as the morning wind began to stir. 'I left Epreto because he was killing your people with machine guns,' he said at last. 'Which, given that he knows as well as you do that you are the same species, seems a stupid and wanton thing to do. But he had reasons for his actions. He has plans. Before I left, he explained them to me. Now I want to know your side of the story.'

'It isn't exactly a "side", Doctor,' said Aapurian. He paused, then waved Eeneeri away. The commander left, flicking his wings in formal salute.

The Doctor watched Aapurian expectantly, the sunlight slowly brightening on his face and his strange clothing.

'You see, there was an experiment,' began Aapurian at last. 'We – our world, ourselves, the very cycles of our lives – are the product of a race of beings: gods, philosophers, call them what you will –'

'The Aapex,' supplied the Doctor.

Aapurian felt his heart accelerate once more. 'How do you know that name?' he asked.

The Doctor put a finger to his chin. 'I saw the name in a book that Epreto let me read. Reekaa's *Compendium*. I recognized them at once. It was hard to tell from the *Compendium* what they had really been up to – the whole thing was cloaked in legends and half-truths. But I could guess.'

Aapurian's heart slowed, a little. He took a sip of the

167

sweet tea, which was now almost cold. 'What was your guess, Doctor?'

The Doctor stood up, began pacing the narrow room, frowning as if he were trying to work out what to say. 'The Aapex weren't a people, exactly,' he began at last. 'They were a corporation. A ... company, of people rather like Epreto. Probably worse than Epreto, because they didn't even have any reason for their ruthlessness except the desire for profit. As far as I can gather, this was some kind of genetic template experiment for the bio-engineering and terraforming of low-gravity planets such as this one. Except that this particular planet is too far from its star to get any useful heat that way, so they had to provide artificial suns.' He paused, met Aapurian's eyes. 'The experiment was almost certainly illegal.'

Aapurian nodded slowly, felt his own face crease into a smile, almost against his will. 'Did you tell Epreto any of this?' he asked.

The Doctor glanced at Aapurian sharply. 'I didn't tell Epreto anything. I wasn't sure he was ready to know about it. Why aren't you surprised?'

'At your description of the Aapex?'

The Doctor nodded.

Aapurian said quietly, 'I have my own ideas. I have had them for some time. You see, I don't entirely represent the Flight.' He hesitated, wondering how much further he dare go. There was still the possibility that this alien represented the Aapex in some way, and was merely dissembling. He was almost sure it wasn't the case, but –

There was a knock at the door. 'Confessor-Senior.' Eeneeri's voice.

Aapurian told him to come in, twisted his body round to look at the door as it opened. As soon as he saw the expression on Eeneeri's face, he knew.

'There is news of Iikeelu.'

Aapurian waited.

'Her body was found in the burning zone below the sun. She was shot dead.' Aapurian thought of Iikeelu; fierce, young, intelligent, beautiful. He thought of the meaningless sacrifice he had let her make. Because there was a chance. Because it had been necessary for someone to take it. 'There were also some fragments of canvas and rope,' Eeneeri went on. 'They might have been pieces of the steamwing, so Epreto may be dead too.'

The Doctor shook his head. 'Knowing Epreto, I'd say it's more likely he got away. He was close to the sun, and he has control over some of its systems. He'll have found a way to escape.' He turned to Aapurian. 'What we have to do is try to get that control back from him. I have some knowledge of Aapex systems myself. If you let me have the necessary materials, I might be able to build a machine which could interfere with Epreto's control.'

Aapurian frowned. He wasn't sure he understood what the Doctor was trying to do. 'What materials will you need?' he asked.

'Oh, just simple electronics. A forty-ZD MIPS system, a reverse double capacitance circuit –' he frowned '– maybe a transionic polarizer.'

Aapurian glanced at Eeneeri, but the commander shrugged.

'I'm sorry, Doctor, I don't think we have these things,' he said. 'Is there anywhere you can obtain them?'

'Well, there's the TARDIS of course, but the Dead have that.'

'The Dead?' Aapurian swallowed, struggled to hide his revulsion. Had this man met and dealt with everyone in the world? How long had he been here? 'How did that come about?' he asked.

'I wish I knew. I left the TARDIS in the forest. When I came back an hour later she was gone, together with one of my companions.' His face shadowed. 'I don't suppose you have any contact with the Dead?'

Aapurian shook his head. 'The Dead shun things of the Sky, and we avoid them. We are irrevocably opposed – I suppose you would say that we are engineered to be so. It might be possible to attempt contact, but there simply isn't time –'

'Then everything is lost,' said Eeneeri from the doorway.

Aapurian jumped: he had forgotten that the commander was still there.

'Not necessarily,' said the Doctor. 'It might be possible to build the device with substitute components. Do you have anything made of copper? It would need to be absolutely pure, and for preference plate-shaped.' He held up a hand. 'About the size of my palm. And for the polarizer . . .' he seemed to think for a moment.

'There are the Temple bells,' Eeneeri pointed out. 'But —'

'Use them,' said Aapurian. 'Doctor, go with Eeneeri. Get whatever you need.' He turned to the commander, shaped his hands into the formal sign of blessing. 'Eeneeri, you have my blessing to give the Doctor any part of the Temple, or any other object within the domain of the Flight.'

Eeneeri looked uncertainly at Aapurian, then at the Doctor. Then he flicked his wings, turned and left. The Doctor flashed a smile at Aapurian and followed.

Aapurian stared wearily at the closed door and hoped that his trust in this stranger would be justified.

Epreto stood in the central chamber of the sun and tried to work out what to do next. Normally he was awed by the vast size of the chamber in which he stood, by the multitude of lights, controls, the pillars of glittering mist reaching to the domed ceiling. But now their size and power gave him no comfort. He was shaking with anger, frustration and — he had to admit it — the residue of fear.

The naieen had almost killed him. They had tried twice, and twice they had come close to succeeding. Epreto had always assumed that the naieen wouldn't go that far, even when their role as leaders of the world was challenged. For them to be willing to kill meant that they knew that Epreto's plan was something more than that — which meant that they probably knew the truth.

Epreto wondered if Gefen and Lofanu had talked to agents of the Flight. It was a possibility he should have considered. But, whatever the reason, one thing was certain. He couldn't risk leaving the sun again. He couldn't leave the fulfilment of his plan for as much as another day. All the carefully worked-out schedules that he had hoped to guide personally over the next weeks would have to be carried out at once. Somehow he had to bring his people here now. Somehow he had to arrange to bring the supplies.

And, most importantly, he had to arrange to poison the Sky.

He thought for a while, then walked to the farmessaging machine and began to compose a letter to Duboli.

Seventeen

The jumbled 'rocks' at the base of the cliff face were warm, almost soft, a reminder that they were part of the living clay that was the Land. Jo was tempted to lean against it, to soak up the warmth and the comfort, but she knew there was no time for that. She had to find the Doctor and – assuming he wasn't already dead – get him back from Epreto and then . . . and then . . .

She frowned, not quite sure what she needed to do after that. Something important. Something that worried her, though she couldn't quite say why. But there wasn't time for that either. She would just have to deal with it when the time came.

The naieen woman was also propped up against the rocks. Whatever had happened in the Sky, it had left her shocked almost out of her mind. Jo had been able to get little sense out of her, and she had quickly fallen asleep. Now, in the growing sunlight, Jo could see that she had been badly hurt. There was a lot of blood on her, and the flesh of her back and her left wing was swollen, marked with long cuts that looked as if they had been made by a whip. She seemed to be sleeping soundly, and even almost comfortably, which Jo supposed was good.

Jo wondered if she should try to find some water for them to drink. She was thirsty herself, and she was sure that the naieen needed water. The rocks where they lay were at the top of a shallow scree slope, beyond which was the sound of surf. Jo had no idea whether the 'sea' here was salt or fresh, but she thought that there might be a stream running into it somewhere. She stood up, searched in the pockets of her jacket, hoping to find something that would hold water. Instead she found the piece of paper – Karilee's map of Epreto's house and, on the other side, his sketch of the Sky showing the places where Epreto was planning to poison it. She stared at the map for a while, remembered Karilee's desperation. *'He's going to poison the Sky. He's going to destroy the world.'*

If they poisoned the Sky it would be the end, Jo realized. Not just for the naieen, but for men, for everyone.

She had to try to prevent it.

She looked at the map and tried to orientate herself. The Rim was a scribbled circle, the sea a wavy snake. Kaygat was marked – at least she supposed it was Kaygat, a simple scribbled sketch of a couple of towers with a K next to it. Near it was a tiny circle, one of seven spaced evenly around the Rim. Between them were seven looplike symbols that she recognized from Epreto's original document: the symbol for the poison. Jo looked around, trying to see something that Karilee might have represented by a circle. Was it in the Sky? She looked up, was momentarily dazzled by the sun.

There was a scuffling sound behind her. Jo looked round, saw that the naieen woman had woken up. She bent down and gently touched the short, wiry fur of the alien's arm.

'What's your name?' she asked.

The naieen woman's eyes fixed on Jo's. 'I'm called –' She seemed to hesitate, then started again. 'My naieen name is Xaai.'

Even names change in the Sky. Jo pushed away the unwanted information, tried not to think about where it might be coming from. 'OK, Xaai,' she said. 'I'm Jo. Now, do you think you can still fly?'

The naieen stretched her wings, winced with pain. 'Maybe. Not far. I haven't . . . they wouldn't let me . . .' She became agitated, her wings twitching.

'Never mind,' said Jo softly. 'Do you know anything about the Sky? I mean, what's up there?'

Xaai shook her head. 'Temples,' she offered. 'The Seven Temples.'

Jo looked at the map. Of course. Seven Temples, evenly spaced around the Rim. And seven sites for the poison, placed neatly in between them. It was obvious. She should have seen it herself.

'Which is the nearest Temple to Kaygat?' she asked Xaai, but the answer was already forming in her own head even as the naieen woman spoke.

'Iujeemii.'

Jo looked up at the blue dome of the Sky, and swallowed. 'OK, Xaai. We have to get to Iujeemii and then we have to fly around the Rim until we reach –' she showed Xaai the map '– here. Can you do that?'

Xaai studied the map for a moment. 'Perhaps,' she said. 'I don't know. But how will you get there? You haven't any wings.'

Jo remembered then that she'd left the pedithopter wrecked halfway up the cliff. She studied the steep slope above them, now brightly lit by the sun. There was no sign of the craft, and it was probably damaged beyond repair anyway.

'I don't know,' she said, trying to hide her sinking feelings from Xaai. 'But we have to do it. There has to be a way.'

'Well,' said the Doctor cheerfully, hammering the copper serving plate into position between the two pieces of cracked ceramic that he'd taken from the Old Gate fountain, 'that's the transionic polarizer taken care of. Now for the tricky bit.' He took a chiming clock from the bench, a delicate antique which featured a complex animated model of the Temple, with its Acolytes, Priests and Confessors. There were hundreds of brass gears and moving copper discs. The Doctor looked the model over briefly, then began pulling it apart with a pair of heavy callipers, checking the distances between various points after every tug.

Eeneeri watched, uncertain and confused. This man

174

seemed very sure that he was right, and in Eeneeri's experience such an attitude almost invariably meant that a person was wrong. Especially in the case of men. But then the Doctor wasn't exactly a man, even if he didn't have wings. His manner, the words he used, even the way he was dressed, all spoke of his alien origin. But did that mean Aapurian was right to trust him? Eeneeri wasn't sure.

The alien looked up from his work and said, 'Ah. Still there, are you, Eeneeri? Look, I need some copper cabling. About six inches of it.' He spread his hands. 'This much. And it has to be insulated. Go and get me some, would you?'

Eeneeri nodded, turned to one of the guards at the door of Aapurian's room. The old confessor himself had gone to a meditation cell to rest.

'One of the bell cables should do,' Eeneeri told the guard. 'Bring it.'

The Doctor was still tweaking at the model he'd taken from the chiming clock. Somehow he had contrived to make it into a dense tangle of copper wires and brass wheels, actually more complex than the original machine. The Doctor tapped it with a finger, and it began spinning. A flicker of blue light drifted between the moving parts.

There was a knock at the door, and the guard returned with a piece of bell cable. He was followed by a confessor in full robes, who pointed a wing at Eeneeri and spluttered, 'I demand an explanation for this! The chimes of Beecii are vital to the contemplation of –'

'Sorry, old chap,' said the Doctor without looking up, 'but we're trying to save the world.'

The confessor looked at Eeneeri. 'What does he mean?'

'Exactly what he says,' said Eeneeri sternly.

Bewildered, the confessor retreated, flicking his wings and muttering under his breath.

Eeneeri met the Doctor's eyes and, much to his surprise, found himself smiling.

'Nearly ready,' commented the Doctor. 'With any

luck, in a few minutes, Mr Epreto will get a nasty shock.'

I hope so, thought Eeneeri. I hope so, for all our sakes.

Duboli breathed in the first stirring freshness of the morning wind, and wondered if the world beyond the Sky would ever be as good as the world below it. From the steering deck of the skyboat he had a clear view across the world. The sea stretched around it, a blue loop fading into a purple distance. The tallest waves sparkled, red-gold in the bright morning sun. Behind him the city of Kaygat rose from the mist, a grey-pink web of towers and roads, glinting with traffic. Ahead, Neef Island stood clear against the sea, crowned with factories, ringed by grey beaches and white surf. The clouds that had hidden the escaping otherlander were retreating beyond the sea, a boiling grey mist already revealing the dark shadows of the Rim mountains.

It seemed strange that all this would have to be destroyed, so that men could live: but Duboli knew there was no choice in the matter. Epreto's evidence was incontrovertible. The fallen suns beyond this Land were smaller than their own sun, true, but the power of their own sun couldn't be infinite. One day it too would die, and, before it did, they had to use it to escape. It all made perfect sense.

But, on a morning like this, surrounded by the beauty of the world, Duboli had to admit he didn't want to do it.

He wondered where the otherlander had gone. He was pretty sure the pedithopter had headed out to sea, but of course it could be anywhere now. And there were other 'thopters up, both in the city and on the island. He didn't think there was much chance of finding the alien now.

'Sir!' Hanu's voice, from the cabin hatchway. 'There's a message from Mr Epreto!'

Duboli hesitated. For a moment he wondered if he should just sail on, on to the Rim mountains. Claim he was searching for the otherlander. Claim anything – but just take a day away from it, a day to see for the last time the beautiful world he was going to destroy.

176

But Hanu was walking across the deck, a piece of rolled paper in his hand. Reluctantly, Duboli took it.

Duboli – The naieen know our plans. They have tried to kill me. We must act at once. Take the skyboat and release the Dead agent to the Sky. One site will have to do – there is no time for the full plan. I have signalled all our people to meet at the sun tonight, so that we may leave the world before morning – Epreto.

Duboli had to read the message twice before its meaning registered properly on his consciousness.

This was it.

This was the last morning.

There were no more plans, no more preparations, no more regrets. There was only action.

He turned to Hanu. 'Are the supplies we obtained from the Dead in the hold?'

Hanu nodded. 'Mr Epreto had them transferred last night from the steamwing.'

Duboli nodded. 'Set the sails for an easterly climb. We have new instructions.'

As Hanu raced around the deck, adjusting the rigging for the new course, Duboli held the tiller and looked around at the last morning that would ever break over the Land and under the Sky.

The man was huge, almost as big as the Unpromoted had been. Jo didn't suppose that he had long to live. He sat, with his back to Jo, apparently guarding the cluster of pedithopters and small skyboats anchored to thick wooden posts at the top of the cliff.

She crept forward, keeping low in the soft mossy grass, her eye on the nearest of the pedithopters. All that held it in place was a chain with a simple padlock. Or, at least, Jo hoped it was a simple padlock. She slipped a hand into her pocket, made a last check to ensure that the skeleton keys were still there.

Then she waited.

After about a minute had passed, Xaai appeared at the top of the cliff, her wings flapping heavily. They had managed to find a stream with some fresh water, but Xaai was still dirty with blood and ragged-looking. As Jo had expected, the man guarding the 'thopters got up in surprise.

'Madam Flyer! What's the matter? Why –'

He broke off as Xaai soared above the chained 'thopters and crashed awkwardly on the ground perhaps fifty yards away. Jo hoped that the yelp of pain was as faked as the crash, but rather suspected it hadn't been.

Poor Xaai, she thought.

The guard was already running across the low grass to investigate. Jo waited until he reached Xaai and began talking to her, then darted forward and went to work on the lock.

Xaai had wanted to simply tell the man the truth about what was happening, but Jo had decided that they couldn't take that chance. There were too many things that might go wrong, too many questions that might be asked. For all they knew the man might work for some branch of Epreto's organization. Whatever Xaai was telling the man now, it was certainly holding his attention. Jo took nearly thirty seconds to break the lock – she counted them, with a rising sense of panic – and he didn't look across once. Then Jo jumped on to the 'thopter, pushed her feet on the pedals. The machine rattled across the grass and the man at last looked up.

'Hey – stop!' he called.

But it was too late. The wings snicked down and the machine lifted off, flew above the guard's head. Ahead, Xaai too was airborne. Jo grinned to herself, then winced when she saw the expression of pain on the naieen woman's face.

'Are you OK?' she shouted into the wind.

'I think so.' But Xaai's voice was tight with pain. 'I can fly, anyway.'

But how far? thought Jo. She wondered if it would be better to leave Xaai behind. She looked over her shoulder at the fast-shrinking patch of grass and the high trees around it. Xaai certainly couldn't rest there. And all Jo could see ahead were the tall dead stone towers of Epreto's factories, belching dirty steam.

No. Xaai would have to come with her.

She looked up at the blue dome of the Sky, the faint smudge of blue-grey that Xaai had told her was the Temple of Iujeemii. It seemed a very long way, and the poison site was even further. Jo looked at her new friend flapping her long, stiff wings, and hoped that both of them would have the strength to fly that far.

Aapurian felt a little more rested in the warmth of the sunlight streaming through the many-panelled windows of the meditation room. It was ironic, he thought, that he should be comforted by the very thing that was currently sheltering his enemy. But then, life itself was an irony. A joke in the face of the darkness.

Now who had said that? Had it been Leetiim? Or Coneeturrian? Certainly it had been said in the last century or two. Part of the *Grikal Chronicos*, perhaps?

'Confessor-Senior.'

Aapurian reluctantly extracted himself from his reverie, and found himself looking at Eeneeri's face, peering around the vine-tangled doorway of the meditation room. Strangely, the commander too seemed more relaxed.

It was something about the Doctor, Aapurian decided. A magic he had.

'The Doctor's device is ready.'

Aapurian got up slowly. 'I suppose I'd better see it.' He stepped forward and took Eeneeri's arm. They walked from the room into the relative darkness of the Temple interior.

After a few steps Aapurian became aware of a buzzing sound, like a swarm of flies, and a metallic clicking. 'Is that the device?' he asked. He felt a strange, crawling premonition, but couldn't be sure of the source of his uneasiness.

They reached his room at last. The Doctor had turned

179

the table into one vast machine, full of moving copper parts and strange blue light. Lengths of bell cable were strung out to various parts of the walls and ceiling. The blue light crawled along these too, like a fluid.

The Doctor was crouched in the middle of it, turning a piece of copper over in his hands. 'Right way up or upside down?' he muttered. 'Eeny, Meany, Miny, Mo –'

'Doctor?'

The Doctor seemed to shake himself, then looked up. 'Ah! Confessor-Senior! I was just repeating an old Venusian nursery rhyme. Aids the concentration, you know.'

There was a loud popping sound from the apparatus, and the air filled with the smell of ozone. The Doctor hastily pushed the copper object he was holding into the middle of the crowded machinery.

There was another popping sound, then a long, steady hum.

'Is it working correctly?' asked Aapurian. All he really wanted to do was sit down. But all the available chairs and couches had been incorporated into the apparatus, so all he could do was stand in the doorway, leaning on Eeneeri for support.

The Doctor was reaching into various parts of the apparatus. Metallic clicks issued from it, followed by a strange high-pitched squeak.

'Well, the first information burst went out all right,' said the Doctor.

Aapurian frowned. 'What has burst?' he asked. 'Is everything all right?'

There was another squeak from the machine. The Doctor turned and smiled at Aapurian. 'That's it,' he said. 'We have control over the systems. What do you want to do with the sun?'

Aapurian struggled to get his thoughts in order. What was the most important thing to do? 'Evict Epreto – no, wait. Seal the sun off. Don't let anything get in or out.'

'And stop it from moving,' added Eeneeri.

'Might be a good idea to disable the weapons systems as

180

well,' muttered the Doctor. He was already fiddling with something that looked as if it might once have been part of a clock mechanism. Mechanical chimes issued from the machine, followed by a third squeak, much longer than the first two. Blue sparks trailed from the copper surfaces.

The Doctor examined the machine once more, then nodded. 'That seems to have worked all right.' He said, smiling. 'Gentlemen, I believe we have won.'

But Aapurian felt that sense of foreboding again. It had been too easy. Far too easy. 'Are you sure, Doctor?' he asked.

'Quite sure,' said the Doctor. 'The signal has been sent, and acknowledged by the starship – by the sun, I mean. Nothing can possibly go wrong now.'

Everything happened in less than five seconds.

The alarms started sounding, and the booming voice that the sun used in what it deemed to be emergencies started to speak about some kind of intrusion. For a moment, Epreto thought that the naieen were actually trying to attack the sun. Then he realized that it wasn't possible. The sun was at full brightness. They wouldn't be able to get within ten miles of it.

By the time Epreto had thought about that, and started to ask the systems what was really happening, all the lights had gone out. He finished the question anyway, but there was no response.

He rushed to the controls, which were still illuminated, and punched out a message on the emergency keyboard. He'd used this on the last but one fallen sun he'd found, and, though it had taken some time to work out how to use the thing, in the end he'd got a lot of useful information.

But this time all the sun said was, 'Attempted software intrusion. Countermeasures in force. Please wait.'

Epreto asked again, got the same response. He bunched his fists in frustration. What was wrong with the thing? What was a 'software' intrusion?

'What is happening?' he bawled.

Then the lights came back on.

'System restored.'

Epreto took a deep breath. 'Source of intrusion?'

A map appeared, with the source marked in red. Epreto didn't need to wait for the accompanying surveillance picture to come through to know where the source was.

'The Temple,' he muttered. 'Of course.'

He told the system to power up its weapons, then watched the target spots form on the old test sites around the Rim mountains.

'New targets,' he told the system. 'Coordinates of source of system intrusion, and all similar structures.'

He waited for the target spots to come up, made sure that they were the Seven Temples and not cities or other structures lived in by men.

He realized as he waited for the weapons to power up that he should have done this as soon as he'd got inside the sun.

'Full power,' reported the system.

Epreto nodded. 'Open fire,' he said softly. 'Continue until targets are destroyed.'

'Now that's odd,' said the Doctor. The copper machinery in front of him was chiming again, but this time the sound was discordant, confused. Aapurian's sense of foreboding returned, with a renewed intensity.

There were more chimes.

'The starship systems seem to have – oh, I see.' The Doctor looked up at Aapurian. 'This isn't going to work as well as I'd hoped,' he said. 'We're going to have to get closer to the sun. In fact –'

'Confessor-Senior,' said Eeneeri suddenly, his voice high with alarm. 'The window – the sunlight –'

He didn't need to say any more, because Aapurian could see for himself. The window was blazing like a tiny image of the sun itself. The light, which had been seeping through on to the wall, had become burning bright.

The Doctor had noticed too. He'd begun to move, was on his knees by the window, pulling it upwards.

'Quickly!' he snapped. 'Out through here!'

'But that's going in to the sunlight!' said Eeneeri. 'We'll be burnt alive!'

'We'll most certainly be burnt alive if we stay here!' snapped the Doctor, almost pushing the commander towards the window. Eeneeri just made it through the frame, his bandaged wing scraping painfully on the polished surround.

'Confessor-Senior,' said the Doctor. The sunlight was now so bright that it was hard to see his face silhouetted against it.

But Aapurian had already made his decision. 'I can't fly far enough, Doctor. Leave me here.'

The Doctor met his eyes. 'We may need you.'

'I doubt it,' said Aapurian. 'I did all I could. The rest is up to you.'

The Doctor's jacket had begun to smoulder. He hesitated for one more second, then nodded at Aapurian and dropped through the window into the open air.

Aapurian closed his eyes. He was glad he was going to die in this way, alert and knowing that the end was coming. He began repeating the last words of the philosopher Coneeturrian, in the way he had always intended to do when the time came.

'World, I hope I leave you better –' The heat was intense enough to dry his throat, and there was smoke in the air. He began to cough. '. . . *better than I came to you,*' he finished silently.

But he knew that he hadn't, despite all that he had done.

There was a violent snapping sound as the timber walls exploded into flame.

I only wish I knew how it will end, he thought, and died.

They had been flying for hours, and Xaai was exhausted. Her muscles no longer ached: they were like belts of dead leather, unable to respond. She was amazed that her wings remained spread, kept beating. Far below, the Rim forests — the cold forests where the Dead were said to walk — were wreathed in evening mist.

'I need to rest!' she called to Jo, though she knew that there was no chance of that now until they reached the Sky.

Jo glanced over her shoulder and smiled. 'Not much further!' she shouted back. 'Only a couple of miles!'

Xaai looked up at the Temple of Iujeemii. It still seemed a long way above her. By some trick of her exhausted eyes, it seemed to be brighter than the Sky around it, as if illuminated by an enormous lamp. As she watched, the light got brighter still. Xaai realized that it was a real light, no illusion. It had to be real, because it was shining on only one side of the Temple. Was it sunlight? But why was it so bright?

Xaai wasn't quite sure what happened next. The light became unbearably brilliant, and then it was as if the wind suddenly started blowing upward. There was a sound: a huge sound, as if the Sky itself was breaking open. Instinctively, Xaai flexed her wings harder, fighting the updraft. Ahead and above, she saw Jo turning her head, staring at something behind them, her mouth open; then suddenly the wings of her friend's pedithopter collapsed and she was tumbling upward.

Xaai strained harder against the updraft, felt herself gaining. Below, the ground seemed to have got darker, further away. The light had changed, as if the sun had gone out. The wind blew harder, until it was pulling her head back. Pieces of loose material slammed into her, and then something heavier. She could feel the bones of her wings snapping. Dark clods of clay rushed past her eyes, and the ripped leaves of the trees.

Suddenly it was over, and everything was still. For a moment Xaai was hovering, buoyed up by the air currents, then she started to fall. She tried to spread her wings, gain control, but only received jolts of pain from broken bones and shredded flesh.

This is how I die, thought Xaai. Just as I intended to last night. But why? What did I do wrong?

She looked up, to see what had happened to Jo, but she was no longer visible in the haze of light and smoke. Above, the Sky looked strange, as if someone had painted a white flower across it. In the centre of the flower, smoke was still shifting, filled with glittering fragments.

And the Temple of Iujeemii was gone.

Xaai stared, and stared, and stared, and finally, with a great effort, looked over her shoulder at the sun. She was surprised to see it still shining, though partly shrouded in dust and ice.

Had that light really come from the sun? Had it been anything to do with the man – Jo's enemy – Epreto? She remembered, quite suddenly, that she had known Epreto as a man, that he had been there in the fallen sun.

'Is it my fault?' she asked, as she fell through the swirling air. 'Could I have stopped it?'

But the ground was very close now, and Xaai knew she wasn't going to live long enough to hear the answer to her question.

Eighteen

Captain Mike Yates was glad to be back on duty. It felt good to have a definite set of orders again after the undefined vagueness of the past few –

Hours? Days? Weeks?

He wasn't sure about that.

Mike decided it didn't matter. He checked ahead, saw that the forest was thinning out. He could see the lamplit windows of a farmhouse, moving in and out of the gaps in the trees.

Find out what's gone wrong in the world above the Land. Take the necessary action.

Those were his orders. He didn't know what 'the necessary action' was, but he knew that it would become apparent once he'd found out what he needed to know. All his orders were with him, but his mind wasn't going to be burdened with every possibility until he knew the truth.

So logical, so simple, so ordered. If only life in UNIT had been like that.

Mike glanced back at his squad, still filing through the trees, their steps silent on the soft, level plain of fallen leaves. They were all kitted out in full combat gear, camouflage jackets and trousers, boots, backpacks. The kit had been Mike's idea, and it had worked: in the dim light, the men looked almost as if they were still alive.

Good.

In the backpacks were supplies of damp, malleable clay to keep the men mobile away from the protective shade of the forest. Mike reckoned that the supply would last about a day, which should be long enough for them to get to the centre of the world and the childforest if they needed to.

Of course, they might not have that long. And hopefully they wouldn't have to go that far.

Night when it should be morning. Bright flares from the sun. The Temples have been destroyed.

It didn't sound good.

There was a sound ahead, a low rustling, a man's whisper. Mike tensed, wishing that the Dead ran to providing guns. But the clay hands of the men, held together as they were with wood-nerve fibre, were far too clumsy to work the triggers of such weapons, even if they'd had any. So he put up a hand to halt the squad and waited.

Suddenly the man bolted, running across the fields clumsily, half falling in the ploughed-up soil. Mike grinned to himself. There were some advantages in being Dead, he decided. But it was a shame the camouflage hadn't worked better.

He gestured the squad onward, his mood suddenly serious again. They had a job to do, and they had to do it quickly.

Outside the forest, the air was colder and drier. Mike could feel the wind flaying moisture from the surface of his face, and at once realized another advantage of the camouflage clothing: it would protect them from dehydration, to some extent at least. Nothing could hurt them, of course, now that they were Dead, but if they dried out too much they would stop functioning, and wouldn't be able to continue with their mission. Mike didn't want that to happen until some results had been achieved.

He looked up. Far ahead, over the misted bay, he could see the lights of Neef Island, tall factory towers and squat workers' houses. He turned his attention to the Sky, but saw nothing. No Temples. No lights at all.

Raising the sensitivity of his eyes to the limit and examining the ground in front of him, Mike could see why. The ploughed-up soil of the field was covered with scattered pieces of debris: copper bells, pieces of charred wood, scattered fragments of glass. A gleaming copper wing stood upright in the middle of the field, part, perhaps, of a ceremonial statue.

Destruction, thought Mike. War. It was all so stupid. Why couldn't people see that it was easier to be Dead?

He led his squad around the edge of the field and along a drainage ditch. It was almost dry, but the clay at the bottom of it was still wet enough to maintain a pleasant dampness in the air. Mike's head was still above the level of the field, and he kept his eyes open, turning his head in a regular 360-degree motion to make sure he didn't miss anything. But there was no movement, only the silent lamplit windows of the farmhouse, the distant factory towers, the charred debris.

Then Mike saw the pedithopter. It was lying in a fallow field on the other side of the ditch, half hidden in the long grass. Mike realized at once that there was something strange about it.

It wasn't charred.

Wrecked, yes, but not burnt. The oilcloth of the wings would have been destroyed completely in any fire. So it had been in the air, away from the Temple, at the time of the disaster.

He nodded to the men, then scrambled out of the ditch and through the long grass towards the downed machine. As he approached he saw the dark shape inside the wreckage. A body? If so, he could take it to the Dead. The information might be useful.

But it was only an item of clothing. A black jacket.

Jo Grant's jacket.

Mike felt something that, if he had still been alive, would have been shock. But there was no need to be shocked, he told himself. Jo was already in contact with the Dead. As long as he could find her body, there would be no problem. He could take her back to the forest, and she could be recovered. Her information, he guessed, would be particularly important.

And – yes – it would be nice to work with her again.

* * *

Eeneeri crouched over the Doctor, shivering with pain. The cold wind of the Rim mountains cut through his body, making his wounds sting. Outside the narrow crevice where they sheltered, it was all but dark. The normal lights of the Sky were extinguished, the Temples all destroyed. Only a few drifting boats and the dim light from the distant city of Kaygat told Eeneeri that the world was still there at all.

Very soon, Eeneeri knew, it probably wouldn't be.

He was amazed that he had survived the destruction of the Temple at all. His injured wing had hampered his flight. All he could remember was light, moving air, the shrieking of dying naieen. Then a shadow had moved over him, protecting him from the worst of it: the Doctor, with his strange manmade wings.

Now Eeneeri was protecting the Doctor, not from the wind and heat but from the cold.

Not that the Doctor seemed all that bothered by it. He was working on something with the same small warbling device he had used to assemble the machine in the Temple. The something was small, and square, and it glowed. The Doctor appeared to have constructed it from various objects he had found in his pockets. One or two Eeneeri recognized from the Temple; others clearly had stranger origins.

'What will it do, Doctor?' asked Eeneeri, trying not to show his fear. If it called the fire down on them again . . .

It could hardly be worse than what was going to happen anyway.

'Do? Well, I'm hoping it'll call the TARDIS to me.' A pause. 'Then again, it might not work. But I don't see any other way of getting to the sun in time to prevent Epreto from leaving, do you?'

'Not for us,' said Eeneeri. Here on the Rim they were at least a night's flight away from the sun. 'Perhaps others . . .' He let the words trail away, suddenly aware of how much had been destroyed. The Seven Temples. All the naieen in the world, except for a very few who might have been flying.

189

The wind suddenly felt colder than ever.

'Yes, we're not alone in this,' said the Doctor with a smile. 'Mike's very resourceful. I'm sure he's trying to do something about Epreto now. But I don't want to rely on that.'

Eeneeri asked who Mike was, but the Doctor didn't reply. Instead he applied the warbling device to the small machine he was constructing.

There was a flare of bright light, as if a lamp had been lit inside the machine. Eeneeri saw a tiny, illuminated image form, like the reflection of a bright room in a mirror. The room was white, and had walls carved in a pattern of circles. There was a strange, angular shape in the middle of the room.

'Is that . . . the sun?' asked Eeneeri.

The Doctor shook his head. 'No, just the TARDIS, I'm afraid. Now I don't know if I can risk trying to –'

He lifted the device to his lips and said quietly, 'Jo? Jo are you in there?'

Eeneeri could only stare, uncomprehending. What was the Doctor trying to do? No one could possibly be in the small box, so the Doctor must be trying to talk to someone in the picture of the room. But how could he expect to do that?

'Jo?' He turned to Eeneeri. 'Oh, well. It looks like she's not aboard any more. I suppose I couldn't really expect her to be, after all this time. But I did tell her to stay put, you know.' He shook his head slowly, then returned his attention to the machine. 'Let's see if we can operate the dematerialization circuit manually.'

There was a flash of light. Eeneeri winced, expecting the worst, but all that happened was a clatter of metal, then darkness.

The Doctor muttered something that Eeneeri guessed was a curse, though he didn't understand the language.

'Doctor?' he asked.

'It didn't work, Eeneeri,' said the Doctor quietly. 'I'm sorry, but I'm going to have to leave you here. I know where the TARDIS is now, and I've got to go to her, since I can't get her to come to me. And it's too far for you to fly in your condition.' A pause. 'I can leave you this.'

There was a small flare of light and a crackling sound. Eeneeri jumped back as a brightly coloured shape expanded across the ground, spreading over his feet in a warm wave.

'It's a blanket made of the same material as my wings. Wrap it around you and it'll keep you warm until morning.'

There were more crackling sounds, and Eeneeri saw the Doctor's wings taking shape, their strange fabric the same bright orange colour as the blanket.

A hand touched his. 'Well, goodbye old chap. And good luck.'

'I think it's you that needs the luck, Doctor.'

The Doctor didn't reply, just dipped his wings and jumped into the air. Eeneeri watched the pale shape rise until it disappeared into the new darkness of the Sky, then wrapped himself in the alien blanket and waited for the morning that might never come.

The poison provided by the Dead glowed slightly in the dark, an eerie pinkish-grey light seeping through the strange transparent material of its packing. Duboli hadn't expected that. He supposed it was made from one of those plants in the childforest that had the same phosphorescent quality, but that didn't make him feel any better about it.

He glanced up at Hanu, sensed that the older man too knew the seriousness of the moment. Around them, the deck of the skyboat was dimly lit by gas lamps. It rocked slowly in the regular waves of turbulent air breaking against the Sky. There were no other lights, anywhere. Morning had been replaced by night after the destruction of the Temples: night, final and absolute.

Duboli reached up from the deck rail and touched the soft, cool surface of the Sky itself. The tiny rough shells of Sky barnacles scratched his fingers.

I don't want to do this, he thought. It's wrong. So

many people — so many living things — will die.

But he could hear Epreto's voice, almost as if the man were standing next to him. 'They'll die anyway, you fool. We have a chance of long-term survival. It's our duty to take it.'

'Yes, but —' muttered Duboli.

'Sir?' asked Hanu.

Duboli felt his flesh grow cold. 'Open the package,' he said quietly.

Hanu opened the package, shredding the transparent material with his huge hands. Duboli kept one hand on the Sky, almost as if comforting it. The boat shuddered, once, as the random movement of the wind drove it against the surface.

Inside the pack was a single solid block of the luminescent substance. Duboli picked it up, found that it was cold, and slippery, like ice. He held it for a moment, letting it chill his flesh.

The boat shuddered again.

'I do this for the sake of life,' he muttered. 'In the long term.'

He slapped the block of poison against the surface of the Sky.

It was night, though Xaai didn't remember the sun fading. There was still some light, dim, artificial, from somewhere behind her. Xaai tried to turn and look at it, but she couldn't make her body obey her. She'd decided that her back was broken: that was probably why she didn't feel much pain. In fact, she felt curiously warm and comfortable, as if she were afloat on a sea of soft wool.

Soon, she supposed, she would fall asleep. Well, there were worse ways to die.

She was trying to remember her time in the childforest, because she'd heard that you were supposed to remember all the stages of your life before you died, so that you could understand it as a whole. She looked at the nearby trees of the Rim forest and tried to recall climbing on huge branches in the warm, humid half darkness of the distant childlands, but no memory came to her. Perhaps, she thought, she would have to wait until the very end.

There was a sound behind her, the faint crunch of boots on soil. With a great effort she half turned her head, and saw a squat figure approaching, wearing pale clothes and dark knee-length boots.

A man? No. He walked too slowly, too awkwardly, and his face was too dark.

There was a stab of pain in the back of her head, and she had to lower it to the soil. When she opened her eyes again, she saw the figure standing over her.

No. Several figures. All of dark clay below their strange clothing.

The Dead. Of course. She had fought and fought to fly, she had dreamt of flying all her life as a man, but she had still ended up amongst the Dead. Somehow, now, that seemed as if it had always been inevitable.

Perhaps this was what was meant by seeing your life as a whole.

The leading Dead reached down. She wanted to tell him that it could wait, that she was in no pain, but she couldn't speak. The Dead gently put its hands around her body, then tightened its grip and lifted her up. Instinctively, she tried to struggle. But her body made no response. The world swung around her, and there was a brief, sharp pain in her skull, before a white mist filled her vision.

Xaai's last thought as a living being was: why are the Dead wearing clothes and boots?

When Jo woke up, she was still falling.

She remembered falling. She remembered the Temple imploding above her. She remembered thinking: it's imploding, not exploding, because all the bits are going inward. The Doctor taught me that.

She didn't remember anything else.

Hello.

Jo opened her eyes, and saw the stars.

She blinked, but they didn't go away, just kept wheeling in pin-bright succession across her vision. Real stars, smudgy nebulae, a faint band of silveriness that might be the Milky Way.

Or another galaxy, of course.

Hello. I am the Sky.

Jo swallowed, opened her mouth, discovered she could talk. 'Ahhm . . . I'm . . . Jo.'

Jo. A pause. *Jo, do you know what is happening to the world?*

'I was rather hoping you could tell me that.' Jo reached out towards the stars. Her hand touched a soft, cold barrier, and the image of stars blurred for a moment. 'Where am I?'

On the outside of the world, in an Emergency Rescue Capsule. I will return you to the world if you can present a satisfactory account of your activities.

'Well, I, er . . . I came here with the Doctor. I'm from another Land – that is, another planet. We came here by accident. We didn't intend to stop –' Suddenly she remembered something. 'They're going to poison you! They're going to poison the Sky! I have a map . . .' She reached into her jacket pocket, discovered that her jacket wasn't there any more. 'It was between the Temples – exactly between the Temples. They're going to poison you so that they can steal the sun."

I see. Thank you for that information. A pause. Jo felt the slight tug of acceleration, and the stars were eclipsed by something huge and dark.

The world, she realized. The world where she had been living for the last few days.

Then: *I think you are too late. The poison has already been released. Structural integrity will break down in three point seven hours.*

Jo swallowed. 'Can't you do anything about it?'

My chemical synthesis facilities are no longer functional.

'I'll bet the Doctor has some that are,' mused Jo aloud. Then she came to a decision. There was only one part of this thing that she didn't yet understand, and that was what had happened to her in the forest when she had first arrived, and how she'd got to Kaygat.

'I need to get back to the world,' she told the Sky. 'I need to go back to the childforest.'

I can take you back to the world. But where is the childforest?

Jo sat up, felt the soft coolness of webbing restraints against her body. 'You really don't know much about what's going on down there, do you?'

I am a semipermeable antiforce glucite membrane. I have no other function.

'Well, I *do* have another function. And I make my own choices about it,' said Jo. 'And so should you,' she added.

The Sky was silent for a moment, as if considering her words.

What can I do to help you? it asked eventually.

'I need some answers,' said Jo. 'Sky, take me back to the Land. Put me down in the childforest. Directly below the sun.'

Nineteen

'Gentlemen, the sun no longer exists. Welcome to the starship!'

Epreto had rehearsed the speech for a long time but somehow, now, in the stress and confusion of the night, it wasn't going right. The audience filled the central chamber of the sun, crowding between the angular machines with their flickering lights and the tall columns of vapour: young men in their stiff coats, the captured naieen in their cages, middle-aged industrialists like Epreto himself, and the heavyset boatmen that he intended to use for manual labour wherever they all ended up. Everyone looked nervous, surprised, uncomfortable. Many seemed to have been roused from sleep. The naieen were almost hysterical, screaming in their high-pitched voices like animals. No one had yet come with the children; Epreto had not heard what had happened to the childforest party and was wondering if he should leave them behind.

He could see Duboli at the back of the crowd, but the man's face was expressionless. Epreto wondered if something had gone wrong with the poisoning of the Sky. There hadn't been anything in the farmessage he'd sent to suggest that, but perhaps he'd wanted to speak face to face. Epreto tried to catch his eye, but failed: Duboli seemed to be staring into an emptiness somewhere between, or beyond, the glittering machines of the starship.

A ragged scatter of applause made Epreto realize that he had paused too long in his speech, and the audience had assumed that he wasn't going to say any more.

'Most of you will be aware,' he said quickly, 'that we

have had to advance our departure, because certain elements amongst the naieen have become aware of our plans. Let me assure you now that the naieen have been dealt with.' The desperate keening from the cages rose in pitch, becoming almost unbearable. Epreto swallowed, then raised his voice to something near a shout and continued. 'We will be leaving the world in two hours or less. We will be travelling to a new world, a world such as this.'

He touched a switch under his hand, and a prearranged projection appeared in the middle of the air behind him. Green, fertile land appeared, low hills retreating into a seemingly impossible distance. A second picture showed a surf-fringed island rising from a blue sea, with other islands in the background. Again, the view seemed to go on forever. Several of the audience gasped in surprise: they'd seen the pictures before, of course, but not like this, in three dimensions, hanging in the air almost as if they were real.

'It may not be like that, you know.'

The voice came from the back of the huge chamber, somewhere near the main doors, and it was disturbingly familiar. Epreto looked up, saw the alien figure of the Doctor standing at the top of the ramp that led up to the doors. He was tossing an orange ball from hand to hand, and frowning.

Somehow, Epreto wasn't surprised that the otherlander had managed to survive. He didn't look like the sort who was easy to kill.

'Doctor!' he called, trying to keep the nervousness out of his voice. 'Welcome aboard! We will be glad to have your assistance.'

The Doctor marched forward, pushing through the astonished crowd.

'And I will be glad to have your assistance,' he said, 'in putting an end to this insane endeavour before it goes any further. We need to get an antidote to the poison you have placed in the biological element of the Sky, and we need to reprogram this starship so that it reverts to its function as a sun.'

With difficulty, Epreto managed to laugh. 'You always did have such wonderful timing for your jokes, Doctor. But unfortunately –'

'This isn't a joke.' The Doctor had reached the platform by now. He turned to the audience, gestured at the images behind him. 'Mr Epreto, I'm afraid, has no more idea where he's going than you do. These pictures have been taken from the starship's memory, but the places they show may well not exist any longer. Even if they do, they probably belong to other people. You won't just be able to land there and live in peace. You'll have to make compromises, strike deals. If you're lucky you might be accepted. If you're unlucky, you might run into some version of your former creators and be destroyed without compunction.' He paused, folded his arms. 'Let me explain to you what you are.'

'No, Doctor,' said Epreto in a low voice. 'They don't need to know this.'

The Doctor glanced at him, said nothing.

'Please,' begged Epreto. 'We have to succeed. The world could not go on as it was.'

The Doctor shook his head slowly. 'I'm sorry.' Then he returned his attention to the audience and cleared his throat.

'Everyone here is the result of an experiment. An experiment conducted by the Aapex Corporation of Mina Fourteen, one of the most grasping and unscrupulous business entities of their era. This planet, that you call the world, was taken over by Aapex about four thousand years ago to conduct a series of illegal terraforming experiments. The experiments probably weren't intended to run for all that long, but the Aapex Corporation went bankrupt shortly after the experiments were started and, since no one's ever been back to check on you, it's a reasonable assumption that all the records were lost or deliberately destroyed. In short, you were abandoned to your fate.' He paused, pulled at the lapels of his jacket. 'Now, I can understand why you want to get away from here. The set-up of this world seems to you arbitrary and nonsensical. Carnivorous children, an enforced

198

policy of cruel competition as men, then retirement in the Sky for the lucky – and under the ground for the unlucky. And of course the sun will die eventually. It wasn't intended to last forever.' Another pause. Epreto wondered whether he should intervene. But to remove the Doctor from the platform would involve using force, and he was reluctant to do that in front of the others, whilst the Doctor was only talking.

The Doctor continued: 'Mr Epreto has probably told you that the suns of other Lands died. He probably didn't tell you why. That's because he doesn't know, at least not for sure. But if he'd looked at his own history – the legends contained in Reekaa's *Compendium*, for instance – he would quickly have realized that it wasn't because they broke down.'

There were a few surprised intakes of breath from the audience. Epreto noticed that Duboli was staring at the Doctor, his big childlike eyes wide.

'No,' said the Doctor. 'They were destroyed. Destroyed by the civilizations living beneath them when they broke up in conflict – exactly the same conflict that you're engaged in now. You are destroying yourselves, not saving yourselves. Your only chance of survival is to reverse your actions and try to live with each other. Your civilization has survived for four thousand years; it should be possible for you to carry on surviving almost indefinitely.'

Epreto had heard enough. 'And allow the naieen to have dominance over men again?' he snapped. 'Do you think that's fair? A just way of ordering the world?'

The Doctor turned to him and said mildly, 'Mr Epreto, I don't like it any more than you do. But you can't just make it go away by wanting it to be different. Whether you like it or not, you have to work for change.'

'I have worked for it,' said Epreto. 'I have worked so hard –'

'Yes, but not the right kind of work. You need some-thing more advanced than steam engines to escape from the biological trap you're in. In the short term, you just have to accept it.'

'No!' shouted someone in the audience. 'We can't accept it!' The cry was taken up generally, drowning out the shrieking of the caged naieen.

'You see, Doctor? I'm not the only one who believes that things should be changed. I'm merely their spokesman.'

The Doctor shrugged. 'Spokesman or not, popular or not, what you're doing is wrong. And I propose to put a stop to it.'

Before Epreto could reply, the Doctor had jumped down from the platform and had his hands over the emergency control keyboard. They moved so quickly that they hardly seemed hands any more, just a flicker of dancing fingers over the dark material of the keys.

Epreto jumped down after the Doctor, intending to push him aside, but it wasn't that easy. The Doctor dodged him, moved around some of the cabinets, and resumed his attack from another control panel.

'Stop him!' roared Epreto, furious now. 'He will destroy everything that we've worked for!'

He saw Duboli moving, levering his young, light-weight body across the top of the control cabinets. The small man had drawn a pistol; belatedly, it occurred to Epreto to do the same.

Then he thought of a better idea.

'Starship: identify the person at panel C as an intruder,' he instructed.

'ID system inoperative,' came the response. 'System suspended: awaiting software evaluation.'

Whatever that means, thought Epreto. He aimed the pistol at the Doctor, but the otherlander was gone, running for the rear doors to the central chamber. One of Epreto's followers was chasing him, waving a short sword. Epreto saw Duboli jump through the doors ahead of him. He followed, leaping clumsily over the cabinets, regretting suddenly his age and size.

Outside there were several corridors leading off, their walls shining in bright, almost gaudy, colours. The Doctor had chosen one that led down – towards the escape hatches, Epreto suddenly realized. He was moving incredibly quickly, drawing ahead of all of them. Epreto drew his pistol, fired, but the bullet went wide. Epreto could have sworn that the Doctor had actually dodged the bullet. He increased his pace, hoping to get near enough for a better shot, but was stopped dead by the sight of Duboli in front of him.

The man was aiming his gun at Epreto's chest.

'What −?' he began.

'Don't you see he's right?' gabbled Duboli. 'Don't you see that killing the Sky was a mistake?' There were tears on his face. 'And the Temples − all those naieen − all those *people* . . .'

Epreto stared at him. 'Mr Duboli,' he said. 'We agreed that −'

'Well I've changed my mind!' Duboli's voice had broken: it was squeaky, hysterical. It was as if he had prematurely changed into a naieen, or changed back into a child. 'You don't have the right − we don't have − no one has −'

'Quite right, Mr Duboli.' The Doctor's voice. 'No one has the right to kill.' Epreto looked up from Duboli's face, amazed, and saw the Doctor standing a pace behind the small man. A couple of other men, including the sword-wielder, were watching from a safe distance, evidently confused.

'Mr Duboli,' said the Doctor calmly. 'There's no need for this. Let's end all the killing now. Give me the gun.'

Duboli didn't move.

Epreto glanced towards the other men, gestured with his eyes at Duboli.

Duboli looked away, for a fraction of a second. In that instant the Doctor moved, his hand chopping at Duboli's shoulder. Duboli dropped, with a surprised expression on his face. The gun clattered to the floor.

'Thank you, Doctor,' said Epreto quietly.

'Will you reverse what you have done?' The Doctor's voice was level, his gaze steady, serious.

Epreto shook his head. 'You know I cannot do that.

Will you reverse whatever it is that you have done to the starship?'

The Doctor solemnly shook his head.

Epreto gestured to the two men, but, as they stepped forward to seize the Doctor, he moved. He seemed to do no more than brush the men aside, but they both dropped to the floor unconscious, and the Doctor was gone, half running, half flying down a helical stairway that led to one of the escape hatches. Epreto set off after him.

He didn't really expect to catch up with the other-lander, and was startled when he almost fell over him at the bottom of the stairway, and saw him struggling with a piece of glowing electronics inside a hastily removed panel. Epreto jumped back, so as to give the Doctor no chance to move, then drew his pistol.

'I'm sorry Doctor,' he said, 'but I must ask you to come with me.'

The Doctor's response was to thumb one of the switches on the device in his hand.

At once, the floor disappeared under him, and he started to fall. Epreto stepped forward and managed to grab the Doctor by the collar. The Doctor's hand flew up and hit Epreto in the stomach, winding him; he fell over, but managed to keep his grip on the Doctor's collar. He staggered to his feet, clutching his stomach with his free hand, then realized that all he was holding was the Doctor's empty jacket. The man was falling some twenty yards below. He turned to look at Epreto and smiled, then suddenly frowned and began twisting frantically in the air, patting his pockets.

'Epreto!' he called. 'My wings!'

Epreto saw the piece of orange material, hardly larger than a coin, lying on the edge of the open hatchway, and recognized the colour. It was heavy when he picked it up, but unbelievably small to unfold into a pair of wings. Yet there were wings embossed on it, and the Doctor could do other unbelievable things.

Epreto held it up over the open hatchway. The Doctor, now nearly fifty yards below, nodded frantically and beckoned. Below him was the darkness of the childforest, shrouded in a faint, oddly luminous mist.

Epreto hesitated.

The otherlander had saved his life.

But the wings would set the alien free. Free to do more sabotage. Free to finish what he had started.

No.

The fate of the world was more important.

'I'm sorry, Doctor,' he muttered. He gave a last glance to the now-distant falling figure, then pocketed the wings and walked away.

Tuy was there.

Xa recognized his friend, though it was hard to say how. He couldn't see him or hear him, couldn't smell him or touch him. Yet he recognized his last friend, Tuy, the man that he had killed. And he knew that Tuy was well, and happy, and whole.

Xa thought, I would like to be that way too. I don't want to fly any more. There is nothing but pain in flying.

Tuy nodded (invisibly). *I know.* There was a curious echo in the voice (which wasn't a voice), a quality of many voices, as if Tuy were more than Tuy.

There is something I/we need you to tell me/us, said Tuy's many voices.

And Xa knew at once.

'She said Epreto was going to poison the Sky!'

Yes. That is what we needed to know.

There was a pause. Xa became aware of a sound: someone breathing. The breathing was close to him, as if he were sitting next to the person, and it was laboured, wheezing.

Quite suddenly, the soundless voices of the Dead resumed.

– *Epreto has betrayed us* –

– *he said the other Lands were marching on us* –

– *and he took the Landkiller to poison them for us* –

– *but he lied* –

– *but he took the Landkiller to poison the Sky* –

203

— and destroy all of us —

The breathing sounds grew louder, until Xa became aware that they were real, that they were coming from his own body. He felt pains in his chest, in his arms, in his wings, and realized that he was alive.

Alive, and a naieen. A naieen woman called Xaai.

'I didn't want to fly again!' she shrieked, and this time she could hear her voice in her ears. 'I have had enough suffering!'

'I'm sorry that you are alive.' Tuy's voice. 'It had to be done.'

Xaai opened her eyes, and could see Tuy's living clay form towering over her in the darkness, wearing strange pale clothes and boots.

No. Not strange. The same as —

'You killed me!' she shouted. 'Why am I alive? What's happening?'

Another voice spoke. 'I'm sorry, but we need you for a mission.' Xaai turned her head, saw a man who, even in the dark clay that was the Dead imitation of flesh, looked different from the others. Smaller, yet heavier, somehow.

'A mission?' asked Xaai.

'Yes. If the Sky dies the experiment will have to be aborted. So we need somebody to take our poison out of the Sky. To save the world from the destruction that Epreto planned. And that person has to be able to fly.'

Jo watched the canopy of the forest move closer, a ghostly pattern of leaves and branches and hanging fruit, with here and there an eye glinting in the beam of the pod lights. As the pod brushed through the canopy, she could see furry bodies retreating into the shadows.

Abruptly, the pod stopped.

Jo frowned. 'What's happening?' she asked.

A small red light began blinking inside the membrane wall of the pod.

Then it began moving upward again.

'No!' said Jo, beating at the membrane. 'Where are we going?'

The beams that had been illuminating the forest snapped off, and for a moment everything was dark. Then Jo saw that the lights were now shining upward, illuminating a small bright speck falling far above them. As Jo watched, the speck resolved itself into the figure of a man. With a shock, Jo recognized the frilly magenta shirt and shock of white hair.

It was the Doctor.

At the same moment, the pod seemed to lose interest in him and started to descend towards the forest once more.

'It's the Doctor!' Jo shouted. 'You've got to save him!' She hit out at the pod walls, but her fists just bounced off the cold membrane and the pod continued moving downward away from the Doctor.

'Sky!' yelled Jo. 'Sky! Listen to me!' But there was no response. Frantically Jo looked around for something that might be a control system for the pod. She could see a collection of bunched, gel-like wires, and something that might have been a joystick, but the webbing that was holding her in place wouldn't stretch far enough to let her touch them, and she wasn't sure whether they really were controls anyway. 'Sky!' she yelled again. But it was no use.

Then Jo realized that the pod wasn't moving away from the Doctor at all. In fact, the Doctor was slowly catching it up.

Very slowly.

He was moving towards the pod at little more than walking pace now.

The machine was *matching speeds*.

Jo felt a wave of relief. She grinned, and waved. The Doctor raised his eyebrows, and mouthed something she couldn't quite lip-read. The top of the pod opened, iris-like, and warm, forest-scented air rushed in, followed by the Doctor. He landed smartly in the middle of the pod and smiled at Jo.

'I thought I told you to stay in the TARDIS!' he said.

Jo jumped forward and hugged him impulsively. 'Aren't you glad I didn't?'

The Doctor patted her back. 'Well, yes, I suppose so. Thank you very much.'

Jo detached herself. 'I didn't do it. The pod did it all by itself.'

'The pod being . . .?' The Doctor was running a finger along the wall membrane and frowning.

'Part of the Sky.' She explained about the Sky, which led to explaining about the poison, which led to explaining about Karilee and Epreto, which led to explaining about Mike.

Then she burst into tears.

The Doctor took her hands, said quietly, 'He might not be dead, you know. The Land has strange powers here –'

'I know,' interrupted Jo. 'The Dead. But Karilee said . . .' She broke off, confused. 'I don't know. I've spoken to the Dead. I think.'

She was starting to remember things. She looked away from the Doctor, stared out through the membrane. Branches drifted by, starkly illuminated by the pod's lights.

'Spoken to them?'

Jo shook her head, feeling uncomfortable. 'Sometimes I've . . . I've just known what to do. But it was the wrong thing. I think –' she bit her lip, turned back to the Doctor '– it might be my fault that Mike died.' The tears were in her eyes again.

The Doctor took her hands. 'No, it wasn't. It's natural to feel guilty when someone close to you dies.' He paused, and a shadow crossed his face as if he was remembering something painful. Then he shook his head and went on. 'But it's not real. From what you've told me, there was nothing you could do about it. You must try to put it behind you.'

As the Doctor finished speaking, there was a gentle bump and Jo again felt an inrush of warm air, this time humid and clay-scented. They had landed on the forest floor.

Jo led the way out of the pod on to the soft, leaf-littered ground.

206

'Why did you tell it to land here, Jo?' asked the Doctor.

Jo frowned. There had been a reason. Hadn't there?

Yes. Of course.

The Dead.

And it was better still, now that the Doctor was unexpectedly with her. She looked around at the tree trunks that surrounded them, huge walls of wood springing directly from the clay. She saw the figures already forming from the wood, the blue eyes glinting in the pod lights.

'Jo?' asked the Doctor. 'Jo, what are you doing?'

'You need to understand, Doctor,' said Jo gently, as the figures stepped forward towards them. 'You need to understand what I understand. You need to be Dead.'

Twenty

_____

For the first time, it seemed, Xaai was truly flying. The Land had vanished into the darkness below: the Sky was still in darkness above. There was nothing here, now, around her, but air, cold, buoyant, rippling air, sliding across her remade skin.

Even if I die, she thought, this moment has been perfect. This moment has fulfilled all of my dreams.

Silently, she thanked the Dead, and clutched their precious burden closer to her chest. The capsule felt warm: the soft silver-blue light emitted by the antidote shone through the transparent casing and was reflected on the skin of her wings as they moved. She watched the light, moving as if it were a part of the air, and felt a surge of hope. For herself, for the Dead, for men, for everyone.

After a while Xaai became aware of the faintest of lights ahead. At first it might have been no more than blood pricking the back of her eyes, tricking her vision, but after a while it became real, a wash of pinkish-grey light across the Sky.

A reflection? she thought. But the Land, with its city lights, was hidden by cloud.

Gradually, she realized that it was the Sky itself that was glowing, and that there was something sick about the glow, an illness.

She beat her new wings harder, churning the cold dry air and holding the antidote capsule even more tightly than before.

— soft —
  — soft warm —
    — soft warm comfort —

– soft warm comfort darkness –

'Never mind about all that. I need access to the TARDIS immediately.'

– why do you –?

– how do you prevent –?

– you should be part of the softwarmcomfortdarkness –

'Well I'm sorry, but I'm not. I'm a Time Lord, you know. I'm not quite as digestible as Miss Grant. Now can you stop this nonsense and take me to the TARDIS? It's vitally important that –'

– the TARDIS is your vehicle –

– you will wish to leave in your vehicle –

– but we can't let you leave –

– not before you have helped us to prevent –

'I know what you want to prevent. I'm trying to prevent it myself. Now if you'll just listen instead of playing silly games with telepathic pseudoviruses, we can actually do something about it. I need the TARDIS because it contains control mechanisms I can link to the software codes I've prepared on Epreto's ship – that is, on the sun. I can control it, and stop him from leaving or from doing any more damage. Do you understand that?'

– we understand that you will help us –

– if you are promising to help us –

'I promise.'

– then we will bring the TARDIS to you –

– we will bring it as quickly as possible –

– but you must promise not to leave us –

– please do not leave us –

– please –

– the Dead need you, Doctor –

The main doors were closed, and the starship was ready.

At least, Epreto hoped it was ready. His fingers shook a little as he punched instructions into the keyboard, instructions that should produce a description of every instruction that had been received in the last day.

He wished he understood the machines better. Sometimes, they seemed as if they were rational beings in their own right. They spoke to him about events and made their own decisions, which usually seemed reasonable in the light of the available evidence. But at other times they used words that Epreto didn't understand, or behaved in ways that seemed to make no sense. Sometimes, inexplicably, they refused to function at all.

At the moment everything seemed to be working, but the question kept running through Epreto's head: how much had the Doctor done? He'd had only seconds at the keyboard. Surely he couldn't have done much in that time.

But he had done something, and the starship wouldn't tell Epreto what it was. The same stubborn message appeared in the air above the keyboard: 'No access to recent input files. Awaiting software review.'

Which meant that something was wrong. But Epreto had no idea what it might be.

He turned and paced back to the platform where he had made his speech. His recruits – and the screaming, caged naieen – had gone. Epreto had hastily appointed Hanu to take Duboli's place and sent everyone to what he had called their 'cabins'.

Duboli was roped and tied to a chair, here, on the platform, where Epreto could watch him. He'd thought about killing the man, but couldn't quite bring himself to do it. Not to coldly stand there and shoot him. He hadn't enjoyed the killing of Gefen and Lofanu, and this would have been worse, without anyone to share the blame, or to strike the final blow.

Duboli looked up as Epreto stepped on to the platform. 'You're not going to succeed,' he said quietly. 'You know that. The Doctor won't allow it.'

'I told you, the Doctor is dead,' said Epreto irritably. 'And anyway, we can't reverse the poisoning of the Sky.'

'The Doctor seemed to think it was possible. We should ask the Dead.'

Epreto looked at him, stared into those huge, childlike eyes. 'Mr Duboli,' he said. 'You are under arrest for treason to the cause of men. I don't require your commentary on my actions.'

'Whatever you say,' said Duboli. His voice remained quiet and level.

Epreto felt a chill of unease. Perhaps what he was doing was wrong after all.

No. Duboli was just trying to manipulate him. He shook his head slowly, turned to a scanner where a light was flickering.

The voice of the sun – no, the voice of the starship, Epreto reminded himself – spoke, the sound booming through the huge space of the chamber: 'Movement has been detected near a designated secure point. Display follows.'

Epreto saw a patch of darkness, like a floating shadow, appear in the main display space. With a shock he realized that the 'designated secure point' was an area of the Sky where the poison had been placed. He could see the dim red glow of the destructive agent, spread across a wide area of the Sky. The dim winged shape of a naieen moved across it.

Epreto told the starship to show him a closer view. The naieen got larger, but more grainy. He could see that it was carrying something in its arms. Something dark, like clay, with a pale blue-silver light at its heart.

Epreto remembered what Duboli had said about the Dead. How they would know whether the poisoning of the Sky could be reversed. Obviously they thought it could.

Epreto knew that this was something he couldn't allow.

'Target weapons systems,' he muttered.

A flickering red light appeared above the naieen's chest.

'No!' said Duboli, from somewhere behind him. 'Let it be! The Dead know –'

'The Dead know nothing!' snapped Epreto. 'They are no more than losers in the battle for existence. We are the winners!' He turned back towards the image. 'Starship: prepare to open fire.'

* * *

Confused, Jo watched the Doctor talking to the Dead. He was sitting cross-legged, in the centre of a ring of Dead, obviously quite at ease. Part of her was glad that they hadn't taken him: another part of her wished that they had, so that her instructions could have been completed.

But, if the Dead didn't want them completed, that was all right, wasn't it?

Jo wasn't sure any more, and that was part of her confusion. The other, bigger, part of it concerned bringing the Doctor to the Dead at all. She had done it because the Dead had told her to. But it still felt like betrayal. How could she possibly have believed it was in his best interests?

She wanted to talk to him about it, but he was too busy talking to the Dead.

'You sent a naieen to fly up with the antidote?' he was asking.

'– Yes. We had no one else –'

'– no one we could trust –'

'– no one else who could fly –'

'– could have done with a helicopter really.'

Jo stood up, very suddenly. She recognized that last voice.

'Mike!'

One of the Dead turned slowly. It didn't have Mike's face, and was far too big to be Mike, but it nodded nonetheless. 'Hello.'

'You aren't dead!'

'I am Dead. But I'm –'

'– alive!' Jo jumped forward, took the warm brown clay hands. 'Mike I'm so glad I didn't kill you. I'm so glad you're still there –'

She was interrupted by a loud cracking sound. Mike whirled round, but his Dead body was clumsy compared with his human self. The Doctor was much quicker. He was on his feet and at the source of the sound before Jo had even realized what it was.

One of the huge trees had cracked open, revealing

the TARDIS, sticking forward out of the splintered wood like a pulled tooth. It looked as if it might topple forward at any moment, but the Doctor was standing under it, ignoring the danger. He was already unlocking the door.

It opened, and the Doctor stepped inside.

Mike looked back over his shoulder at Jo, and Jo could imagine the expression that would have been on his face if he'd still been human. She grinned.

The Doctor poked his head out of the TARDIS door. 'Come on, Jo. And you, Captain Yates. We have work to do.'

The Sky was very close now. The pinkish-grey glow was all-pervading. It seemed to pulse from Xaai's eyes through to her brain, making her sick and confused, as if the poison could spread by sight alone.

Or perhaps through the air.

Best not to think about that.

She beat down with her wings again, suddenly aware of a curious warmth and light in the air. Her skin tingled, then burnt.

Was the sun shining again?

The heat on her skin grew, becoming painful. A light, dull and red but incredibly hot, glowed sunward.

Then Xaai realized.

'No!' she gasped, and beat down with her wings against the heating air. She turned to the malevolent sun. 'I'll reach the Sky first!'

But the heat was searing her eyes, searing her throat. Her muscles began to convulse from the pain, and her wings began to lose their grip on the air.

'No!' she yelled again, but the light only brightened more. Suddenly all the air was burning, all the air was pain. She wrestled with the air, tried to escape the heat, to hide just for a moment. In the improved light she could see that the Sky was only a hundred yards away. Perhaps less. If she could just keep going . . .

But the ruby light got brighter still, brighter beyond

belief, beyond the possibility of survival. The last thing that Xaai felt was the shock of heat and flame as the capsule containing the antidote exploded, sending her tumbling away from the Sky.

Then her flesh caught fire, and Xaai died.

Twenty-One

Mike gazed at the tiny, flickering image on the TARDIS scanner. He could just see the shape of a naieen body in the middle of the flames, but it was fast disintegrating into ash. He quickly calculated the time that would be needed for the Dead to make another naieen body – or preferably several – and knew that it wasn't enough.

'We have to do *something*,' said Jo. 'We can't just let him destroy the world.'

The Doctor was leaning over the console, examining the readings on various instruments there.

'I can tell you what I'd do if I was still in UNIT,' said Mike.

The Doctor gave him a curious glance. 'You are still in UNIT, Captain Yates.'

Mike would have blushed, if he'd had blood to blush with. Instead he looked down at his huge, inhuman, wood-coloured body and said, 'I don't feel as if I'm still in UNIT.'

The Doctor was stroking his chin. 'Yes, I can see that we'll have to do something about that.'

Mike wasn't sure whether he wanted that to happen or not. Being Dead was good. It felt . . . more definite, somehow, than being human. But he didn't say anything, because he wasn't sure about it, and he knew it would upset Jo if she thought he wanted to stay here.

But before he could even consider the idea of staying there was the little matter of saving the world.

'We should load a large squad of the Dead aboard the TARDIS,' he said, 'then materialize in the control room of the sun. If there are enough of us, it won't matter what weapons Epreto has. We'll overrun him in the end.'

'He's bound to kill some of you,' the Doctor pointed out.

Mike pushed his stiff clay face into a shape that he hoped was a smile. 'The Dead aren't afraid of dying, Doctor,' he said.

It wasn't quite true. Not in his case, at least. The Dead would be able to make another Mike Yates, of course, but it wouldn't be the same, somehow. *He* would be dead.

Wouldn't he?

He became aware that Jo was talking. 'We'll need to take the antidote to the Sky as well,' she said. 'It's no good getting control of the starship if the Sky's going to collapse anyway.'

The Doctor nodded his agreement, then muttered something about coordinates and returned his attention to the controls.

Mike frowned. For some reason travelling to the Sky didn't quite seem to make sense. A few minutes ago, getting the antidote there had been important, but now something about the situation had changed. He tried to work out what it was, but couldn't.

He needed to consult the Dead, he realized. He needed further orders.

But there was no need to get the Doctor alarmed and start him asking questions. Especially when Mike didn't know any of the answers yet.

Aloud he said, 'I'll start rounding up the men, Doctor.' That ought to sound fairly innocuous, he thought.

Sure enough, the Doctor only nodded vaguely. Jo didn't respond at all, but sat in one of the chairs, apparently lost in thought.

Good.

Mike walked out of the open doors of the TARDIS, into the familiar, comforting humidity and warmth of the forest. The other Dead were standing against the huge trunks of the trees, waiting.

216

Yes, thought Mike. This is my home now. This is my world. These are my people.

He was certain about it now.

He walked up to them, happier with his life than he had ever been before, and ready to receive his new instructions.

Kimji Duboli watched as Epreto talked to the machine that governed the sun. He moved his hands slowly against the bonds that held him to the chair, making a picture in his head of the shape of the knots, searching for weaknesses, for some way of freeing himself.

A startling clarity had come to him since he'd heard the Doctor speak: everything that hadn't made sense before was now perfectly clear. Poisoning the Sky had felt wrong because it was wrong. All his life since he had left the childforest, Epreto had been the centre of Duboli's world. The man who gave the orders, the man who was always right.

Now Duboli knew that Epreto had been wrong all the time.

And every part of Duboli's mind, all the crystal determination, all the strength he could summon, were dedicated to preventing Epreto from destroying the world.

He moved his hands against the ropes again, felt something give way. He logged the sensation, reviewed the picture of the knots he had made in his head, and realized that he was nearly free.

He looked around the control room, across the strange metallic cabinets and the shimmering columns of light, looking for something that was solid, something that he could lift, that he could carry.

Something that he could use as a weapon.

Jo watched the Dead troop into the TARDIS with a sense of misgiving. The Doctor had told Mike that he could pilot the 'old girl' into Epreto's control room without any difficulties, but Jo wasn't so sure, and the Doctor's show of businesslike fiddling with the controls wasn't increasing her confidence. Once, she would have trusted the Doctor to do anything, but now . . .

Now she was sure that *he* wasn't entirely confident. She could tell, from the slight uncertainty of his movements around the console, from the grim expression on his face. He really didn't know if he could make the TARDIS do it.

'Doctor,' she said quietly, 'we don't have to use the TARDIS.'

He glanced up. 'There isn't time to get there any other way. Besides, Epreto would shoot us down.' He glanced at the Dead, still thudding through the console room and out through one of the many internal doors. Mike was directing them, steering the column between the litter of chairs and electronic equipment. He had managed to shape his clay face into a semblance of his human self: it seemed incongruous on the huge wood-coloured body.

'We could use the pod,' said Jo.

'It isn't big enough.'

'We could put the TARDIS in the pod, and tell the Sky to move the pod towards the sun. Then we can use the starship itself to reach the Sky. I don't think Epreto can shoot the pod down. I don't think that the starship can fire on anything to do with the Sky, or Epreto would have done it ages ago. He wouldn't have bothered with all this poison business.'

The Doctor raised his eyebrows and grinned, then put his hands on Jo's shoulders.

'You know,' he said, 'that's a pretty good piece of deductive work. I think I might make a scientist out of you yet.' He signalled to Mike, who clumped over and listened whilst Jo explained her plan.

'What happens if he does fire on us?' said Mike simply.

The Doctor shrugged. 'We'll be safe enough in the TARDIS. She's virtually indestructible. She'll have to dematerialize, of course, but we'll be no worse off than we are now.'

Mike still seemed dubious, though it was hard to tell

218

from the dark, carved-looking face. 'If you say so, Doctor,' he said at last.

Jo grinned. 'I'll go and talk to the Sky,' she said.

She pushed out through the doors. Outside, she was amazed to see that the ground had collapsed for hundreds of yards around, leaving long, rough pits of raw earth. A pale light issued from the broken ground, supplementing the light from the open door of the TARDIS. The huge tree trunks were pocked with holes, as if they had been eaten away. Fallen leaves and sticks covered the ground and more were raining down all around. Wood groaned, cracked. Jo realized that the Dead were destroying the heart of the forest to produce their army: destroying the heart of the Land itself. She wondered how much would be left of the world after this final battle.

The pod had fallen on to one side, but the doorway was still accessible. Inside, she said, 'Sky? Can you hear me?'

There was no reply.

'Sky?' She felt a rising embarrassment. The only time she had spoken to the Sky from the pod before was when she'd thought it wasn't going to save the Doctor, and it hadn't replied then. Why had she supposed that it would now?

Then a voice spoke: a human voice, faint, half hidden in static. 'This is the Sky.'

'Sky, we need to –' but Jo broke off, because the Sky was still speaking.

'– only emergency systems are available. Repeat: total failure is imminent and only emergency systems are available.' The voice faded into the static.

'How long?' asked Jo.

No response.

'Sky, how long to failure?'

Still no response.

Then even the static faded, and there was only silence.

Shivering slightly, Jo stepped out of the pod into the half-dark forest, wondering how she was going to tell the

Doctor that all her reasoning had been wasted and he was going to have to get the TARDIS to work after all.

Then she heard a rustling in the leaf litter ahead of her, and a low whooping sound. Something moved against the faint light from the distant TARDIS. It was too small to be one of the Dead.

Her embarrassment and disappointment vanished, and were replaced by a chill of fear.

The low whooping sound was repeated, then echoed to either side of her and behind her. She turned, saw the glint of huge eyes, the faint outline of a monkeylike body with ribbed wings.

They were the children, she realized. The children of the childforest. The carnivorous stage of the species.

And they were hungry.

The whooping got louder, and Jo saw the gleam of long teeth. She backed away, brushed against a furry body, which hooted as if laughing. She turned, and then they were all around her, their wings flapping, their whoops drowning out all other sound.

In panic, Jo looked back towards the pod, hoping for sanctuary, but it was covered in the pale bodies. There were even some of them moving inside it, as if they were eating it from within.

A heavy weight descended on Jo's shoulders, and furred wings beat against the side of her head. She raised her arms, tried to pull the thing off, but it was impossible to get a grip on the writhing fur. Claws raked into her hands.

She screamed.

Twenty-Two

Once he had freed his hands, Duboli waited. His legs were still tied, and to untie them he had to have a moment unobserved. But Epreto had returned to the platform and was watching the spread of the poison across the Sky.

Duboli watched too.

It didn't seem to have covered a very large area, but the centre of the area was now a deep, angry red, almost as if it were on fire. Duboli was sure he could see it moving. He imagined it breaking, imagined the air rushing out through the break, the Sky falling like a rumpled blanket all over the Land.

Everything dying. Men, naieen, children, screaming and burning and dying. Cities crushed, forests and hills flattened. The Land itself destroyed.

And it would be his doing. His fault. Not Epreto's. Because he was the one who had poisoned the Sky.

The starship spoke. The words were all but nonsense. 'Critical membrane state detected in immediate vicinity. Plotting escape course.'

Epreto frowned, clearly no more sure of what this meant than Duboli was. He stroked his beard, pulling at the heavy gold rings threaded there.

'Is the Sky about to break open?' he asked.

'Yes,' responded the machine. 'First breach estimated to occur in three point four minutes.'

Epreto smiled and stepped down from the platform.

Duboli leant forward and began to untie his legs from the chair. He knew he had to do something, and do it now.

221

Even though it was probably too late.

Mike ran, as fast as he could in his clumsy body. His shadow wavered in front of him on the uneven ground, cast in the light from the torch that the Doctor was carrying.

The scream had come from the direction of the pod, so Jo must still be there. He could hear a commotion there now: whooping sounds, the rustle and thud of moving bodies. Eyes glinted in the torchlight.,

'Mike!' shouted the Doctor, from behind him. 'Mike! Hold this!'

Mike turned, saw the Doctor offering him the torch. For a moment he considered refusing, arguing, telling the Doctor that he was the expendable one. But there was no time for that. Jo might be injured, might be dying.

He took the torch, and at the same time heard a despairing wail from behind him. 'Mike! Doctor!'

'It's all right Jo!' The Doctor was plunging forward into the mass of furry bodies, holding something in his hand, something that glinted in the light. The children whooped and chittered and screeched, but slowly they retreated from the Doctor, leaving a clear space. Jo was visible in the middle of it, muddy and battered but otherwise apparently unhurt.

'Nice children!' said the Doctor. 'Watch the pretty colours!'

Mike saw then that what the Doctor was holding was a brightly coloured, multifaceted plastic cube. He flung the cube into the air with one hand, caught it with the other.

The huge eyes of the children watched.

The Doctor threw the cube again, signalled to Jo whilst the object was still in the air. She struggled upright and plunged out towards Mike. On the way the Doctor touched Jo's shoulder and muttered something in her ear.

'He says we've got to bring the TARDIS. He'll keep them entertained.'

Mike stared at her, then looked at the Doctor, who was now pulling coloured handkerchiefs from his pockets. The children's huge eyes watched him steadily.

But Mike didn't suppose that the party tricks would work for long.

'Are you OK?' he asked Jo.

She nodded, wiped some clay from her forehead. But her hands were shaking.

'Come on, then,' said Mike, putting as much reassurance as he could into his half-human voice. 'We've got a job to do. For the Dead, as well as for the Doctor.'

Jo looked into his eyes for a moment, then nodded. 'For the Dead. Yes.'

Mike wondered then whether to tell her about the new orders.

He decided that it would wait.

Duboli had almost reached the torch, almost got hold of it, when Epreto saw him. The big man moved with incredible speed, almost flying over the two bulky cabinets that separated them.

Duboli made a grab for the makeshift weapon, missed, and fell against one of the cabinets. From the corner of his eye he saw Epreto leap, his heavy body silhouetted against one of the columns of shifting vapour. Duboli dodged, rolling on the cabinet top, hitting controls at random. The starship itself seemed to shift under him, and its huge voice began speaking.

For a moment, Epreto was distracted, looking around him wildly at the flickering displays that were coming to life in the control room.

Duboli made another dive for the cabinet where the torch lay. This time he made it.

He was scrabbling at the torch, trying to get a grip on the metal, when a huge blow knocked him flying, He saw Epreto, fists clenched, eyes bulging with fury, bracing himself against the cabinet, ready to leap after him.

Duboli hit the ground, rolled, jumped. But he wasn't fast enough. Epreto landed on top of him, pinning him to the steel floor with a knee against his chest.

The starship shifted again, and a huge mechanical roaring sound began. The floor trembled.

'No!' begged Duboli. 'You have to listen to me!'

But Epreto's hands were reaching for Duboli's throat. Suddenly, shockingly, he growled.

'You're wrong,' he said. 'I have to fight.' Saliva drooled from his mouth. 'I have to kill.'

And then Duboli understood. The constant stress of the last few days must have brought on Epreto's urge to fight.

Epreto was being Promoted.

He flailed from side to side, but it was useless. He couldn't break Epreto's grip. Helplessly he watched the claws breaking through Epreto's flesh, and the older man's hands moving across his chest to rip out his heart.

Four of the Dead carried the TARDIS, shouldering it like an oversized coffin. Jo walked behind it as they approached the pod, watching the assembled children nervously. The Doctor was juggling with a long ivory-handled cane and several of the brightly coloured cubes, leaping about as he juggled, only just catching the objects as they slowly tumbled in the air around him. The children watched, wide-eyed.

Somehow, they looked more human. Perhaps it was because their wings were folded. Or perhaps it was simply because they weren't trying to eat anyone. But Jo still kept close to the heavy wood-clay bodies carrying the TARDIS, claiming the double protection of the Doctor and the Dead.

The procession was only yards short of the pod when the children suddenly seemed to notice it. There was a chorus of whoops and growls, and they leapt away from the Doctor and on to the TARDIS. Then, the spell broken, they seemed to notice Jo again, and bared their fangs.

The Doctor shouted something. The Dead clouted the small bodies aside, bowling them away, causing them to screech with shock and pain. But more of them kept coming, springing out of the darkness around until the air was full of furry bodies, huge eyes, long teeth.

Jo saw the TARDIS toppling towards the ground. Then the torch went out.

For a moment she blundered around in the darkness, colliding with things that might equally have been children or the Dead. The Doctor was still shouting. Then Jo saw a line of light appear in front of her.

A door. The TARDIS door, opening.

She struggled forward towards it, but a child landed on her shoulders, and she felt claws rake at her shoulder, tearing her dress. She pushed at the thing, felt it lift away. Then she saw Mike holding it. He broke its neck and threw it aside. Then something pushed Jo, hard, and she was stumbling through the doors of the TARDIS and into the console room. The TARDIS shuddered, tilted. Some of the ranks of the Dead who were in the room swayed and wobbled, like skittles clipped by the ball, but they all succeeded in righting themselves.

Jo looked round, saw that the Doctor was behind her, still clutching one of the coloured cubes he'd been juggling with. It was covered in blood.

'The scanner, Jo!'

Jo flicked the switch and watched the scanner screen. The TARDIS was in the pod. She could see a couple of the Dead in there, with several children clinging to each one.

'It's a shame, you know.' The Doctor was looking at the bloodstained cube in his hands. 'They're only children, after all.'

'They tried to kill me!' objected Jo. But the part of her that was Dead knew the Doctor was right. They were only children. Hungry. And confused by the darkness, by the failure of the sun.

The TARDIS doors swung open and Mike stepped through it, his wood-clay body a little misshapen, and covered in scraps of fur and blood. 'Now what?' he asked simply.

The Doctor was lying on the floor, prising one of the panels off the console. 'If I can just get the field generator program unit linked up to the biomorphic glucite links on the pod, we should be able to pilot it manually.'

'Pilot?' said Mike. 'That sounds like a job for me.'

The Doctor glanced up at him. 'Well, yes, possibly. But you'll have to do something about those hands if you're going to work the controls.'

Jo looked at Mike's hands and saw that they were little more than crude lumps of clay, the fingers barely able to move separately. Mike wriggled them a few times, then shook his head. 'If I concentrate, I should be able to do it,' he muttered.

As Jo watched, the hands thinned out, gained a finer bone structure. Knuckles appeared, and even crude sketches of fingernails. Jo was vaguely aware that she should be afraid, but she knew it was only happening because Mike was Dead.

Mike flexed his hands again, and then the crude mouth on his face curved into a smile. 'That ought to do it,' he said. 'Right, Doctor, what do you want me to fly?'

The Doctor pulled a device out from the console, a messy, cobbled-together-looking thing, made of flickering objects that looked like blobs of melted plastic lying in a tangle of wires, with something that looked like the front of an old radio tacked on. Cables trailed from it inside the console. The Doctor began unplugging some of these, but he left others connected as he carried the device out of the TARDIS doors into the now sealed pod.

Mike followed him. Jo stared after them for a moment, then looked at the serried ranks of the Dead still waiting, silent and patient, in the console room.

Their blue eyes flickered.

And, quite suddenly, Jo became aware that the Dead were speaking to her.

   – *the situation has changed* –
   – *the experiment has failed* –
   – *so the orders have changed* –
   – *here are the new orders* –
   – *orders which must be carried out without fail* –
   – *orders which must be carried out whatever the cost* –

226

After a moment, Jo nodded, understanding the truth at last.

It was so simple, once you knew.

Epreto knew that he had lost at the same time as he had won.

He lay on his back in the huge, bright control room, the taste of Duboli's heartmeat still on his tongue. He felt incredibly tired, and at the same time at peace, at peace in a way he had never felt as a man.

He heard footsteps crossing the room, a slow, heavy tread. A face peered down at him.

Hanu.

'Sir?'

There was no need to say anything, thought Epreto. The truth was obvious. Everything he had done was wrong: everything he had sought to achieve, a mistake. He had destroyed the world because he was afraid of growing up.

But somehow that didn't seem to matter.

Hanu was speaking again. 'Mr Epreto, the sun is moving. What should we do?'

Die, thought Epreto. That's all that remains to us.

But even that didn't seem to matter. He was fulfilled.

He would die happy.

He would die with wings.

As the pod climbed and the branches of the forest thinned out, it became obvious to Mike that there was something wrong with the Sky. A pink glow was visible through the canopy, a sickly light silhouetting the branches, giving the leaves a grey-brown tone. The glow was brighter in some parts of the Sky than in others. As the canopy thinned, he could see that pieces of the Sky were falling, brightly glowing, or perhaps burning. In the distance, tall flames rose from parts of the Land, moving with a slowness that was almost majestic. A layer of smoke was visible, glowing dimly in the eerie light.

'It looks like we might be almost too late,' said the

Doctor, looking around at the mess. Then an expression of alarm crossed his face: 'The starship has gone!'

Mike nodded, but kept his attention concentrated on the Sky. The starship certainly wasn't where it was supposed to be. He scanned the area, and after a moment saw the dark, circular silhouette some twenty degrees away from the zenith, in the direction of Kaygat.

It was moving.

Mike estimated the speed, then glanced down at the Doctor's control panel. The Doctor had explained the function of the various plastic knobs and small metallic levers, but it had been too much for Mike to take in at speed, even with the greater concentration of the Dead.

'How do I change the bearing?' he asked the Doctor.

The Doctor too had spotted the sun, and was staring at it, a frown on his face. 'It's going to collide with the Sky.'

'That doesn't matter as long as we get there first,' said Mike. 'Now how do I –'

The Doctor reached across and tweaked something that looked like the volume control of a radio, and the pod lurched sideways. Mike had a brief view of the forest canopy from above. He saw the corpse of a naieen entangled in the branches, one wing smouldering, the body being eaten by a couple of children.

He looked up, checked their new bearing, then took the controls again. The pod accelerated rapidly.

Mike became aware that Jo was standing behind them, just outside the TARDIS door. The TARDIS took up most of the space in the pod: there was only just room for the three of them to stand on the floor in front of it.

'Are we going to make it?' asked Jo.

'I don't know, Jo,' said the Doctor. 'All we can do is hope for the best.' He stepped back, put an arm round her.

A piece of Sky fell past them, no more than a few hundred yards distant. It wasn't exactly burning: instead it seemed to be radiating discrete bursts of pinkish light.

The Doctor stepped forward again and stared at it with interest. 'That's it!' he said suddenly. 'Of course! It's all one system!' He turned to Jo. 'Jo, get the Pulse Control Meter from the console room.'

'The what?'

'Pulse Control Meter! Top right hand drawer! Bright yellow!'

Outside the pod, the piece of Sky had fallen out of sight. Ahead, darkened farmlands burnt. Mike adjusted the alignment of the pod, pushed up the slider that controlled its speed. The burning landscape rushed below; above, often concealed by smoke, the sun moved slowly across the dying Sky. Mike kept his eyes on it as far as possible, making occasional course corrections. Gradually it came closer.

Behind him he could hear the Doctor talking to Jo inside the TARDIS, and intermittently the high-pitched warble of the sonic screwdriver.

The pod began to rock from side to side, in response to the increasingly fierce air currents. The distant flames almost reached the Sky now: Mike could see that the factories of Kaygat and Neef Island were burning. The city itself was obscured by a pall of smoke.

There won't be any survivors, he thought.

Which was as it should be, of course. The new orders from the Dead had been quite clear about that.

The pod rocked again and Mike became aware that the Doctor was standing beside him. 'How long –?' he began.

Then there was an explosion of light. The Sky flared blue-white, and the air around them was suddenly full of burning fragments. The Land below vanished in the screaming light.

Directly ahead, the sun was blazing at full power.

Twenty-Three

'Quick!' yelled the Doctor. 'Into the TARDIS!'

Mike could already feel the heat drying the clay of his body. The Doctor's clothes were smouldering. Mike pushed the Doctor through the door, then followed him in. Jo was sitting next to another of the Doctor's cobbled-together pieces of circuitry, an expression of shock on her face.

The Doctor hit the door control on the console, but the doors wouldn't close. They jammed, with a wide strip of the killing light still shining through them.

'The cable!' yelled Jo. 'The cable to the pod controls!'

The Doctor yanked at it, but it wouldn't give. The doors were open only a few inches, but the light coming through them was bright enough to burn the clay of the Dead that it fell on. The air began to smell of smoke. Mike saw flickering blue eyes, became aware of messages of pain and confusion.

The Doctor was holding a metallic object that looked a bit like a spanner. 'Stand back, everyone!' he shouted.

Then the air itself seemed to scream.

The cable exploded in a shower of sparks.

And the doors shut.

The Doctor chopped a hand down on the dematerialization switch, and the time rotor began to move.

Then he turned to Mike and Jo with a grin, waving the spannerlike object. 'Sonic monkey wrench,' he explained. 'Works every time.'

Jo grinned back, and even Mike had to smile.

But then Jo said, 'We are going to the sun, aren't we?'

The Doctor turned his attention to the controls. 'I hope so,' he said.

Jo and Mike looked at each other. The TARDIS wasn't in flight, exactly: even Mike could tell that it was already materializing.

Somewhere.

He looked anxiously at the scanner, and was relieved to see a huge, vaulted room filled with consoles and pillars of gas-state circuitry.

The control room of the sun.

'Doctor, you did it!' Jo had taken both the Doctor's hands and was positively jumping up and down with excitement.

The Doctor was smiling broadly. 'Well, I did tell you I'd get the hang of it eventually.'

Mike knew that the time had come to carry out his orders. He didn't like it, but there was nothing he could do. It had been the same at UNIT, sometimes.

Orders were orders.

He looked at the two Dead he'd positioned close to the console, and nodded. They stepped forward and grabbed the Doctor, taking an arm each.

'What the —?' began the Doctor.

'I'm sorry, Doctor,' said Mike. 'But we have our own programme to carry out now we're here, and I can't let you interfere with it.'

The Doctor glared at him, every bit as angry as Mike had expected him to be.

'The experiment is over,' he told the Doctor, trying to keep his voice calm. 'An abort situation has been created.'

'What on earth do you mean?'

It was Jo who answered, speaking gently, a hand on the Doctor's arm.

'It means we have to kill everyone,' she explained. 'And then we're going to destroy the world.'

Twenty-Four

Jo couldn't understand why the Doctor couldn't see it.

'The Aapex Corporation set up the experiment in secret. Obviously they can't risk the results getting out to any unauthorized persons,' she said. 'It's a matter of commercial confidence.' She stared at him, willing him to understand.

But all he did was gesture towards the scanner, which showed the Dead moving efficiently around the control room of the starship, manning positions and heaping up the lifeless bodies of the various men and naieen who had been found on board. Mike was sitting on the platform, in the captain's chair.

'Jo,' said the Doctor gently, 'even if the Aapex Corporation existed any more – and I can assure you that they don't – do you think that "commercial confidence" would be any justification for what's happening out there?'

'We haven't any choice in the matter,' said Jo desperately, trying to avoid his gaze. 'The Aapex Corporation cannot allow its experimental procedures to be released to the general public at this stage.'

The Doctor was shaking his head. 'Listen to yourself, Jo. Listen to the words you're using. They're not yours, are they? They're not Jo Grant's words!'

Jo felt a momentary confusion. 'I . . . I don't know,' she said. 'Some of them are. Look, Doctor, it doesn't *matter*. We have to abort the experiment.'

'And then what?'

Jo glanced at the two Dead holding the Doctor. She shook her head. 'I . . . I'm not sure. I mean, I don't need to know that yet.'

The Doctor struggled in the restraining grip of the Dead. 'Jo! Snap out of it!'

Jo decided that she couldn't stand any more of this. She turned and left the TARDIS, ignoring the Doctor's shouts.

I have to make my own decision, she thought. That's what I said I would do, when I was talking to the Sky.

She walked across the control room of the starship, intending to talk to Mike. But she hadn't got halfway to the command platform before she heard a groan from behind one of the metal cabinets that served as control mountings. She stopped, looked behind the cabinet, and saw a man's body, stained with blood. He had a long beard, full of gold rings, and his body was strangely deformed – as if –

With a shock, Jo realized that the man had been Promoted. Very recently. He hadn't even formed his chrysalis.

She also realized that he was still alive.

His eyes turned slowly to meet hers.

'Help,' he said. 'You must stop them.'

Jo looked at the man again. 'You're Epreto, aren't you?' she asked.

He nodded. 'You must stop them,' he said again.

'Who?'

'The Dead. This is wrong. Everything I worked for was wrong. You have to stop it.'

Jo thought about this for a moment. 'Yes,' she said. 'It probably should have been stopped. But it's all over now. The experiment has been aborted. You must join the Dead.'

The man shook his head weakly. 'Please – you are a man. Don't take their side – there's a club there . . .'

Jo saw it: a piece of metal about half as long as her arm, glazed at one end. She suspected it might actually be a torch.

Jo knew then what she had to do. She had to end this poor man's unhappiness. It was the only useful thing she could do, the only thing that didn't involve thinking

233

about . . . well, about the Doctor, for instance.

She raised the club over the man's head.

'Please . . .' he said. 'Please don't do this to me.'

'It's for the best,' said Jo.

And she brought the club down as hard as she could.

Mike sat in the command chair of the starship, watching the Dead. His orders were pleasingly definite again: ride the starship beyond the Sky, navigate it to the nearest authorized Aapex base, and make your report. In the event of any encounters with unauthorized personnel, destroy the ship and everything aboard, including yourself.

It made sense. It felt good.

He saw Jo, down between the cabinets, clearing up one of the other men, adding him to the heap of bodies.

Good old Jo. You could rely on her. It was a shame about the Doctor, though. Mike hadn't felt good about putting him under restraint. And he felt even less good about what he was going to have to do once the starship was under way.

But orders were orders.

He looked around his men. 'Main engines on,' he ordered. 'Bring up the navigational consoles.'

A steady vibration ran through the control room, gradually gaining in amplitude. The starship began to move.

He looked at each of the men in turn, flickering silent instructions to them with his eyes in the efficient manner of the Dead. But he knew that synchronization using that method was going to be a bit of a problem. He was glad once again that he had been trained in UNIT. He explained what he was going to do non-vocally to each man, then, slowly and carefully, spoke aloud.

'On my mark, blow a hole in the Sky.'

Jo wasn't quite sure why she'd brought down the torch on the deck instead of Epreto's skull. It was against her orders. But it had felt right, somehow.

She leant close to Epreto where he lay in the heap of bodies and whispered, 'I know this is horrible. But just keep still, and they'll think you're dead like the others. I'm going to rescue the Doctor.'

She hurried across the control room, trying not to look at any of the Dead. In particular, trying not to look at Mike. If they guessed that she wasn't obeying orders, she knew what would happen to her.

She was all too well aware that there was no room for mercy now.

In the TARDIS the two Dead were still holding the Doctor, who was struggling grimly.

'Mike has given you new duties in the control room,' she told them. 'Release the Doctor. I'll deal with him.'

The Dead let the Doctor go at once: thankfully the individual units were used to obeying orders without question. The Doctor sagged to the floor, apparently exhausted by his struggles.

Once the Dead were gone, Jo said quietly. 'You were right. We have to stop them.'

The Doctor raised an eyebrow. 'What made you change your mind?'

Jo shook her head. She wanted to say, I nearly killed someone. But she didn't want to talk about it. Not now. Not even with the Doctor.

The Doctor nodded briskly. 'Well, I'm glad that you have, anyway. Now, we need to get this device –' he indicated the machine based on the Pulse Control Meter; a conglomeration of electric parts and yellow plastic blocks '– out of the TARDIS so that it can interface with the starship systems and, if I'm right, with the Dead and the Sky as well.'

Jo nodded, then helped the Doctor lift the machine and carry it out through the doors.

Outside, viewscreens showed the Land still burning, but now in sunlight. Smoke hung over most of it, but to Jo's relief some green was still visible. She pointed it out to the Doctor.

He nodded. 'There's hope, then. But we'll have to be

quick.' He kneeled over the device and began adjusting the positions of the plastic blocks.

A blue light began to flicker deep inside. Jo watched, fascinated. It was as if the light were telling her something – something very important – but she couldn't quite grasp the meaning.

'Hold it, Doctor!'

Jo jumped, looked up to see Mike standing above them. Mike in his dark, sculpted, Dead body, only the face and the voice recognizable. He had a gun in his hand, and the gun was aimed at the Doctor.

'Doctor, I'm sorry but you'll have to turn off that device,' said Mike. 'Now.'

'Captain Yates!' snapped the Doctor. 'You are perfectly well aware that –'

The pistol cracked, and a bullet thunked into the side of the improvised console of the machine. Jo stared at the small hole that it had made. She didn't quite believe that this was happening.

But then she didn't quite believe that she had almost killed Epreto, either.

Mike stepped forward. 'That was your last warning, Doctor.' The Doctor bent over the device and made an adjustment, his eyes on the screen at the other side of the starship control room.

'Mike!' called Jo. Her voice was shaking. 'You know the Dead can't reconstruct the Doctor. If you kill him he'll just die!'

'I haven't any choice,' said Mike. 'We can't allow the Doctor to control the starship.'

'Then destroy the device, not the Doctor!'

'He'll make another device. You know the Doctor, Jo.'

Yes, thought Jo. I know the Doctor. I know that he's trying to save people, and the Dead are trying to destroy people. I know that the Doctor would never, never kill you, Mike, or me, or anyone he cared for just because of orders – and neither would . . . and . . .

And neither would Mike Yates.

She had to convince him somehow, make him see what was really happening, just as she had seen it after she'd almost killed Epreto. 'Mike,' she said. 'This is wrong. We've got it all wrong. Don't do it.'

Mike ignored her. 'You've got a count of five, Doctor,' he said. The gun was steady in his wood-clay hand.

The Doctor made another adjustment to the Pulse Control device. The blue light got brighter, its flickering more urgent. Jo stood up and put herself between Mike and the Doctor.

'Get out of the way, Jo.'

'No. I won't. What you're doing is wrong.'

Jo's head jolted back, and she saw a thin trail of smoke coming from the gun.

Mike had shot her.

He was staring at the gun, his blue eyes flickering with light.

'It's wrong, Mike!' said Jo. Blood thundered in her ears, and her knees crumpled under her. 'Mike! Don't —'

Her vision misted, her throat clogged with blood, and the world faded away into darkness.

Twenty-Five

Mike stared at the blood running from Jo's forehead, at the grey-white flesh of her face, unable to believe what he had done.

He had shot Jo.

He had killed Jo.

Killed her, just because she didn't agree with what the Dead had decided.

The Doctor was leaning over Jo's body. He glanced up at Mike with a fury on his face that Mike had never seen before. With a violent shock, he realized that the Doctor's fury was directed at him. He felt as if his clay body were breaking open, but he couldn't move, couldn't speak.

He watched the Doctor roll Jo over on to her back and begin resuscitation.

'Doctor, I . . .' he began. He wanted to tell the Doctor that he hadn't wanted to kill Jo, that he had only been trying to stop her from betraying the Dead, but the words seemed inadequate, wrong.

'Mike!' The Doctor spoke in between his breaths into Jo's lungs. 'Medical kit! In the TARDIS!'

Mike didn't hesitate, but ran through the TARDIS doors.

'Cabinet! Top left drawer!'

Mike made for the cabinet, opened the drawer, and found what appeared to be a standard UNIT medical kit.

Outside, the Doctor was still trying to breathe life into Jo. He took the medical kit without a word, and opened it to reveal a small machine covered with flick-ering lights. He put it over Jo's body, then shot a glance at Mike.

'There's too much damage to her brain, Mike. I can keep her alive, but she'll be a vegetable for the rest of her life.' The fury had gone from the Doctor's face, had been replaced by an icy calmness which was even more terrifying.

Mike told himself that all non-Aapex personnel were going to die anyway. Including the Doctor – and Jo, if she didn't choose to join the Dead. So it didn't matter.

But he couldn't quite believe it.

'Just give me a chance to prove that I'm right, Mike,' said the Doctor softly. 'Give yourself a chance to look at the evidence.'

Mike was confused. 'What evidence?'

The Doctor returned his attention to the device. 'The evidence stored on this starship, Mike. The evidence from Aapex themselves.'

Mike hesitated. He lowered the gun, then raised it again.

He became aware that he had an audience. The tall clay figures of the Dead were all around him, looking down. Their blue eyes flickered and their silent voices filled Mike's head.

– *we are awaiting the order you were to give* –

– *you are no longer giving the order* –

– *you must give the order soon* –

– *there can be no delay now* –

– *the Doctor should be killed* –

– *Jo should be killed* –

– *all non-Aapex personnel are now unnecessary* –

'Shut up!' yelled Mike. 'Let me think!'

He managed to turn away from the flickering eyes and look at the Doctor again.

The blue light inside the device flickered.

And Mike received the message.

Starship AAPEX 09879/LJ.

Message Stored: AAPEX System General Instruction.

Dated: present minus 2347.54 years.

To: All personnel and those acting on their behalf.

Message Text: Experiment AAPEX 6cJ##47 is hereby

terminated and all products of the experiment which may be deemed sentient beings are hereby chartered as free citizens of the Eyriearchy.

Message ends.

'It doesn't make any sense!' protested Mike.

But, dimly, he was aware that it did. The authorization codes were correct.

The orders had been changed.

Mike turned slowly and looked at the images of the world on the starship's screens. Smoke. Flame. Ruin.

'It's not too late?' he asked.

'No,' said the Doctor softly.

Mike turned to the Dead and passed the message on nonvocally to each of the waiting men in turn.

The response from each one was the same.

– what do we do now? –

'What do we do now?' Mike asked the Doctor, when he had finished.

The Doctor stood up, and his face broke into a smile.

'Well,' he said, gesturing at the images of the world around them. 'I think we have some repair work to do.'

Epilogue

The fifth sun was rising when Jo at last felt well enough to walk out of the TARDIS and into the landscape of melting ice. Eeneeri and Xaai were there, resting on the small patch of cleared earth around the TARDIS, his head nestling against her spread wings. A few other naieen were flying close overhead, watching the slow track of the clean new sunlight across the Land. A small radar-type dish attached by a cable to the TARDIS also tracked the sun, presumably controlling it, or at least making sure it didn't get out of control. Jo looked at the lashed-up electronics attached to it, and wondered that something so apparently primitive had managed to activate not only the repair systems of the Sky above the original Land, but the five suns of the other, dead Lands as well.

The World was going to be a lot bigger now.

The Doctor was talking to Mike. Jo watched the conversation nervously, not quite daring to come close enough to hear. The Dead had managed to revive Mike's original body, just as they had Xaai's, but this Mike had no memory of the events since he'd died.

Had no memory of killing Jo.

She wondered whether the Doctor would tell him. She wondered whether Mike ought to know that he was capable of killing her – and then she wondered if that was true, anyway.

It hadn't really been Mike.

Had it?

Mike was turning away from the Doctor, walking towards her, his dress shoes slipping on the frozen ground.

She looked at his face, and guessed what the Doctor had said.

'The Doctor told me who shot you.'

Jo nodded, blushed, looked at the ground. 'It wasn't too bad. The bullet glanced off my skull. I'm OK now.' She took his hands. 'It's OK, Mike, really it is.'

Mike shook his head. 'I still don't think we can trust Epreto. How can a man who can kill someone in cold blood be left in charge of a world?'

Jo looked up at the Sky, where Epreto was flying above the others, his eyes, no doubt, on the miracle of the slowly rising sun. She felt a sudden surge of relief. Mike didn't know. The Doctor hadn't told him.

The secret was safe.

'Epreto's different now,' she said. 'He understands that you have to work towards change. Anyway, he's naieen. He can't kill anyone any longer. They don't, you know.' At least not usually, she thought.

Mike looked stubborn for a moment, then shrugged. 'Well, it's the Doctor's business, I suppose. I was out of it.'

There was a distant crashing sound: they both jumped and looked around in alarm, but then Jo realized.

'It's only ice,' Jo said. 'A big chunk of it. Melting.'

They were both silent for a while. The sunlight was becoming hot now, but the air was still cold. A breeze was starting up. Jo heard the faint dripping of water, the crackle of the slowly melting ice.

'Do you reckon we'll ever get to Karfel?' asked Mike.

Jo shrugged. 'I don't know. We never got to Metabilis Three.'

They both laughed.

'You never know where you're going to end up, or how long it's going to be for, do you?' asked Mike, looking at the TARDIS.

'No,' agreed Jo. 'That's the worst thing about it. You don't.' She almost added, I'm not sure if I want to do it any more. But she decided to leave that discussion for another day.

242

'Cup of tea?' asked Mike.

Jo grinned. 'You bet!'

Mike grinned back, then walked away and into the TARDIS. Jo watched him go, and wondered if he knew where the Doctor kept the teabags.

Then she wondered if she would ever tell Mike that he'd killed her. Probably not, she decided.

But you never knew.

Epreto landed on the spur where the Doctor was standing, surrounded by dirty mounds of snow and pools of brown meltwater. The sky had clouded over, covering the new sun, and a strong wind was blowing: it was getting dangerous to fly.

He walked up to the Doctor, who was staring into the distance.

'Did Captain Yates believe you?' he asked.

The Doctor nodded. 'He had no reason not to, really. As far as he was concerned, he was dead, and now he's alive again. It's possible that he might remember what happened in between at some time, but the Dead seemed pretty sure that he wouldn't.' He paused. 'I hope not, because I told him that Jo was dead and could never be revived, to shock him into changing his mind. I don't like to think about him remembering that.' Another pause. 'Thank you, by the way, for agreeing to take the blame.'

'The blame was mine to take,' said Epreto. 'This would never have happened if it hadn't been for my arrogance.' He paused, looking around at the thawing landscape. 'To think that I almost destroyed the world!'

The Doctor turned to him, met his eyes. 'You are still one of the most able and intelligent people here. You still have a duty to guide your people forward. Don't forget that. Just don't assume that the only way forward is the obvious one.'

Epreto laughed. 'I have learnt my lesson, Doctor.'

I hope, he added silently.

Then, disregarding the dangers of the wind, he spread his wings and took off into the singing air. It bounded around his body, rippled under his wings, propelled him into a swaying, wild, effortless climb towards the low grey clouds. Somewhere above them was the sun, but Epreto didn't care about that any more. It was enough to see the Land – this new Land – slowly thawing in the warm, boisterous wind, enough to feel the air streaming around him.

Perhaps, he thought, all I ever wanted to do was fly.

Available in the *Doctor Who – New Adventures* series:

The next Missing Adventure is *The Plotters* by Gareth Roberts, featuring the first Doctor, Ian, Barbara and Vicki.